THE STOLEN MOON

Rachel Searles

FEIWEL AND FRIENDS
NEW YORK

A Feiwel and Friends Book
An Imprint of Macmillan

Feiwel and Friends books may be purchased for business or promotional use.
For information on bulk purchases, please contact the Macmillan Corporate and
Premium Sales Department at (800) 221-7945 x5442 or by e-mail at
specialmarkets@macmillan.com.

Library of Congress Cataloging-in-Publication Data Available

ISBN: 978-1-250-03880-7 (hardcover) / 978-1-250-06654-1 (ebook)

Book design by Véronique Lefèvre Sweet

Feiwel and Friends logo designed by Filomena Tuosto

First Edition: 2015

1 3 5 7 9 10 8 6 4 2

mackids.com

For Liz Briggs, a tough critic
and great friend

CHAPTER ONE

For the fourth time in as many days, Chase Garrety was mad enough to spit nails.

His swift footsteps echoed off the walls of the metal corridor as he rushed through the soldiers' quarters of the starship *Kuyddestor*, muttering dire threats under his breath. How on Taras had this happened again, after everything he'd tried? Asking, begging, threatening—nothing seemed to work on her. He stopped short in front of one of the dozens of identical doors and stabbed at the entry key embedded in the wall. The door slid open almost soundlessly, and he stormed into his sister's bunkroom.

Lilli glared at him from her narrow bed, where she sat hunched with her back against the wall, knees drawn up toward her chin. The tiny chamber was not even two arm spans across, with a wide metal crossbeam on the ceiling that made it feel even smaller.

Chase stood shaking his head, almost speechless with anger. What could she possibly say that would make him understand her behavior? "And?"

She looked down at her wool bedcover and plucked an invisible piece of fuzz. In a barely audible voice, she mumbled, "It was a mistake."

"A *mistake*?" The words came out in a shout. He glanced over his shoulder at the open hallway and hit the interior key to close the door. The last thing he needed was more people's attention.

This time it had happened in the cafeteria. One moment Lilli was sitting at a long table sandwiched between a group of younger children and a handful of soldiers, and the next she was gone. Vanished. Luckily for her, she was so quiet that most people didn't pay much attention to her, and their minds tended to invent a rational explanation when she disappeared—so far everyone just thought she was incredibly stealthy. Nobody knew the truth: that the girl who sat among them wasn't real, that she was just a projection, a "traveling copy" of Lilli's body sent from wherever she actually was.

Until she got bored and withdrew the projection. Just like she had from the observation deck the day before, and the medical bay the day before that, and the fourth-level hallway the day before that. Chase was never there when it happened, but somehow word always filtered back to him about his ninja sister.

"Why? Why do you keep doing this? Eventually someone's going to realize there's something weird going on. They'll figure out you're not normal."

Lilli nipped at a cuticle and gave him a baleful look that made her seem much older than ten. "Nobody saw me go. I'm always careful."

"Careful?" Chase rolled his eyes. "I don't want to hear 'careful,' I want to hear 'yes, you're right, I won't do it again.' If I can manage to open doors instead of walking through them, you should be able to walk around in one single body like a normal person instead of projecting a copy everywhere."

She ran a hand through the choppy blond hair she insisted on cutting herself and didn't answer, casting her eyes at the floor with a shrug. Anger swelled up inside Chase. "You do realize we're supposed to be hiding here, right? Those people who killed our parents, who locked you up in a lab? They're still out there. All it takes is one slip-up, and they'll find us. Do you want that to happen?"

She exhaled sharply, a tiny indication of her own fierce temper. "What do you think? *I'm* the one who knows how bad it really was. I'm the one who *remembers*."

Chase rubbed the spot between his eyebrows. Somehow

she always managed to twist his words into her advantage when they fought. "Lilli—"

"Just leave me alone. Stop trying to be my parent. You're not responsible for me."

But he was responsible for her, even if he was only three years older. He was the only family she had left. And as long as they were living aboard a Fleet starship, they needed to hide the special abilities that had been passed down to them from their parents, a pair of genetically enhanced soldiers created by the Fleet itself. "If you can't control yourself, I'm going to have to tell the captain what you're doing. You're putting him at risk too."

She arched a pale eyebrow, but didn't comment on his formal name for the man who was once Uncle Lionel to them both. Before the attack that destroyed their family and erased Chase's entire memory of their shared childhood. She didn't say anything at all, but she didn't need to. They both knew there was nothing anyone could do to stop her.

The first time Lilli had seen him after the attack that, as far as she knew, had killed everyone in her family, she'd thought he was a clone of her dead brother and tried to stab him. At the time he hadn't even realized that the grief-crazed girl was his own sister. She was still as much a stranger to him now as she had been then. How could he make her see how reckless she was being? "It's dangerous for all of us when you travel. Just—please, promise me you won't do it anymore, okay?"

She gave him a flat little smile and, in a voice crackling with sarcasm, said, "Sure thing, big brother."

And then she blinked out like a light.

Chase yelped in frustration and raised his hands, grabbing uselessly at the air. It was impossible to tell the difference between the real Lilli and her traveling copy—for all he knew, he hadn't seen the real her in weeks. And he had no idea where she was hiding on the ship when she disappeared like this. How had their parents dealt with this wild animal of a daughter? For a brief instant, he was furious with them for being gone, for leaving him alone with her. Then he felt like a jerk.

He whirled around to the door, perversely tempted to phase right through it to show that Lilli wasn't the only one who could break the rules. But he imagined someone walking down the hall who would see him emerging from the solid door like it wasn't even there. Why couldn't Lilli see those kinds of consequences?

He pressed the exit key, and the door slid open. A second later, two soldiers in gym gear jogged past. Chase gave a fierce nod, his point proven.

His own bunkroom was at the other end of the long hall. When he walked in, Parker was sitting at their shared desk, typing furiously with one hand and swiping his fingers over a touchscreen with the other. Without turning around, he asked, "How'd the disciplining go, boss?"

"She did it again, right in front of me!"

Parker paused and half-turned, a smile tugging at the corner of his mouth. He snapped his fingers. "Just like that?"

Chase gave him a dark look. "I need to figure out where she's hiding."

"On a ship that houses over two thousand people? *Pfft*. Good luck." He turned back to his computer.

Chase punched the door key closed and sank onto his bunk.

After the attack on his family, he'd awoken on the planet Trucon, rematerialized from the particle disperser attack that should have vaporized him for good but with no idea who he was, what had happened to him, or why he was able to phrase through solid objects. He was grateful that he'd managed to find the answers to these questions, even though he'd also learned his memory would probably never come back, and that his parents' friend Captain Lennard had given him, his sister, and their friend Parker shelter aboard his Fleet starship. But in the three months since they'd come to live on the *Kuyddestor*, Chase's life had become safe, steady, and endlessly frustrating. Nearly every interaction with the sister he'd fought so hard to save turned into a fight. He'd tried everything: random acts of kindness, asking questions, not asking questions, being attentive, giving her space. Nothing seemed to get through to her, and instead of grounding him, his relationship with her made him feel more adrift than ever.

Chase rose to his feet and walked to the window. Outside in black space, the glow of distant stars outlined a massive patchwork collection of metal structures, the Movala mining colony. For the past three months, the *Kuyddestor* had been protecting the colony from raider attacks—a mission the captain had taken on in order to get the ship far away from Fleet High Command until he could figure out which corrupt arm of the Fleet had carried out a massive attack on the planet Trucon, setting up one of the *Kuyddestor*'s own officers to take the fall. The captain had told a very public lie to save his officer—a lie that showed he, too, knew about the Fleet's deception. Not one day went by when Chase didn't worry about retaliation from whomever it was they'd foiled.

Chase swiped his fingers across the window, which was not, in fact, a real window. Their room was located somewhere deep inside the belly of the starship, and the window was actually a video screen that displayed the view from the observation deck. With each swipe, the view changed quickly to recordings of a scenic forest, a mountain, a twinkling cityscape. One more flick of his fingers, and Chase found himself viewing the inside of the command bridge, where the ship's top officers were hard at work.

"You finally hacked into the bridge camera," he said, only slightly surprised. Parker had already hacked into much more.

"Yeah. I can't get audio yet, but this isn't bad, right?" Parker glanced up at Chase, grinning at his accomplishment.

Chase nodded absently, his eyes locked on Captain Lennard, who strode across the bridge to lean over the shoulder of someone at console. It was the first time Chase had seen the captain in over a week.

Parker reached past him and flicked the screen back to the cityscape scene. "Don't leave it set to that view for very long. If somebody walks in, I don't want them to see what I've done."

"Understood. That's really cool."

"Yeah, well." Parker turned back to his computer. "Unfortunately, the other project's not going as well."

Chase glanced over at their shared desk, which was covered in bits of wiring and an assortment of tools. Parker touched an angled monitor resting amid the clutter and scanned over the day's accumulation of data.

"Nothing yet," he said, stating what Chase already knew. Soon after they'd arrived on the ship, the chief medical officer on board, Dr. Bishallany, had removed a tracking chip from under Parker's scalp. The chip had been placed there by Parker's guardian, a mysterious weapons dealer named Asa Kaplan, who'd created an identical chip found under Chase's skin—although Chase still had no idea what Asa's connection to him or his family was. The captain wanted Parker's chip destroyed, but Parker had insisted he could disable its tracking function inside a one-way radio blocking enclosure, which would still allow him to hunt for its source by intercepting the chip's reply to his former guardian, the man who held the answers to many of both his and Chase's questions.

But after nearly three months no good data had come from the chip, and seeing Parker's face pinched with worry as he tweaked his tracer program over and over, Chase had lost hope in that avenue. Not that there was much he could do to help.

Parker looked over at Chase. "The encryption on the chip seems to be getting more complicated the longer it's been out of my head. Asa might have programmed it to secure itself once it's no longer sensing living human tissue. The answer's there, I just have to find the right way to get to it."

Chase gave a half-smile. "Of course you will." It wasn't that he doubted Parker's genius with electronics—heck, Chase would have as much luck eating the tracking chip to absorb the answers by osmosis as trying to decode it himself—but Asa Kaplan, criminal mastermind, had clearly put all his resources toward making sure he was untraceable. How much progress could a kid hacker really expect to make against him?

"I'll do it," Parker repeated forcefully. "It just takes time." He had a good reason for wanting to find Asa Kaplan—although the man had been his guardian, he'd left Parker tucked away in an isolated compound to be raised by an android, and Parker knew nothing about his parents or why Asa was the one entrusted to care for their son.

But for Chase, the need to know what connected him to Asa was almost unbearable. After Chase's body was vaporized, his molecules had found their way back together in Parker's yard, apparently drawn there by the pull of the matching tracking chip under his own scalp. But after escaping from the Fleet, Chase's parents had lived in hiding on a planet the captain wouldn't even name for Chase—so how had he ended up with Asa Kaplan's tracking chip under his skin?

"Do you think he can tell you're trying to look for him?" Chase asked.

Parker didn't answer—all his attention was back on the computer. He likely hadn't even heard Chase, who began to turn away.

"Ha," said Parker loudly, with one final keystroke. "There. I've hacked into the mainframe so I can use the ship's computing power to analyze the chip's encryption."

All Chase heard was *blah blah blah hacked into the mainframe*. "That easily?"

Parker made a face. "Well, it wasn't *easy*. I've been working on it for a few days. But I've gotta say, I'm kinda surprised at how archaic the technology on this ship is." Seeing Chase's frown, he added, "It's solid, don't worry, but it's not even close to what I had at my house on Trucon."

"Solid?"

"Yeah, it's strong enough, especially the external defenses. Nobody could hack into the ship from the outside—it's locked down tight. But once you're inside, on the local network? I mean, you'd have to be a really good hacker, but the infrastructure is pretty vulnerable."

A prickle of anxiety danced down Chase's spine. Why wouldn't the Fleet fix security holes in its own ship? "Do you think the Fleet did it on purpose? To keep the *Kuyddestor*—"

"No," scoffed Parker. "I doubt the *Kuyddestor* is the only one like this. There are only, I think, eight other Titan-class starships—these are the biggest ships the Fleet has—and they're spread pretty thin. To strip and update one would take at least a year, and the Fleet probably can't afford to lose one of its ships for that long. I'm sure this was top-of-the-line for internal network security when they built it back in the day."

Parker leaned over the desk to peer at the circuit board where he'd affixed the chip and frowned. "I'm going down to the engine room to ask Chief Kobes if he has any extra processing boards lying around. Come with me."

"I've got my appointment in a little bit," Chase muttered. He knew he didn't need to feel embarrassed about his visits with Dr. Bishallany, especially not around Parker, but talking about them made him feel defective. Parker wasn't the one who had to see a doctor once a week to study his own freak body.

Parker pulled him off the bunk and pushed him toward the door. "You've got time. Come on. You can ask around to see if anyone's spotted a skinny little blond girl lurking in any dark corners."

Chase stepped out into the hallway, his mind already back to the immediate problem of getting Lilli under control. "Hey, you think we could spot her now that you've hacked into the camera system?"

Parker tilted his head in thought as he followed Chase into the hall. "Hmm. Not right now. I've only got access to the bridge and the engine room cameras, and there aren't really that many cameras in the hallways."

A trio of boisterous engine room ensigns with their identifying green badges came around the corner of the hall. "Hey, Parker," called out one with a cheerful grin. "You still joining us for a game of Questlords tonight?"

"I dunno, Cutty—I'll send you a message later today," Parker called over his shoulder. A flicker of jealousy passed through Chase. It hadn't taken Parker long after arriving on the ship to make some new friends and establish an easy familiarity with the crew. Not that Chase wanted to play some nerd game with a bunch of dorky ensigns. Parker turned back to him. "Have you mentioned to Maurus or anybody what Lilli's been doing? It'd be easier to find her if more of the crew is helping you look."

"No," said Chase quickly. "I don't want her to get in trouble. I won't tell the captain unless I have to."

"Guess it wouldn't make you any more popular with her either."

Chase snorted. "I don't know if there's anything that can do that."

The next step he took was into sudden and complete blackness.

CHAPTER TWO

Surrounded by the dark, Chase froze, not knowing if the lights had gone out or he'd gone blind or something worse. "Parker?"

"Right beside you." Parker's disembodied voice sounded oddly muted by the darkness. A moment later his fingers squeezed Chase's shoulder.

Chase's heart raced so loudly in his chest, he was sure Parker could hear it. "What just happened?"

"I'm not sure. Power trouble? There should be emergency backup lights along the floor. I don't know why they're not coming on."

"Do you think it's out in the whole ship?"

Parker didn't answer for a moment. "Do you hear that?"

"What?"

"The sound of nothing. There's no airflow coming through

the vents. The whole ship's mainframe must have gone down for the life support systems to crash."

"You mean there's no more air?" Chase asked in a panicky voice.

"There'll be a couple of hours' worth of oxygen in the system. I'm sure this won't last that long."

They stood there for a minute, listening to their own breathing and waiting to see if the lights would come back. "Let's try to get to the canteen," said Chase finally. He took a step, sliding his foot out first to make sure he wasn't going to run into something. As they inched their way down the hall, his other senses sharpened, and he could hear distant sounds of shouting, the whoosh and crash of a door slamming.

Suddenly he noticed something much closer, a sound that didn't quite fit: three sets of footsteps, not two. Adrenaline surged through him and he stopped, heart pounding. Parker's grip on his shoulder tightened.

"Who's there?" asked Chase, sounding bolder than he felt. No one answered, but whoever it was had snuck up on them without a sound. "Lilli, is that you?"

Brief silence. "Yes," came her scratchy voice from the right.

Parker groaned. "Good grief, Lil. Thanks for the heart attack."

Chase reached out in the direction of her voice, but his

hand found nothing. "Are you okay? Come with us to the canteen. I'm sure the captain's going to make an announcement any second now to let us know what's happened."

"Um, not with the power out he won't," said Parker.

"They'll fix it." He hoped Lilli couldn't hear how nervous he was. What if this was the retaliation he'd feared all these months? Was this the precursor to an attack? "I'm sure the engine room's already figuring it out."

"I'll go check," came Lilli's voice.

Chase started shaking his head before he realized she wouldn't see it. "No, wait—"

She didn't make a sound, but Chase could feel her absence and knew that she'd disappeared again. He cursed under his breath.

"Lords, I almost wet my pants when she showed up like that," whispered Parker.

"Yeah, it's a great party trick," said Chase sourly.

Another minute ticked by as they waited, and then the sound of Lilli's breathing filled the air beside them again. "All the power systems shut down," she announced. "The mainframe's rebooting."

"What?" asked Parker. "They just shut down? Impossible. There are backups, and backups for the backups. On top of it the mainframe has its own local power unit."

But what if someone was messing with the mainframe? Chase didn't share the thought. Parker's hack job couldn't have caused a blackout on the whole ship . . . could it?

"Well, Chief Kobes didn't say that exactly. Something about an upgrade and a glitch—"

"There's no 'glitch' big enough to take out the entire power system on a starship, including the emergency lights," Parker interrupted. "It's impossible, there are too many redundancy measures."

"Well, I didn't investigate the problem myself!" snapped Lilli. "Take it up with the engineers if you're so sure of yourself."

As much as Lilli fought with Chase, she was even quicker to butt heads with Parker—which was why Chase usually tried to keep them away from each other. "Calm down, you guys. Whatever happened, they'll figure—"

A door crashed open somewhere down the hall, followed by the rapid pounding of boots against metal. Someone was running toward them.

"Hey!" shouted Chase. "Slow down!"

Whoever it was didn't stop running, and Chase jumped to the side of the hallway as the runner blew past, heaving for air. The footsteps quickly faded out down the hall. Was there some kind of emergency? Chase rubbed his sweaty palms against his pants.

"Jeez, panic much?" growled Parker. "What an idiot. You guys okay? Still here, Lilli?"

Lilli muttered a wordless reply, and again Chase felt the impulse to reach out and squeeze her arm to reassure her that they would be okay. On some level, it made him happy that she'd sought him out in the blackout. But what if she pulled away or snapped at him? It almost felt as though he were reaching out to touch a spiky Goxar alien. "Let's keep going," he said instead.

They were getting closer to the canteen when they heard the tap of footsteps coming up from behind them, walking swiftly but not running. A light swung around the corner of the hall, and a lilting voice called out.

"Chase? Parker? Is that you?" Maurus's face emerged from the darkness, illuminated by a glow of light. The Lyolian soldier held a short white rod that lit the immediate space a few feet around him. His expression was pinched. "Lilli too? Cursed suns of Hesta, what are you all doing out in the hall? You should stay in your quarters when something like that happens."

"If I could tell my orifice from my elbow right now, maybe I'd be there already," said Parker. "What happened to the power?"

Maurus ignored his question. "The captain sent me to find you and take you somewhere safe."

"Why?" asked Chase. "What's going on?"

"We don't know yet. It's just a precaution."

"In case of what?" asked Parker. The same question had popped up in Chase's mind. Was the captain still worried about someone on the ship discovering their secrets? Or had they already been found out?

Maurus turned and waved the glowing rod over a metal box affixed to the wall. "Do you know about these emergency stations? They should always be stocked with phoswhites." He opened the box, where a stack of clear rods rested in a bin, and tossed one to each of them. "Just hit the round end hard against the wall, like this." He demonstrated by whacking a stick against the wall. The echo rang down the hallway as more light filled the space around them. "They're good for about an hour."

Lilli grabbed a rod from the bin and gave it a savage smack against the wall, her eyes glittering in the glow it created. They all took turns lighting phoswhites, until enough light surrounded them that they could see everything for several feet. Beyond that the view dropped off into dense blackness. They moved slowly down the hall, where Maurus led them past the empty canteen. Shouts were being exchanged somewhere in the distance. Chase strained to hear what was being said, but he couldn't make out a single word. When they came to one of the ship's three wide stairways, Maurus pulled the stairwell door open and waved for them to go inside.

"Where are we going?" asked Chase as he passed by.

"Head upstairs," said Maurus. "We'll go to the armory."

Parker looked back. "What? Why?"

"The captain told me to get you somewhere safe. The armory's our best bet."

"But I want to go to the engine room," said Parker.

"I want to go to the engine room," mimicked Lilli in a mocking voice.

A door crashed open above them, and the sound of multiple footsteps echoed down the stairwell. Four grim-faced soldiers marched past and headed through the door Maurus still held open into the hallway, all with their blaster guns out and at the ready. Bringing up the rear was Colonel Forquera, the ship's second-in-command. A frown flashed across his lean, shadowy face when he saw the small group.

"What are they doing out of their rooms?" he asked Maurus in a low voice. Forquera was one of the few people aboard the ship who knew about Chase's and Lilli's unusual abilities and the true reason why they had been taken aboard the *Kuyddestor.*

"Captain wanted me to secure them and get them somewhere safe. I was taking them up to the armory."

Forquera shook his head. "Armory's no good—Poliski's team is out doing a sweep of the ship to check for any signs of external incursion."

"You think this could be an outside attack?" asked Parker. "I highly doubt it."

Chase's blood went cold. Parker had told him that it was impossible to hack the ship from the outside, but maybe someone had found a way. Parker didn't know everything, after all.

Forquera's eyes flickered briefly to Parker. "Take them to the brig. All the cells are empty right now."

"No," said Chase firmly. He'd spent time in that brig before and had no interest in revisiting it.

"Take us to the engine room," said Parker. "I can help fix the problem."

"The bridge—" Maurus started.

"Absolutely not," said Forquera.

"Engine room. Engine room. Engine room," said Parker, like an obnoxious parrot.

"Enough!" barked Forquera. The communicator at his belt beeped, and he looked down at it. "Lieutenant, just make sure they don't get in the way." He turned and continued into the hallway after his men.

As soon as the door closed behind Forquera, Parker crossed his arms. "Engine room."

Maurus sighed. "Please, don't make this hard. You know I'm still under extra surveillance right now." After Maurus was framed for orchestrating the Trucon disaster, Captain Lennard had publicly cleared him of any involvement with the plot, but because he had learned along the way that Maurus actually had covered up his past involvement with the Karsha Ven rebel group when he joined the Fleet, Maurus's return to the *Kuyddestor* had come on the condition that he let himself be monitored.

Parker snorted. "We know nobody's surveilling you right now, there's no power. Besides, Forquera never explicitly said *not* to take us to the engine room." He prodded Chase toward the stairs that headed down toward the engine deck. "Look, Chase is going there, and oh no, there's no way you can stop him. Better keep up so you don't lose track of him."

Chase took a halfhearted step down the stairs, giving Maurus an apologetic look.

Maurus had the flat expression of someone who was about to give in. "If they yell at us to leave, there won't be any objections."

Parker grinned. "They won't ask me to leave. I'll be quiet as a ghost." He gave Chase another prod and then jogged down the stairs ahead of him. "Hey, is it true that Colonel Forquera used to be a smuggler before he joined the Fleet?"

"Where did you hear that?" asked Maurus sharply.

Chase's head snapped to attention. Parker had never mentioned this to him before.

"Just some talk I overheard."

"Do you believe all the gossip you hear?"

"Well, if it walks like a Horga, and talks like a Horga . . ."

Chase frowned at Parker's back. How many other things had he heard about and not shared?

"He wouldn't have been allowed to join the Fleet if he was a smuggler," said Maurus. After a long pause, he added, "I heard he raced in the comet-chaser circuits. So, yeah, he probably ran with some pretty sketchy people, but I doubt he did anything illegal."

"Or maybe he just didn't get caught," said Parker with a sly smile in his voice. "I heard you can still get into the Fleet if you lie about your past."

"Shut up," said Chase. That last comment had been a dig at Maurus.

"Yeah, Parker, give it a rest," mocked Lilli.

"Did anyone ever tell you you're really annoying?" said Parker.

"Enough," said Maurus in a firm voice. "Move aside. I'll take the lead here."

They had reached the bottom level of the starship, the engine deck. The engine room itself was located in the rear half of the ship, but someone had tossed phoswhites on the ground down the length of the hall to light the way. They walked past soldiers prying open doors with crowbars, while other soldiers jogged by them, passing information to one another in urgent tones.

The door to the engine room had been jimmied halfway open, and in the dimly lit space behind it, shapes moved among the shadows. Maurus squeezed inside and pointed for everyone to stand along the back wall.

The engine room was technically an entire suite of individual chambers, but when people referred to it, they meant the big, circular room that ran around the engine core. At any given time there were at least a dozen engineers seated at the consoles and walking briskly from room to room. Chief Engineer Kobes practically lived there full time, reviewing calculations and barking orders. Chase had met him on a few occasions and was always somewhat intimidated by the stout, perpetually grumpy older man.

One of the consoles in the room was glowing, and a group of engineers including the chief stood clustered around it. "We were running a standard system upgrade on the navigation controls, but instead of performing a concurrent reboot like it always does, it crashed the entire mainframe," said Chief Kobes loudly.

"How soon until you get it back up?" crackled a deep voice from a handheld communicator held up by one of the engineers.

"We've had to reboot the whole mainframe from scratch. We're scrapping the update and reverting to the previous version. The reboot time is short enough that there won't be a lapse in any of the life-support systems. All electrical power should be back shortly, although navigation and propulsion might take up to half a day to get fully back online."

Parker stepped forward with a loud, attention-getting cough. Maurus snatched at his arm, but Chief Kobes had already looked up. "Who's back there?"

Maurus spoke up in a hurry. "It's Lieutenant Maurus, sir. Captain sent me to secure these young passengers and take them somewhere safe. Engine room was closest. We'll keep out of your way."

But Parker was already walking past him toward the console, ignoring Chase hissing his name to try to get him to stop. "If it's just a system update that crashed the entire mainframe of the ship, then why are the emergency lights out too? Those should be on a separate network."

Kobes squinted at him for a second. "That's not my biggest concern at the moment. Power will be back up shortly."

"Doesn't it seem kind of strange to you that *all* the lights went out? That would have to override multiple safety redundancies."

"It's a giant starship with a lot of integrated systems, kid. Glitches happen."

"I want a look at that code you were updating with," Parker said.

A growl fit to match his bulldog face came from the back

of the chief's throat. "I don't have time for this. Lieutenant, get him out of here."

Muttering apologies, Maurus grabbed the back of Parker's shirt and shoved him toward the door, waving for Chase and Lilli to follow. When they were back in the dark hallway, he hissed, "Is that what you meant by quiet as a ghost?"

Parker twisted out of his grip. "They're making a mistake. I don't think this blackout was an accident."

Chase's pulse spiked. This was it, the attack he'd been expecting for the past three months. "We should go to the captain and tell him before things get worse. What if we're already under attack? Would we even know if we're being surrounded right now?"

Maurus stopped and raised his hands. "First off, if this were an attack, the best thing to do would be to let the Chief and his crew get the mainframe back online as quickly as possible. Not pester him about technicalities." He glared at Parker. "The second best thing, Chase, is to keep a cool head and not over-react. The captain and the rest of the bridge team have things under control. You saw that Colonel Forquera and his team were sent out to look for possibilities of external incursion. The ship's already on high alert. But you heard the Chief, it was very likely just a problem with a system upgrade. If there's something else wrong with the ship, the engine crew will find it."

Parker shook his head. "They won't be looking for sabotage. They can't expect retaliation for something they don't know about."

"And when this is over, you can investigate the blackout to your heart's content," said Maurus. "But for now, you let the crew do what they were trained to do. They've got the ship under control. You do your part and be a respectful passenger." As if to emphasize Maurus's words, dim blue lighting flickered on overhead. "And there's the emergency lighting."

"Only fifteen minutes too late," retorted Parker, before he turned and headed back to the stairs.

Maurus saw them back up to their rooms on the soldiers' level, where Parker went straight to his desk and checked the connections on his computer before trying to power it back up. The air and regular lighting had kicked back on while they were walking up the stairs. Chase stood behind him, still shaken from the blackout and trying to formulate the question he'd resisted asking in front of Maurus. "Is it possible . . . with all the hacking you've been doing, piggybacking on the mainframe . . ."

That made Parker look up from his screen. "Are you serious? You think *I* caused the mainframe to crash?"

"I know you're good at what you do, but this isn't a house or a cruiser, it's a humongous complicated starship. Maybe you did something by accident."

Parker narrowed his eyes. "A starship's core is nothing more than a great big computer. Sure, it's a computer that makes engines fire and produces gravity and maintains life support, but at the basic level it's still just a very complex computer. That's all. And I know computers better than anyone." He turned his back on Chase and tapped his finger on the desk, waiting for his console to start up.

Chase paced in front of the bunk, restless. As usual, there didn't seem to be much he could do to help. "So what should I do?"

"I don't know," muttered Parker. "Do anything, for once."

Chase stopped. "What's that supposed to mean?"

Parker turned around with the irritated expression that Chase knew meant he was being distracted from what he really wanted to do. "It means you spend every day sitting in this room or you mope around the ship, lurking in the officers' lounge or mooning over a videofeed of the captain. You don't actually *do* anything else."

Chase's mouth dropped open slightly as Parker spoke. "What do you want me to do then, just forget about everything else and make a new life here while I wait either for you to find something on Asa or the Fleet to hunt us down and wipe us out? Should I find some buddies to play a dumb game with? This isn't a home—it's a refuge! And I'm not moping around all day. I have my sister to watch over."

Parker rolled his eyes and turned back to his computer. "Your sister is fine, let her be. Just relax and try to live your life for a while, okay? Find something you like to do and do it."

"I don't even know what I like to do," Chase muttered.

"Ugh, Chase, come on," groaned Parker.

But there really wasn't anything Chase could think of that he wanted to do besides look for Asa and defend himself and the others against potential Fleet attacks. How could he possibly concentrate on anything else? "What can I do to help find the hacker?"

Parker sighed. "Nothing, honestly. Just let me look into the blackout. You heard Maurus. It was probably just a 'glitch' anyway."

"You don't believe that," said Chase.

Parker didn't turn around. "Nope. I'd bet my life on it. I just hope I don't have to."

CHAPTER THREE

Rather than sitting in his room pointlessly watching Parker click on a screen and stressing himself out more by looking for clues in computer code he had no hope of understanding, Chase went out to the hallway to walk off his nervous energy and see if he could learn anything from being out around the crew. The officers' lounge was empty, but that came as no surprise. He'd been walking for fifteen minutes before he realized he'd completely forgotten about his appointment with the ship's medical officer.

Now he stood outside the empty quarters of Dr. Bishallany one floor down on the civilian level, apparently too late. Or maybe the appointment had been canceled—he hadn't bothered to check his messages before leaving his room. After trying the notification key a second time, he stepped back to leave.

The door slid open, but instead of the slight, balding form of Dr. Bishallany, standing before him in the doorway was a girl with long, honey-colored hair who looked about his age. A girl he'd never seen before.

Chase stared at her. *Say something, you dope.*

She waited a moment, raising her eyebrows. "Can I help you?"

"Who are you?" he asked, blurting out the first thing that came to mind.

She crossed her arms. "I'm Dr. Bishallany's daughter. Who are you?"

"I'm ... Chase." Since when did Dr. Bishallany have a daughter? She didn't look anything like him.

The girl leaned against the doorframe. "What do you want, Chase?"

"Um. I'm here to see the doctor?" He said it as if he were asking a question, and then gave himself a mental kick in the pants.

She shook her head. "These are his private quarters. Medical offices are on the third level."

"Yeah, I know." Chase squinted at her. "I, uh . . ."

Behind her, the slope-shouldered doctor hurried toward the entrance. "Chase, hello there. This is my daughter, Analora. She just got here a few days ago." He placed a hand on his daughter's arm. "Chase takes his sessions down here, my dear. I'm sorry, Chase, I should have sent you a message. There were some injuries caused by the blackout, and I'm heading up to the medical bay right now to help out. We'll have to reschedule our appointment."

"That's okay. I was just coming by to check. I figured, after everything that just happened..."

"Walk to the stairs with me?" the doctor asked. He strapped on a wristband communicator, gave his daughter a kiss on the cheek, and stepped into the hallway. Analora gave them a curious look as they left.

"Later, Chase," she said, letting the door slide shut in front of her.

"She lives on Jypras half the year with her mother," the doctor explained as he hurried down the hall. She had to have gotten that blond hair from her mother, because she certainly didn't have her father's bushy black eyebrows.

Chase rushed to keep up. "Yeah, I didn't realize that you, uh..."

As he spoke, the lights flickered, and they both glanced up at the ceiling.

"Looks like they're still ironing things out," said the doctor with an unconvincing chuckle. "I've never been in a ship-wide blackout before. I hope you weren't frightened."

"No," Chase lied. In all the time he'd spent letting the doctor try to poke him with needles to test the limits of his phasing, Chase had grown comfortable talking to him, so he only hesitated a moment before sharing the next bit of information. "Parker thinks someone caused it intentionally."

The doctor rubbed his bald scalp and glanced over. "Why does he think that?"

Chase gave an irritated sigh. There was so much he wanted to say about Parker. "I don't know, because he's paranoid. Because he thinks it's fishy that both the main and the emergency lights went off, and he doesn't think it was caused by a software upgrade like Chief Kobes is saying."

The bushy eyebrows bunched into a frown. "Has he told someone about this?"

"Just Maurus." Chase paused. "I'd go tell the captain, but I'm sure he's too busy fixing everything from the blackout. He's always pretty busy."

Dr. Bishallany stopped in front of the stairwell door. "Don't be afraid of him, Chase. He'll make time for you. Go see him."

After leaving the doctor, Chase wandered through the hallway toward the elevator, navigating with ease the corridors that had been such a maze when he, Parker, and Lilli had first come aboard the ship. The three of them should have been quartered here on the civilian level, where soldiers with families lived, but the captain had insisted on finding space for them in the middle of the soldiers' quarters, where he thought they'd be more secure.

Captain Lennard didn't live on the soldiers' level. His private quarters were up on the second floor behind the main command bridge, so that he had quick access in case of emergency. This also placed him farther away from the ship's escape shuttles, but a captain was never expected to flee his own ship.

As Chase neared the captain's suite, he could hear shouting. When he rounded the corner, he saw the leader of the Movala mining colony, a coarse, ruddy-faced man with pocked skin, waving his hands in an agitated fashion as he spoke. "Our company signed an agreement with the Federation when we set up operations out here that promised uninterrupted Fleet protection. Where is that promise now?"

Captain Lennard stood in the doorway to his quarters, arms crossed. "You know very well that between the instability in the Crayder system, the attacks on the Primus shipping pathway, and the continuing aftermath of the Trucon disaster, there's barely a Fleet vessel to spare these days. The Fleet can't offer you a replacement for the *Kuyddestor* after we leave. You should bring your men in from the outer belt."

Leave? Chase frowned. He knew that the captain had intended to spend at least half a year at the Movala colony. Why was he talking about leaving already?

"The inner clusters are nearly ninety-five percent depleted," snarled the miner. "If we stop mining the asteroids in the belt, we'll have to do four times the work to extract a tiny fraction of what we're getting now."

"I'm sorry, but that's your best option." The captain's voice was firm. "We'll be starting preparations for our departure immediately."

Hurling a storm of angry curses, the miner stalked off toward the stairs. The captain shook his head and turned to go back into his quarters when he spotted Chase. A tired smile stretched across his face. "Hey there. What a day, huh?"

Chase pointed after the miner. "Was he here with you during the blackout?"

"Luckily, no. He just teleported over a few minutes ago after we sent him word that our plans have changed."

Chase hesitated. "Are we really leaving?"

Captain Lennard sighed and nodded. "I'm afraid so." He stepped back to usher Chase into his quarters and gestured for him to take a seat. "Fleet command has ordered us to change assignments. Actually they've been trying to switch our mission almost since the moment we got here. They're sending us to the Galloi star system to help moderate a territory dispute."

Chase sat down on the hard brown couch in the captain's spartan sitting room. "Can't you tell them no?"

"I've already given High Command a long list of reasons

why we can't leave the miners alone out here, but they just keep after us. Pretty soon it's going to look less like wanting to protect the miners and more like insubordination, and I can't risk bringing more attention to the ship than we've already got."

Chase stared at the arm of the couch, running his finger along the seam. "I thought we'd be able to stay out here for a lot longer."

The captain didn't speak until Chase looked up and met his pale, wolfish eyes, and then he smiled. "We haven't been called in to answer questions; this is a standard change of mission. I received the most recent orders from Rear Admiral Shaw, who's been a personal mentor of mine for many years. And the mission isn't a dangerous one. We're escorting a Federation peacekeeping envoy to Storros, which is a peaceful, prosperous planet and an important ally to the Federation."

"But what if it's an excuse?" Chase asked. "What if this was all planned by the people who want to get back at you or Maurus?"

"I don't see how it could be. This conflict with Storros began long before the events surrounding Trucon." Captain Lennard paused, and sighed. "Anyway, I sent word an hour ago that we'd be on our way there within the coming week. There's nothing we can do. We'll just have to be very, very careful."

Hearing the captain's warning, Chase finally remembered why he'd come to visit. "The blackout. Parker doesn't think it was an accident. He says somebody inside the ship hacked the mainframe."

The captain took a moment to absorb this. "Why does he think this?"

"I don't know, he said it seemed suspicious. You know how Parker is about computer stuff. He just said that was the only thing that made sense."

Frowning, the captain said, "Our crew will investigate every possibility."

"But if someone on your crew did it in the first place, couldn't they just cover it up and say it didn't happen? How can you trust anyone?"

"I have to be able to trust my crew. This," he said, gesturing around them to indicate the entire ship, "doesn't work without trust. We all work together, and if someone's acting out of line, they'll be found, believe me."

Chase smiled, but the uneasy feeling in his chest didn't fade. If Parker could hack into the mainframe unnoticed, couldn't someone else do the same?

*   *   *

Chase was in the officer's lounge that evening watching Maurus annihilate his teammates from the expeditionary squad at a Shartese card game when Lennard came on the public address system to announce to the rest of the ship that they were leaving the Movala system. The lounge filled with cheers at the news.

"Huzzah and hallelujah," said Lieutenant Seto, throwing down his cards and flashing his easy grin. "Finally out of the backwater and back to civilization."

"I don't know that I would call Storros civilization, exactly," came a cool reply from one of the officers sitting at a big round table. Lieutenant Karsten Derrick was Chase's least favorite member of the expeds, and not just because he consistently ignored Chase's presence. "Bunch of slugs living in beehives, as far as I can tell."

"Oh, give it a rest," said a sharp-tongued female pilot who Chase knew only as Vidal. "Wherever we go, it's guaranteed to be less boring than here."

Maurus, who had moved back to sit beside Vidal on a hard sofa, fixed his dark eyes on Chase as soon as the announcement was broadcast. Chase was certain he was thinking the same thing: *This could be a trap.* "Storros is actually a pretty enlightened place," Maurus said casually. "They have a rich musical culture."

Derrick sneered. "No, they're just rich, period. Otherwise we wouldn't be rushing across the galaxy to solve their problems for them."

"Well, it's hard to argue with an endless supply of rhenium," said Seto in a wry voice. There was something about his expression that always made it look like he'd just heard a good joke.

"A planet is more than its resources; a planet is its people," said Maurus. "And the Storrians are far more than just a 'bunch of slugs.'"

"Of course you'd say that," sneered Derrick. "Aliens stick up for one another."

Maurus turned on him. "I'll tell you where you can stick something." Chase had learned early on that the word *alien* was a quick path to Maurus's formidable temper. It was moments like these where Chase was reminded of the fact that Maurus was the only non-Earthan among the *Kuyddestor* officers. Most of the officers treated Maurus, if not as a friend, at least with respect, but there were a few like Lieutenant Derrick who scorned him openly.

"I'd like to see you try," snapped Derrick.

"Guys, please," interrupted Vidal as she pulled her long, dark hair into a ponytail. "This whole flirtation between the two of you is getting really boring. Even Chase thinks it's lame, don't you?" She gave him a coaxing smile.

Maurus shot her a warning look. "Don't drag him into this."

She rolled her eyes and offered Maurus her hand. "Then will you escort a gal to the canteen for a hot caff before duty starts?"

He pulled her to her feet, flashing Chase a look that promised more discussion later.

"I can't believe Vidal's into that freak," muttered Lieutenant Derrick after they'd left.

Seto looked after them and frowned. "I think they're just friends."

With a sneer, the blond lieutenant gathered up the cards scattered on the table and dealt to the three remaining officers, ignoring Chase as usual. "Cutty, you in for this hand?"

Ensign Cutler, a funny, round-faced kid and one of the few engine room ensigns deemed cool enough to hang out with the officers, rose from a sofa where he'd been reading something on his communicator. "Do you know how to play seven-card Ambessitari risk?" he asked Chase as he joined the other officers at the table. "Do you want to learn?"

Hanging out in the officers' lounge wasn't as fun when Maurus wasn't around, and Chase had no patience to learn a new game at the moment. He tried to give Cutler a grateful smile. "Thanks, but I think I'll go take a walk."

He stopped by the canteen for a synthesized soy-chitin-riboflavin patty—a scrappy, as he'd learned from Parker—and scanned the long, low-ceilinged room for a glimpse of Dr. Bishallany's daughter. She wasn't there, so Chase took his scrappy to go, munching on the crisp patty as he strolled down the hall. He turned toward his room for a second, but

Parker was there, deep in thrall to his computer, which he had scarcely left since the blackout. He wouldn't be any fun to hang out with. Instead Chase wheeled around and took the elevator up to the fifth floor, where the observation deck was located.

The long room was empty, so Chase descended to the bottom tier of benches and sat directly in front of the glass wall, looking out at the massive mining colony below. Part factory, part living quarters, the colony looked like a ragged conglomeration of white metal warehouses that had been stitched together and left to float in space. Most of the mining work was done at outpost stations in the outer belts of the asteroid cluster, where miners extracted helium-4 from the icy chunks and sent it back to the main station for processing. It was during those long transports that raiders liked to strike, stealing the precious helium-4, but regular patrols of the *Kuyddestor*'s Khatra fighters along those routes kept them at bay. Chase could understand why the head miner was so upset that the Fleet was withdrawing its protection.

A high-pitched sigh sounded to his left, and he looked over to see Lilli sitting beside him. "Hey," he said. "Where've you been?"

Her expression was tense, her gaze fixed on the colony. "We're leaving."

He nodded. "Captain says we can't refuse these orders."

"We shouldn't go," she said in an unusually strident voice. She turned to him, her eyes filled with an urgency that alarmed him.

"Why?" When she didn't answer, he said, "It'll look worse if we don't go. The *Kuyddestor* still answers to the Fleet, or at least it has to seem that way."

Lilli shook her head fiercely. "It's too dangerous."

Something about her attitude riled Chase. "I don't understand why you're so worried about safety now, after all the times you've pulled your disappearing act since we got here."

Lilli gave him a condescending look of such disgust it might have been funny, if he thought she had even a shred of a sense of humor. "You still think I did that on purpose?"

Oh, that's right, it's always just a "mistake." The words were on the tip of his tongue, but he stopped himself from saying them. One thing he'd learned in all their bickering was that she never backed down, and it was up to him to bite his tongue and defuse the conversation before it escalated into a skirmish.

"Hey, I need to ask you something," he said, changing subjects. "From, um, back when we were still living with Mom and Dad, before I lost my memory?" Her eyes narrowed, and he rushed to finish his question before she decided to disappear. "Do you remember . . . What did I like?"

"What did you *like*?" she repeated, her face paused in a look of cautious disbelief.

"Yeah, like, what did I enjoy doing? Did I have hobbies?"

Lilli blinked a few times. "Um. You liked to do these stupid puzzles. I mean, Mom and Dad were always giving us these long, complicated puzzles to do, and you really liked them. I was never any good at them." She frowned. "Oh, and you liked camping. You and Dad used to go on camping trips together. He called them your boys' wanderings. You'd spend weeks preparing for them. Mom said she couldn't tell who was more excited about them, him or you." Her voice trembled on the last sentence.

Beside him, Lilli's hand rested on the bench, and he laid his own hand over her cold fingers. He couldn't look at her. His fingers sank to the bench as hers disappeared, and she was gone.

So he liked puzzles and camping, and both activities were linked with his parents. This had been his life only four months ago, and now he had nothing but questions and worries and a sister he couldn't connect with. Chase rested his elbows on his knees and looked out at the black space beyond the mining colony, and tried to pretend he was okay.

CHAPTER FOUR

The *Kuyddestor* pulled up stakes and left the mining colony two days later. Deep space travel was much different in a massive starship than it had been the times Chase had experienced it in a cruiser. He barely noticed when the ship made folds, bending space around it to leap through unimaginably gargantuan parsecs of the cosmos. Aboard the ship, everyone was in an uproar of preparation. Announcements blasted through the loudspeakers, calling different groups to readiness reviews, or reminding soldiers to install the latest system updates to their mod software.

Chase sat in his room, sorting through the contents of an emergency bag he'd put together after the blackout, mainly just a few phoswhites and some packaged rations from the canteen. He kept it near the head of his bunk, to feel like he was at least doing something to be prepared. Everyone else on board was eager to start the new mission—even Parker, who claimed that the new location would give them a much better chance of making headway with his microchip search. It seemed like Chase was the only one with any apprehensions about leaving the Movala system—well, he and his nearly nonexistent sister.

Maurus had asked Chase to meet him in the officers' lounge at 1700 hours so they could go to dinner together. Chase had planned to bring Parker, but Parker had gone off to the engine room that afternoon and wasn't back yet, so at 1658 hours he headed into the hall alone. On his way he stopped by Lilli's room to see if she wanted to join, but she wasn't there either, which irritated him more than he liked to acknowledge. What kind of trouble was she getting into right now? As he walked his mood darkened, until he arrived at the officers' lounge with a scowl on his face.

He hit the entry key, and the door slid open on an empty room. Chase sighed in disgust. Maurus had forgotten and gone to dinner without him.

"Surprise!" cried a chorus of voices coming out of nowhere.

Chase stepped back, confused, and the view of the empty room shimmered and vanished—a hologram projection—revealing that the room was actually packed. There was Maurus and Parker and Lilli, along with Vidal and Seto and a dozen other young officers and pilots. A confused smile touched the corner of Chase's mouth.

"Happy birthday, Chase!" Parker grinned and waved excitedly at the table. "We made you a real cake!"

"Today's my birthday?" Chase asked. An unsettled feeling mixed with the pleasure of the surprise.

Awkward laughter filled the room, and Maurus stepped forward and put his arm around Chase's shoulder. "Lilli told us, and the captain confirmed your birth record."

This, Chase knew, was a lie—there was no public record of his birth. But everyone on the crew knew about his amnesia, which was woven into the captain's cover story about him, Parker, and Lilli being orphans of the Trucon disaster. "Where is the captain?" he asked, looking around.

"He said he'd try to come, but he didn't make it in time for the surprise." Maurus squeezed his shoulder. "Sorry if this was a huge shock. We figured you didn't remember your birthday, but thought this would be the best way to learn about it, right?"

"Are you going to cut this cake or what?" asked Vidal.

Chase glanced around the room again. "Shouldn't we wait for the captain?"

"Don't worry about that," said Maurus. "Go ahead and cut it—we'll see if Vidal can bake as well as she claims."

"Real cake!" repeated Parker, his eyes locked on the confection. "Chocolate!"

"Disrespectful though, isn't it?" Lieutenant Derrick unfolded himself from a chair, speaking not to Chase but to Maurus, his face arch with disdain. "We should wait for the captain."

Maurus glared back, his dark eyes sparking for a challenge.

"Let the kid cut his cake, jeez," said Seto, turning his toothy grin on Derrick, who rolled his eyes and looked away. Sometimes it was hard to tell if Seto's cheerful cluelessness was authentic, or if underneath that grin he knew exactly what was going on.

"Here," said Vidal, handing Chase a slim melamine knife. He looked around the room, flushed. He'd grown comfortable hanging out in the officers' lounge, but it was different with everyone's attention focused on him. For a moment, he stood frozen with the knife in his hand. Maurus began to reach toward his hand, to take the knife away, and with his cheeks burning, Chase lowered his head and began sawing into the rich chocolate frosting.

Vidal helped him hand out plates with slabs of cake on them, finally taking over so that he could enjoy his own piece. He took a seat on a couch, balancing the plate on his lap, and dug in, closing his eyes in pleasure at the first moist, decadent mouthful. Parker was right—real food was always light-years better than synth.

"Mmmm," said Ensign Cutler from a nearby chair, his eyes closed in delight as he ate the cake. "This reminds me of my mom's cooking back on Ueta. She always made us birthday cakes."

"You're from the farmlands, Cutty?" asked Maurus. "How on Taras did you end up in the engine room?"

"What, you think farm boys can't learn to code?" Cutler said with a grin.

Parker was already scraping the last of the frosting off his plate with the edge of his fork. "Jeez, Parker, there's more," said Chase. "Have another piece."

Parker rose from the chair. "Don't mind if I do."

Maurus squinted up at him. "Wow, you've really grown since you came here, haven't you?"

It was true—Parker had sprouted up several inches over the past three months, as if the atmosphere aboard the *Kuydd-estor* encouraged growth. For him at least—not for Chase, who had already been shorter than Parker and now felt positively dwarfed.

"Cheers to you, Chase," said Vidal, who sat in the corner with her friend Lieutenant Chiao. "How old are you now?"

"Fourteen," said Chase. The same age as Parker—at least for a few months.

A flat little voice rang across the room. "No, you're not."

Everyone turned to look at Lilli, who sat perched on the arm of a chair, balancing a plate with an untouched piece of cake on her knees. It was rare that she spent time in the officers' lounge, and rarer still that she spoke. She looked at everyone defensively, shrinking back into herself.

Please don't vanish, please don't vanish, thought Chase. "What do you mean?" he asked.

She stared at him for a moment. "You're thirteen."

"No, I *was* thirteen. Now I'm fourteen."

Lilli shook her head. "You were twelve. Now you're thirteen." Chase began to say no again, certain she was wrong, but she interrupted him, reciting facts rapid-fire. "We celebrated your twelfth birthday last year. Mom surprised you with a blackberry tart instead of a cake. We packed up our dinner and ate a picnic at the lake. I *remember* this."

Heat rushed over Chase's face. Why had he thought he was thirteen? Because Parker had guessed that was his age, and he'd never even questioned that assumption. It wasn't like he'd ever had a reason to talk to anyone about his age. He looked around the room and saw pity on everyone's faces. They didn't know everything about him, but they knew enough to feel bad for the boy with no memory. A boy who couldn't remember his last birthday.

Slowly he set his half-eaten cake on the table. When he raised his gaze, the first thing he saw was Maurus's dark eyes locked on him. The second thing he saw was that Lilli was no longer sitting on the chair. She was no longer in the room at all, but no one had noticed that she'd vanished.

He felt like he was going to explode.

Maurus stood up quickly, setting his empty plate down. "Chase, will you come with me?" Without waiting for a response, he guided Chase out of the quiet lounge and into the hallway, where they walked a while without speaking, their footsteps ringing on the metal floors.

"You've had a harder time adjusting to the ship than Parker has," Maurus finally said.

Chase said nothing at first, placing his hands briefly against his burning cheeks. "He's got all these friends already, and interests. . . . I just—I don't know what to do. What am I supposed to be doing now?"

Maurus hesitated. "Adjusting to your new life. Getting reacquainted with your sister. Building new memories for yourself."

"How do I do that? Am I supposed to forget about everything that happened to me? Stuff like this always happens and gets thrown back in my face."

"It will always be a part of who you are. But as time passes and you learn more and grow more, hopefully the experiences you have will fill you up and make your amnesia seem like a smaller and smaller part of you." Maurus looked ahead. "On Lyolia, belief in fate is a very strong part of our culture. I think you have a very special fate, and the unique events of your life will bring you closer and closer to it."

It was strange to hear Maurus sharing this deeper, philosophical side of himself. Chase tried to think of something to lighten the conversation and move away from the topic of fate. "Yeah, I'm definitely special. I'm the only person I know who has a birthday and gets a year younger."

Maurus smiled and squeezed Chase around the shoulders with one arm. "Do you want to go back to the party?"

"Do I have to?"

"No. Go ahead—I'll tell them the captain called for you."

"He's not coming down to the party, is he?" Chase felt silly for even asking.

Maurus's smile twisted into a regretful look. "No, but you should go visit him on the bridge. I'm sure he'd like to wish you a happy birthday."

Chase shrugged. He already felt stupid enough about his age blunder—he didn't want to interrupt activity on the entire bridge just because it was his birthday. He left Maurus and headed for the stairs, but instead of going up he went down, farther and farther until he was deep in the lower part of the ship somewhere near the engine room, an area he wasn't as familiar with. He wandered the dark metal corridors of the lower halls, looking for anything that might possibly be Lilli's hiding place, but there were too many doors and hallways and ladders to search. Finally he found a dark entryway and sank down against the wall. He closed his eyes and rubbed them. Wherever Lilli's hiding place was, he wasn't going to find it. She'd just stay hidden forever, which was probably the way she wanted it.

Soft footsteps came down the hall and stopped beside him. Opening his eyes, he expected to see his sister and was surprised by the sight of long golden hair—and puffy red eyes. Analora stared back at him in surprise. Her cheeks were shiny with tears.

"Are you okay?" he asked.

"No," she said bluntly. "Are you?"

Chase shrugged and sighed, looking at his hands on his knees. After a moment, Analora came over and sat beside him on the floor. "Sorry, that was a dumb question. Nobody just sits by themself on the floor of the engine deck hallway if they're feeling awesome."

Chase gave a half-laugh and paused, trying to think of something to say. "What are you doing down here?"

"Just walking around. Remembering stuff. I used to play down here with my friends."

Chase looked around at the sterile hallways. "It doesn't look like a ton of fun."

A wistful look crossed her face. "You'd be surprised. When we were really little, when my mom still lived on the ship and I was here all the time, we'd pretend to be defending the ship from raiders. Or sometimes we'd pretend to be the raiders. It was pretty great. Then my parents split up and I started having to go to Jypras half the year, and when I'd come back it would always be something new, a different kind of game." She sighed. "And now they're all gone."

"Your friends? Where are they?"

"Genevieve's parents got transferred to another ship. Samir was older than the rest of us, and smarter than the rest of us, so he went off to university. And Dany . . . he got sent to Fleet academy." Her voice threatened to break. "I went to the engine room to see Chief Kobes—Dany's his son—and he told me he's back on disciplinary status. I can't even message him."

"I'm sorry," said Chase awkwardly.

"No, it's okay," she said, wiping her eyes. "It's stupid of me to sit here and bawl about losing my friends to someone who doesn't know them or me, really." She took a deep breath. "So what's your story?"

Chase hesitated. He'd assumed that she at least knew his cover story about being an orphan from Trucon, but maybe the doctor hadn't told her. Or she hadn't asked. So he told her the sanitized, crew-friendly version of his life story in brief.

Analora's face grew still as she listened to him speak. "That's awful," she said quietly when he was done. "I followed the Trucon events in the news when it happened. I can't even imagine what it was like for you."

Chase shook his head. "It's weird, I don't even remember

my parents. I don't know which I'm sadder about—losing them, or not even remembering who they were to begin with. My sister's here now too, but I don't have any memories of her either. We don't really get along."

"That sounds horrible." She stretched her legs out beside his.

"I guess when you lose the things that matter to you, it kind of feels like you don't know who you are anymore. With or without amnesia."

Analora nodded. "I know that feeling for sure." She knocked her foot companionably against his and smiled at him. "Maybe we can hang out, then, and be a little less lonely."

"I'd like that." Chase returned her smile, and his spirits brightened for the first time that day.

CHAPTER FIVE

Lying in his bunk in the early morning, Chase watched the view from the observation deck on their video screen as a smaller vessel pulled up alongside the *Kuyddestor*. After three days of travel, they had stopped at the edge of the Galloi star system for a rendezvous with a Federation envoy ship, the *Falconer*. In the officers' lounge Chase had overheard that the ambassador sent by the Federation was coming aboard this morning to meet with the captain.

"Do you understand what it is we're supposed to be doing on this mission?" he asked.

The sound of rustling sheets came from the top bunk. "Escorting some peacekeepers," mumbled Parker, half asleep.

"Yeah, but what are they keeping the peace about?"

Parker sighed and rolled over. "This planet we're going to, Storros, wanted to terraform one of its moons, so they hired some workers from another planet in their star system to do it. But then the people from this other planet were pretty happy with the terraforming work they'd done, so at the end they were like, hey, we're gonna just stay here, okay? Bam, conflict. Honestly, you should watch the news once in a while."

Chase rolled his eyes. "Couldn't they just share the moon?"

"If you were having a house built, would you invite the contractors who built it to live in it with you afterward?"

"A moon's a lot bigger than a house."

"Yeah, but the principle's the same." Parker's feet dangled over the edge of the top bunk, and he dropped to the floor and slouched toward his desk. Between working on his microchip and sorting through data about the blackout to look for anything suspicious, nearly all his time lately was spent in front of the computer.

Chase got out of bed and started changing into the clothes he'd left lying on the floor. "So we get to Storros tomorrow?"

"I suppose so. Or maybe later today." Parker started fiddling with a jumble of tiny wires he'd brought back from his last visit to the engine room.

Chase walked to the desk and leaned over to watch Parker laying out each thin wire as he untangled them. "Did hacking into the mainframe help you with the Asa stuff at all?"

"It did, but then I needed to get a more accurate signal reader. I just finally got the right stuff to build one." He kept working, head bent over his desk.

"I'm going up to the observation deck for a closer look at the Federation ship." Chase paused. "Wanna come?"

Parker shook his head, not looking up. "Nah."

Chase slipped out of the room and headed down the hall, but not toward the observation deck. His path went toward the teleport chamber. If someone were trying to entrap Captain Lennard or anyone else on the *Kuyddestor*, the ambassador would be the first possible suspect. Catching a glimpse of the man might not tell Chase much about him, but it was a start.

The room to the teleport chamber was open, and the only person inside was the officer manning the teleport console. Chase groaned internally when he saw who it was. Corporal Liadan Lahey, with her limp brown bob and permanent sour expression, was probably the unfriendliest person on the entire ship—surpassing even Lieutenant Derrick. Swallowing his apprehension, he tried to stroll casually into the room.

"Hey, are the Federation people here?" he asked.

Corporal Lahey looked up from her console with an insta-scowl, pursing her lips. "It's none of your business. Get back to your quarters."

Chase tried again. "I was just curious if the ambassador's on the ship."

"What part of 'get back to your quarters' did you not understand?" Her eyes shrank to angry slits. "Get out of here, or I'll have the MPs escort you off the deck."

Chase opened his mouth to say something, thought better of it, and turned back to the hallway. He knew Parker would have had some kind of smart response for this, but he didn't feel safe risking it, nor could he think of anything halfway clever to say. He was certain that Corporal Lahey was one of the soldiers who'd been sworn to secrecy about Chase's status aboard the ship. He didn't think she knew about his ability, but she'd been one of the few people present when Captain Lennard had accused Chase of being a clone—before Chase proved him wrong by surviving the vaporizing beam of a particle disperser.

Chase headed back down the hallway, thinking he might go to the officers' lounge instead, when a door slid open on his right. He froze as three MPs walked out, followed by a tall, dark-haired woman and two men.

"I do of course appreciate you putting your ship and crew at our disposal with such short notice," one of the men was saying in an overly gracious tone. His face was plump and saggy, and the receding knot of hair on the top of his head was obviously dyed an obnoxious mahogany. He ran his hands over a wide, soft belly that bulged under an expensive-looking caftan.

"It's only our duty, Ambassador," said a familiar booming voice. Captain Lennard followed them out of the room, giving a slight frown as he noticed Chase in the hallway, and continued, "I'll have the crew begin prepping the ship immediately."

Chase frowned. *Prepping the ship for what?*

The ambassador smiled at Lennard in a condescending fashion. "We'll send over a crew of our own people to help with the preparations."

The tall, bony, raven-haired woman beside the ambassador caught sight of Chase and cocked her head. "Is there a large civilian population on your ship, Captain?" she asked in a deep, mellifluous voice.

"Some of our older soldiers have families on board," Lennard said curtly.

The woman took a few steps toward Chase, eyeing him with a curiosity that made him regret coming to the conference level of the ship. "Hello there," she said. "Who are you?"

Chase gulped and looked to Captain Lennard.

"He is one of a small number of cadets we took on board after Trucon," Lennard explained. "His parents were killed in the disaster."

"My dear boy," said the ambassador loudly, shaking back the sleeves of his caftan to spread his hands in a way that Chase guessed was supposed to look welcoming. "Please know from me personally that the Federation acknowledges your loss with great sorrow. *You* are the Federation." His words were slick-perfect, delivered as though he'd spoken them hundreds of times. "Come, Ksenia, we must be getting back to the *Falconer.* Captain, we will rendezvous with you again once we are in Rhima's orbit."

"I'll escort you to the teleport chamber," he said, giving Chase a stern look as he walked past.

Chase hurried away down the hall, but he paused to look back as the group entered the teleport chamber—all but Ksenia, who lingered in the hallway a moment longer, staring directly at Chase.

✳   ✳   ✳

Parker spun around in his seat as soon as Chase got back to their room. "What did you do?" he asked, eyes alight.

Chase stopped where he stood. "What?"

The message flashed on the screen: *Chase Garrety please report to the bridge immediately — end message —*

Busted. The captain must be furious with him for snooping on the meeting and letting himself be seen by an outsider—and not just any outsider, but someone from the Federation. What a dumb mistake.

"What's that all about?" asked Parker. "Chase?"

But Chase had already turned, sweat beading on his forehead, and walked out of the room without answering.

The elevator ride up to the bridge seemed to take forever. On the second floor, directly across from the elevators, was the double-door entry to the bridge. Chase took a step toward it and paused. He'd only been on the bridge a couple of times, and then as a guest—not summoned. He didn't have a badge, so he had to press the notification key and wait to be identified and allowed inside.

The command desks on the bridge were organized in three tiers, all facing a huge video screen. The screen was split into six quadrants—one a feed of the mining colony, two with navigation charts, two filled with scrolling data, and one with the videofeed of a blond woman whom Chase recognized as Parri Dietz, a well-known intergalactic news anchor. In the front tier, the navigation officers sat relaxed, their duties relatively few as long as the ship was orbiting the colony. In the middle tier, the safety and weapons officers sat alongside Colonel Forquera, who glanced back at Chase and resumed the conversation he was having. And in the back tier, Captain Lennard sat at his wide console, with the communications and tactical officers at his side.

Without turning, the captain spoke. "So, you're curious about the peace talks, are you?"

"Um, I just thought maybe..." Chase paused, hoping the captain would start talking again and let him leave the sentence unfinished, but Lennard said nothing. Instead he barreled ahead with the questions that eavesdropping had left him with. "What are we prepping the ship for? Why was the ambassador telling you what to do?"

The captain turned his chair and examined Chase, frowning slightly. "Chase, what do you know about the Federation?"

"They . . . run the Fleet?"

The captain suppressed a smile and looked at the officer beside him, a young woman with light auburn hair cropped short and dark brown skin. "Lieutenant Thandiway, do you take your orders from the Federation?"

"No, sir," the lieutenant answered.

"Does Admiral Cort take his orders from the Federation?"

"No, sir. Separate but united."

"Separate but united," Lennard repeated, looking Chase directly in the eyes for impact. "The Federation and the Fleet are—how much galactic history do you know?"

Chase shook his head. He knew his parents had intentionally kept him unaware about the larger universe, in what was apparently a misguided attempt to shelter him from its dangers. And studying history hadn't exactly been a big priority since he'd come onboard the *Kuyddestor*.

The captain sighed. "I apologize. I'd planned on setting you kids up with a tutor once you got settled, and I'm afraid I dropped the ball on that. I'll put in a crew request once this mission is over." He paused and interlocked his fingers. "Let me see how well I can explain this. Before there was a Federation, about a hundred years ago during the Expansion Era, all the planets operated independently of one another. There were a few individual alliances between planets, but no overarching governing body or regulation structure.

"When the Ganthas star system was discovered—Qesaris, Ueta, Senica, and Trucon, four habitable planets, none of them with preexisting civilizations—it was like this incredible jewel in the middle of the galaxy, and many planets rushed to claim one for themselves. Very quickly this escalated into fighting and became the Ganthas War, which dragged on for years and nearly ruined entire civilizations. In the aftermath, the planets left standing with the fewest losses made the decision to create a governing body for the known universe."

"Which planets?" asked Chase.

"The strongest ones, which we now refer to as the alpha grade planets. It was at this time that they also created the civilization grading system. Now, the Federation needed some sort of body to enforce its regulations, but the alphas were unable to agree on how to organize this, so Earth, who had the largest and most advanced spaceforce, offered to establish the Federal Fleet, with the agreement that officers from other alpha civilizations would be trained and incorporated over time. This promise wasn't actually put into action until very recently, when the officer interchange program began."

"That's how Maurus got into the Fleet, right?" asked Chase.

"Exactly. But do you understand the relationship between the two? The Fleet operates in conjunction with the Federation, but it's run independently. That said, there is a lot of crossover—many former Fleet officers retire to work for the

Federation. Officially, neither body has any say over what the other does . . . but there is an undeniable degree of influence."

"So who's in charge here, the Fleet or the Federation?"

Captain Lennard pushed his chair away from the console. "The Federation is heading to this conflict to mediate a disagreement between two Iota civilizations, and our role here is to support and protect their representatives. That means helping out wherever we can. What you overheard was that Ambassador Corinthe has requested that we host the first round of peace talks aboard the *Kuyddestor*. Both sides insist on sending an entire delegation, and the *Falconer* isn't big enough to accommodate them all."

That sounded like a lot of strangers aboard the ship at one time. Chase didn't say anything, but his panic must have showed on his face. "This is a good thing, Chase," said the captain, softening his tone a bit. "We have a higher level of security aboard the *Kuyddestor*, which means everything will be under our control, and everyone will be safer.

"I'm going to be busy making sure these negotiations go smoothly, so I might not always be available when you need me. If I'm not, you can go to Colonel Forquera with any problems you have, okay?"

Chase glanced down at Forquera, who was still talking with his crew and didn't give any sign he noticed that his name had been mentioned.

The captain leaned toward Chase, waving him to come closer and dropping his voice. "But more importantly, Chase, I need you to promise me that you'll stay on the soldiers' level during the talks tomorrow. There are already a lot of non-*Kuyddestor* personnel onboard right now to help out with preparations, and tomorrow there will be five times as many strangers on the ship. I need you out of sight, for safety's sake. Same goes for your sister and Parker. I need you to keep an eye on them."

Chase started to shake his head. "Lilli's impossible to keep track of. I never know where she's at."

"Then today it's your job to find her, and make sure she understands how important this is."

Chase wanted to explain how she'd been hiding, but that would require talking about her traveling within possible earshot of the bridge crew. "Okay."

"Promise me you'll all keep out of sight, okay?"

"I promise."

The captain smiled. "And I promise you that nothing will go wrong tomorrow."

But somehow, the captain's promise didn't make Chase feel any better.

CHAPTER SIX

Chase sat alone in the canteen running his fork through a plate of greasy synth biryani, wracking his brain for ideas on how he could find his sister before the peace talks began. He hadn't planned on eating alone, but Parker had come with him to get lunch and then left to take his plate back to the room and keep working. Chase scooped up a forkful of rice and stuck it in his mouth just as he realized that someone was standing across from him. Analora pushed her hair behind her ears and smiled at him as she sat down.

"Hey," he said, gulping quickly. "I haven't seen you around."

She shrugged. "I've been catching up with my dad. He always wants to hang out together all the time when I first come back here. Takes a while before things get back to normal."

"Ah." He stirred his rice awkwardly, and set his fork down. "We're supposed to arrive at Storros tomorrow. Are you excited?"

She shrugged. "I guess. I doubt we'll be allowed to go visit Storros ourselves. The Storrians have a super strict immigration policy."

It hadn't even occurred to Chase that they might ordinarily have been able to go visit a planet they were stationed near. "How many planets have you been to?" he asked.

"Oh, gosh, a lot." She began counting off on her fingers. "Earth, Jypras, Banafiel, Namat, so about four origin planets, plus maybe half a dozen colony planets."

"Did you ever go to Trucon?"

She grew quiet. "Yeah, my mom and I went there once for a conference in Rother City." She looked cautiously at Chase. "It was a nice place. Very sunny."

Chase had only meant to find a planet in common that they had both visited, but he realized she thought he was from Trucon. Desperately he tried to change the topic. "So, what's Jypras like?"

"It's all water," she said, shaking her head. "How do you like living on the *Kuyddestor* now?"

Chase placed his napkin over his plate as he considered this. "It's okay. I don't have much to do, besides my appointments with your dad. The blackout last week was kind of exciting."

She grinned. "I slept through it. Time adjustment from Jypras." She looked at the walls around them. "I guess the old girl needs to go in for a tune-up."

Without thinking, Chase said, "Parker thinks somebody hacked the power grid."

She frowned at him. "Who's Parker?"

Before she even asked the question, Chase regretted saying Parker's name. He liked having his own secret friend, someone he could just pretend to be normal around without all the baggage of his past that Parker and everyone else knew about. "Uh, he's a friend," he muttered.

"Why does he think someone hacked the power grid?" She wasn't going to let this go, Chase could tell.

He sighed. "He's pretty good at hacking and electronics and stuff like that, so he's been trying to figure out what caused the blackout."

Analora leaned forward, her curiosity fully piqued. "Why didn't you mention him before? Is he from Trucon as well? Can we go see what he's doing?"

"Um, Parker doesn't like to interact when he's working on something. He doesn't really like people at all, actually." Well, at least the first part was true.

"Oh." Analora's face fell.

Chase's mind raced for a way to grab her interest again. "Oh hey, I met the ambassador," he said. "Corinthe. He was on the ship."

"Really? Did you hear they're hosting the peace talks on the *Kuyddestor*?"

"Yeah." After thinking it over more, Chase had decided that this did make him feel slightly better about the mission—if the *Kuyddestor* was such an important part of the process, the Fleet really couldn't do anything bad to them. "The captain ordered me to stay on the soldiers' level the whole time. He thinks I'll...get in the way or something. So I'm not going to get to see anything."

"Oh. Well, that stinks." Analora fiddled with his empty tray, looking like she was thinking hard. "There are ways around that, you know."

"What do you mean?" asked Chase.

She gave him a sly grin. "I know every inch of this ship, and all its secrets. Trust me—there's a way."

※　　※　　※

Standing in a narrow back hallway on the soldiers' level near the ship's maintenance offices, Chase watched as Analora wedged a knife stolen from the canteen into a panel of the wall, popping it loose. Behind was a black crawlspace with a bracket of wires running overhead.

Chase crouched and stuck his head through the opening, looking down the dark tunnel inside. "We're going in there?"

"Behind the walls there's a whole other *Kuyddestor*," said Analora. "The maintenance corridors. You just have to know the right places to get to them."

"How do we get out again?" In the back of his mind, a voice that sounded suspiciously like Parker's said, *You phase through it, dummy.* But he couldn't do that with Analora around. She thought he was normal—he didn't want her to see that he was actually a freak.

"We can push this panel back out from the inside. This hall's usually empty, so we just have to be sure to come back to the same spot. I've never been caught." She held the panel steady with a knee as she looped her hair up on top of her head. "Get in and head to the right. I'll be behind you."

Looking quickly up and down the hall, Chase crept inside the wall. The crawlspace was dark and dusty, but as he scuffled along, his eyes adjusted and he realized there were ventilation spots every so often that let a tiny amount of light through. Behind him, he heard Analora get inside and pull the panel shut. He glanced back at her once and she flapped a hand, waving him onward.

After a few minutes, the crawlspace ended, but someone had cut a neat hole in the metal, and he crept out into an open space. As he waited for Analora to join him, he looked around. They were now in a tall, narrow corridor that curved and disappeared in the distance. Square utility lights sunk into the wall every few meters provided dim light, and the air was hot and smelled like wax and hair.

Analora clambered out, rubbing the dust off her hands and grinning.

"Where are we?" he asked in a whisper.

"We're in the maintenance area, beside the ship's air filtration and climate control." She placed a hand on the tall wall beside them. "This is the influx chamber."

"How do you know all this?"

"My friend Dany knew the ship better than any of us. We used to come back here all the time, and he'd explain where we were and how everything worked." Her voice sounded soft and happy describing these memories, and Chase felt a tiny twinge of jealousy toward this person he'd never met.

They walked along the wall of the gigantic influx chamber. At one point the closed crawlspace beside them curved back into the wall, creating a little alcove. Chase squinted at something crumpled in the corner. "Hold on," he said. He crouched in the corner and picked it up, shaking out what appeared to be a woolen Fleet standard-issue blanket.

Chase squeezed the blanket, suddenly feeling ill. Could *this* be where Lilli spent her time hiding—in a dark corner inside the walls of the ship? He felt around on the floor and up around the pipes running along the wall, but there were no other clues as to who might have left the blanket.

"Is everything okay?" asked Analora.

"How big is the interior maintenance area, the whole thing?" Chase asked. "Could we walk through it all right now?"

"Oh, no way. It's huge, and not all the parts are connected. There are a bunch of different entry spots we used to use."

How would he find out where Lilli hid? There had to be a million places like this one. Chase looked down the long walkway in despair. Did she even come back to the same spot, or did she hide all over the place?

"Come on." Analora grabbed the metal rung of a ladder embedded in the wall. "Let me show you how to get to the conference level."

Watching Analora navigate the maintenance corridors and the randomly placed ladders that connected them, Chase grew more and more impressed with how well she knew the interior of the ship. "The best way to get up and down levels is in the rear of the ship, where the energy core is," she told him. "The core cuts through from the lowest level up to, I think, the fifth? It's inside an insulation chamber, but the outside of that chamber has entry points and ladders. We're at the wrong part of the ship to get to it right now, though."

They climbed up to a level where Analora said the teleport chamber and conference rooms were located and walked along another musty corridor, this one longer and darker, until they reached another crawlspace with the end cut out.

"Did you do this?" asked Chase as he pointed at the hole, although he already had half an idea what the answer would be.

"It was Dany. A couple have been found and patched, but most of his modifications are still here."

"Didn't he get in trouble for cutting up the ship?"

"Dany didn't like rules," she said simply.

They moved along the crawlspace, Analora leading the way this time. She paused in front of each group of ventilation slits, peering out to see where they were. At the third, she pulled her head back sharply, peered out again, and turned to Chase with wide eyes.

Look, she mouthed.

He squinted through the ventilation holes, at what appeared to be the entrance to a meeting room. Two armed MPs stood guard outside the room, but a third person stood there as well—a blond woman in a suit, adjusting her hair. Something about her looked very familiar, but Chase couldn't immediately place her. She removed an item from her pocket and held it out at arm's length from her face, where it hovered in the air, a flat disk that faced her. She cleared her throat, and that's when Chase realized who she was.

"This is Parri Dietz, coming to you live from the IFF *Kuyddestor*, where tomorrow the first round of peace talks in the

Storros/Werikos conflict will take place. Federation Ambassador Royben Corinthe is leading the process, with representatives from both parties seated at the table. More details as the story emerges. Back to you, Boris."

Parri Dietz paused a moment and then plucked the disk out of the air. "Did you get that? Okay. I'll have something more for you in a few minutes. No, this isn't going to take long—this one's just a formality." She stuffed the disk in her pocket and turned away, heading down the hall.

Grinning excitedly, Analora motioned to Chase that he should head back the way they came. It wasn't until they'd both climbed out of the crawlspace that she grabbed his arm and said, "Good stars, did you see who that was? We're going to be on the Universal Newsfeed!"

"Not *us*," said Chase cautiously. The last thing he needed was his face plastered on newsfeed screens across the galaxy.

"Well, no, but the ship—and probably people we know. This is so exciting!"

Having located the conference level—and being unable to top the excitement of seeing Parri Dietz on the ship—they headed back down to the soldiers' level, to exit where they came in by the maintenance offices. Analora went first so she could open the right panel, but she was halfway out of the wall when Chase heard her say a surprised "Oh!"

Tapping footsteps approached in the hallway. By the time Chase climbed out of the wall, the ambassador's colleague Ksenia stood before them, a half-smile on her face. "Well, this is interesting," she said in her rich voice. "What exactly are you doing?"

Analora's face was scarlet. "Just playing around."

Pushing aside his first impulse, which was to turn and run like a chicken, Chase went on the offensive instead. "What are you doing down here? These are the soldiers' quarters."

"Ah, the young Trucon survivor," Ksenia said with a curious smile. "Hello again. Perhaps you can help me—I seem to have gotten lost in my search for your utility officer. My translink is malfunctioning, and we don't have any spares of this particular model on the *Falconer*." She smiled and tapped her ear as she said this.

Chase had no idea what she was talking about, but Analora pointed down the hall toward the elevator and told her, "Utility office is on the sixth floor."

"Ah, there's the problem—I always mix up six and seven. They sound so similar to me." She smiled, but Chase felt like her dark eyes were examining the two of them. He glanced away, uncomfortable. She waved a graceful hand at the panel that still hung half open on the wall. "We can keep your little adventure to ourselves. Thank you for your help."

As Ksenia strolled back down the hall, Analora lifted the panel again, and Chase helped her fit it back in its place. "Well, that was embarrassing," she said. "I didn't even hear her footsteps."

"Do you think she was really looking for the utility office?" asked Chase.

Analora frowned. "What else would she be doing?"

They walked back toward the staircase that Analora would take down to her quarters. Chase kept his voice low as they passed his room, and didn't point out that that was where he lived. They had nearly made it to the stairs when the door to the officers' lounge slid open, and Parker stepped out. Chase clenched his teeth and uttered one of Maurus's curses in his mind.

"Hey, I was looking for you! I think I found—oh, who's your friend?" A smile curling across his face, he extended his hand toward Analora. "I don't think I've seen you around here before?"

"You must be Parker," she said, smiling sweetly as she shook his hand. "I've heard about you."

Parker frowned. "Unfortunately, I can't say the same."

"Well, I'm Analora and I need to get home to dinner." She stepped backward out the door.

"Nice to meet you, Analora who needs to get home to dinner."

"Same to you!" She stopped before she headed into the stairwell. "See you tomorrow, Chase!"

"You bet!" he called in a cheery voice, not looking over at Parker until the door closed.

"Found a new friend?" asked Parker, leaning against the hallway wall.

"I met her a few days ago."

"Huh. Interesting."

"You've made some friends on the ship too."

"Never said I hadn't. I was looking for you so I could tell you I finally got a pingback on my chip this morning. I wasn't able to trace the location, but it's something."

Excitement immediately washed out Chase's irritation. "Really? That's awesome."

"Yeah, well, don't get too excited just yet. It's still not enough to find Asa."

"But you're closer now."

Parker nodded. "He's out there somewhere. We'll find him."

They started back down the hall toward their room. "Oh hey," said Chase. "I just saw Parri Dietz upstairs."

This caught Parker's full attention. "What? She's on board?"

"Yeah, I guess she's here covering the peace talks."

"I can't believe she got permission to come on the ship. She's the top news anchor in the galaxy—not to mention the best looking." Parker waggled his eyebrows. "Did you talk to her?"

Chase gave him an incredulous look. "What do you think? Would this face look good on the five o'clock news?"

"I didn't mean interview, geez. What would she want with a skinny thirteen-year-old like you?"

Chase pressed his lips together and stopped speaking. Parker had decided that the best way to show Chase he didn't care about him being a year younger than they'd thought was to make fun of Chase's age constantly—which only made it worse. Parker nudged his arm. "Come on, buddy, I'm just joking. You know I don't care if you're one or two or ten years younger than me."

Says the guy who's turning fifteen in a few months, thought Chase. He hit the entry button and went straight to his bunk, ignoring Parker's apologies.

"Well, maybe not ten years. I can't really see myself hanging out with a four-year-old. But seriously, get over it. It's not like knowing your real age means—"

Parker went silent. After a few moments, Chase looked up at him standing in the middle of the room with a look of frozen shock on his face. "What?"

Parker dashed to his desk, ruffling through papers and equipment, overturning files and keypads.

Chase walked up beside him, catching a circuit board that was about to tip onto the floor. "What is it?"

Parker turned to him, pale. "My microchip. It's gone."

CHAPTER SEVEN

Chase watched numbly as Parker tore apart his desk, shoving wires and equipment to the floor as he searched for the missing microchip. "How long were you out of the room?" he asked.

"I just went over to the canteen for something quick to eat, but I ran into Cutty there and ended up going to the lounge with him to play cards for a while. When were *you* last here?"

Chase sat on his bunk, trying to remember. "I . . . I don't know. I left the room before lunch, when you were still down in the engine room."

"Was this error message scrolling?" Parker asked, pointing at the screen.

"Um. Something was scrolling."

Parker rolled his eyes. "You're no help. I'm going to the armory to report it stolen." He turned and charged from the room before Chase could say another word.

Chase started sorting through the mess that was left on the desk, sliding wires and boards into little piles. Who would have wanted Parker's chip? Had Parker stumbled onto something chasing after this imaginary blackout hacker and made himself an enemy on the ship? Or was it someone from outside the ship who'd snuck on board with the crew preparing for the peace talks? Could it have been the reason Ksenia was down on the soldiers' level? But what would a Federation employee want with Parker's microchip—was he a target?

Out of habit, Chase turned on the video screen and flipped through to the bridge. The captain wasn't there—probably busy with the preparations on the conference level.

The door slid open, and Parker walked in with Colonel Forquera, speaking rapid-fire as they entered. Parker looked up and froze, his eyes going wide.

"What?" asked Chase. As soon as the word passed his lips, he knew. Parker was looking past him, at the video screen. At the bridge.

"What is that?" asked Forquera, his voice dangerously low.

"It was like that when we moved in," said Parker quickly. "I figured it was standard."

"That's a lie." The colonel's eyes traveled over the messy desk and scattered equipment. "What are you building in here?"

"You know all this." Parker swept his arm around the room in frustration. "I've been working on reverse tracking my microchip. You know, the one that was just stolen."

But Forquera was already on his communicator, calling the master-at-arms for MPs and a software specialist. Parker's eyes were angry laser beams, fixed on Chase.

Master-at-arms Poliski, a brutish man with a tiny nose and floppy blond hair, showed up personally with three members of his crew. Feeling ill about what he'd caused, Chase watched them standing tight-lipped around Parker's desk as the specialist went through his files, uncovering just how much Parker had hacked into.

"Do you think his hacking might have caused the blackout?" murmured Poliski to the specialist.

The specialist nodded. "Most definitely. He got into nearly every system."

"Oh, that is such garbage!" shouted Parker. "I'm the only one on the ship who was investigating the blackout!"

"How did you break into the mainframe of the ship?" asked the specialist. "Who was helping you?"

"Helping me?" asked Parker indignantly. "I knew more about hacking by the time I was five than you ever will."

Shut up, shut up! thought Chase. Did Parker really need to brag about how easily he was able to break the rules?

"You're completely oblivious to what's really going on," Parker continued. "There's a hacker on the ship, a really good one—almost as good as me. That's who caused the blackout. Ask Chief Kobes, I've been helping him. I'm the only one who can help you find who it is."

"I'm supposed to believe a kid is the best hacker on this ship?" asked the specialist, smirking, as the MPs swept everything from the desk into boxes.

Parker whirled around on him. "You learned about software code, what, from teachers, from books? I learned from an android. When I was two. I *think* in code." He stepped up in Poliski's face. "Aren't you even going to do anything about my stolen chip?"

The master-at-arms gave him a sardonic nod. "We'll look into it."

Forquera, standing at the back of the room, shook his head as the crew carted away their boxes full of Parker's equipment. "I'll take this news to the captain. He'll decide what to do." The door closed behind Forquera as he left, and Parker looked back at his empty desk, clenching his fists.

"You'll get it all back," Chase reassured him. "The captain will—"

"Will what?" snapped Parker. "Will take time out of organizing the peace talks between two planets to make sure I get my way? Why did you have the bridge on the screen? You knew I was going to look for help!"

"I just . . . forgot," Chase admitted.

Parker ran his hands through his hair and squeezed his skull, groaning. "Chief Kobes won't even let me in the engine room after he finds out about this. I need to go talk to him before someone else does." He dropped his hands and turned on Chase. "You're coming with me this time."

Chase had to hurry to follow Parker's swift march to the elevators, and when they'd taken them down to the bottom floor, Parker walked so quickly on his long legs that Chase practically had to run to keep up. In the engine room, a group of green-badged ensigns sat gathered at a cluster of consoles. Chief Kobes paced behind them, hands clasped behind his back, and watched them work with his standard dissatisfied expression.

"I have to talk to you," said Parker in unnaturally loud, strident tones. "I need your help."

Chief Kobes glanced up at him. "I haven't got time for you right now, Parker. We're doing trainings all day here. Stow it 'til after tomorrow."

"Please." The strained quality in Parker's voice made Kobes look over at him again. "The MPs have taken all my stuff. They're accusing me of all kinds of things I didn't do. You know I didn't cause the blackout. I've been helping you investigate it!"

With frightening alacrity, the chief engineer crossed the room and grabbed Parker by the arm. He pushed him into an empty corner, and Chase was close enough behind them to see the real fear that flashed through Parker's eyes.

"Helping me investigate?" growled Kobes. "Getting underfoot is what you've been doing, and I've been tolerating it because the captain told me to give you some leeway. Whatever you've been up to with all the junk you've been taking from my engine room, you'd better hope to the high-handed heavens that you didn't cause the blackout, or I personally will make sure that you are removed from this ship."

"I was helping you," said Parker. The surprised hurt on his face moved Chase to anger. No wonder Dany Kobes defied the rules, if this jerk was the father he'd grown up answering to.

"Parker didn't cause the blackout. Someone on your team probably did, and you don't even know who it was." As soon as he'd blurted the words out, Chase regretted them.

Kobes turned on him, his eyes wide and threatening. "Both of you. Out. Don't come back."

Parker tore free and stormed out of the engine room, his face flushed. Chase hurried after him. "Hey, we'll go talk to the captain. He'll fix this."

"Leave me alone, Chase. Don't try to help." Parker stormed toward the stairs, slamming the door behind him as he left.

He couldn't talk to Captain Lennard now, but after the

peace talks were over, he was sure the captain would make sure that Parker got his equipment back, especially if he was able to show that he hadn't caused the blackout. That still didn't answer the question of who had taken the microchip. On his way back to their room, he took a detour to pass by the conference room and check if Ksenia was still on the ship.

The conference room door was open, and he could hear voices inside. He pressed himself against the wall to listen, ready to phase through and hide if need be.

"I won't allow it," came Captain Lennard's voice. "I gave you permission to cover the peace negotiations, that's all."

"But, Captain, the galaxy wants to hear his side of the story. And yours." Chase recognized the smooth, well-modulated voice—it was Parri Dietz. What was she still doing on the ship? "You made yourselves inaccessible immediately after the situation was resolved, and we never got to hear the story in Lieutenant Maurus's own words."

"It will turn into a witch hunt," said Lennard. "I won't expose my soldier to those kinds of risks."

"Captain, it's been months now—the galaxy has moved on from the Trucon disaster. I'll make it a short interview. Five minutes—ten, tops."

"Permission not granted, Ms. Dietz. Now kindly remove yourself from my ship and let me get back to work." Lennard left the room, speaking into a commlink on his wrist. "Poliski, send someone down to the conference room to escort Ms. Dietz off the ship." He didn't even notice Chase standing by the door.

Parri Dietz stayed in the room, but Chase could hear her speaking in a low voice. He knew he should leave, but he kept listening, trying to figure out what she was saying. It surprised him when she stepped out a moment later and quickly turned to face him.

"Hello," she said with a pleasant smile. Her cool blue eyes sparkled. "What's your name?"

He'd learned better than to give his real name to strangers. "Corbin."

"Say, Corbin, do you know where I could find Lieutenant Maurus?"

Why was she so interested in Maurus? Was it really just a news story, or was she looking for something more? His name had been cleared, and the last thing he needed was someone dredging up his role in the Trucon disaster and airing it on the galactic news all over again. "No," Chase said harshly. "Leave him alone."

✳   ✳   ✳

When Chase went to bed that night, Parker was already in the upper bunk, turned toward the wall so Chase couldn't tell if he was sleeping or sulking. He whispered Parker's name a few times but got no response.

He pulled back the thin Fleet-regulation quilt and climbed into bed. Tomorrow he would find Colonel Forquera and argue on Parker's behalf. Together they would hunt down his microchip and bring the thief to justice. He rolled over and slid his hand under his pillow. His fingers touched something hard and crinkly, and he pulled it out. It was a piece of paper.

Chase jumped out of bed and went to the video screen, swiping it on so he could look at the paper in the dim glow of the screen. When he saw what was written on the paper, he gasped.

"What are you doing?" muttered Parker.

But Chase didn't answer, staring at the words on the slip of paper.

Sorry about the microchip. I can tell you everything you want to know about your parents and Asa Kaplan. Meet me tomorrow at the Rostanna in Lumos.

-A friend

CHAPTER EIGHT

"We're going to Lumos." These were the first words out of Parker's mouth when he read the note that Chase had discovered under his pillow.

Chase set the note on the desk and stared, still not quite believing what was written on it. "We have to take this to Colonel Forquera. What's Lumos?"

"It's a city on Storros." Pulling a jacket on over his pajamas, Parker paused. "I think it's the capital, actually. But we're not taking this to Forquera. The captain needs to see it."

Chase didn't argue. "We're supposed to be hiding out in our quarters tomorrow. He's never going to let us leave the ship."

Parker gave him a steely look. "This person has my microchip. I have no other way to pursue Asa—it's our only chance to learn anything. Are you really going to let anyone stop you?"

Chase knew what Parker meant. The possibility of answers, of a mysterious friend who could help them, was an opportunity he couldn't fathom passing up.

"We'll make him see how important this is," said Chase.

Parker shrugged as he hit the exit key on the door. "And if he still says no, we'll go anyway."

*　　*　　*

Captain Lennard came to the entrance of his quarters in his shirtsleeves, collar and cuffs unbuttoned.

"What is it, boys?" he sighed. His tired eyes were surrounded with stacks of wrinkles. His gaze rested on Parker. "Colonel Forquera told me what happened. I can't give you back your equipment, Parker. That was a very serious—"

"Did he tell you someone stole my microchip?" Parker interrupted.

Chase held out the scrap of paper. "Someone was in our room. They stole Parker's chip and left me a note."

Frowning, Lennard took the paper and read it for what felt like a very long time. He took a step back. "Come inside."

They sat across from him at his desk and explained everything that had happened that day. Parker did most of the talking, skimming over some of the details when it came to how he hacked the mainframe. When he was done, Lennard nodded gravely, rubbing his eyebrows.

"I don't have a lot of manpower to spare tomorrow because of the peace talks," he began slowly. "But I'll send a small expeditionary squad down to Lumos in the morning to see what they can find."

"We're going with them," said Chase.

Lennard shook his head. "I can't let you go. We don't know who left that note. This could be a trap."

"You're not *letting* us go?" said Parker. "What gives you the authority to keep us here? You're not our father."

"I'm not, but as your self-appointed guardian, I'm certainly going to be calling the shots until you're a little more self-reliant than fourteen," Lennard snapped.

"You think we're going to get kidnapped? You know no one can catch him, right?" Parker threw his hand in Chase's direction. "Invincible superboy, remember? What are you worried about? The person who contacted him isn't going to come out unless he shows up anyway."

"If there's something of merit to this note, the exped squad will find out. That's what they're trained to do. I'm not sending children after some anonymous thief."

"What am I supposed to do?" Chase burst out. "Sit here and wait for news? Do you remember what I went through to get here? I'll be safe. Nobody can trap me."

"Chase, I understand—" the captain said gently.

"No! Look at me." Chase raised his hand and plunged it into the desk, phasing through wood and paper and whatever else the captain was storing in his drawers. "Do you know what it's like to wonder every single day who my parents were and why they were killed and if there's ever anything I'll be able to do about it? I am trapped on this ship with this weird body and all these questions, and I know you put yourself at risk to let us stay here, but please, please don't make me stay here and miss the only lead I've ever gotten and may ever get."

Lennard sat quietly for a minute, looking at the desk where Chase had phased through. Finally he nodded. "Chase, be at the teleport deck at five hundred hours. You'll go down with the expeditionary force—I'll make sure it's Maurus's squad. You will do exactly as you're told by the squad leader. If you're told to leave, you will leave. Parker, I'm sorry, but you're right. Chase is less vulnerable than you. I can't let you go along."

Parker fumed, realizing he'd set himself up to be excluded. "Whatever," he mumbled, standing up to leave.

He didn't speak to Chase at all on their way back to their quarters. They turned off the lights and climbed into their bunks silently, but Chase was so wound up with the idea of going to Storros the next day, he couldn't sleep.

"Parker," he whispered. "How am I going to find this person?"

For a moment Parker didn't answer, and Chase thought he might be asleep. "I wouldn't worry about it," came his tired voice. "Whoever it is, they'll definitely be looking for you."

＊　　＊　　＊

Chase grabbed a synth croissant from the canteen on the way to the teleport chamber, wolfing it down in the elevator as he tapped his foot nervously. He'd only ever taken a teleport twice before that he could remember, and the second trip hadn't gone so well—malfunctioning to place him a good hundred meters away from where he was supposed to appear. He tried to reassure himself by noting that that had happened a long time ago, and this was a different teleporter.

He paused outside the chamber door, listening for voices to make sure he wouldn't be the only one in the room with Corporal Lahey. He could hear someone laughing, so he entered.

His heart sank when he saw who was inside. Lieutenant Derrick leaned over the console, talking to Lahey. To Chase's surprise, she was actually smiling. They both spotted Chase at the same time, and their smiles dried up on their faces.

Derrick stood up straight, scowling. "What are you doing here, kid?"

Before Chase could formulate an answer, voices sounded in the hall, and a second later Maurus entered the chamber with Lieutenants Vidal and Seto.

Maurus cast a scathing look at Derrick. "*He's* not on the mission, is he?"

"Of course not," said Vidal in a no-nonsense tone. "Derrick, you're here to supervise escort duty for the peace talks, right? When are the guests supposed to start arriving?"

Pulling his glare away from Maurus, Derrick turned to Vidal and said stiffly, "Any time now."

"Then we should get out of your way." Vidal approached Chase, holding out a folded piece of soft, light gray material and a tiny silver object shaped like a horn. "You'll need these for the mission."

"What are they?"

She picked up the silver horn. "The translink goes in your ear. Hold still." She reached out and gently tipped his head to the side, placing the silver object inside his right ear. For a moment it tickled as the device expanded and settled into his ear canal, and he squirmed.

"It's an automatic interpreter. You'll need to be able to understand what anyone's saying," said Maurus. "Not everyone speaks the common language." He started speaking in another language, the sharp, fluid tongue that Chase guessed was his native Lyolian. Almost simultaneously another voice rang inside his head, drowning out what he could still hear in his left ear: "This is the language I spoke growing up, and now you can understand it."

Chase cocked his head. "I hear two voices. It's hard to pick out the translation."

"It just takes practice. Pretty soon your ear with the trans-link will become dominant and you won't even hear the other voice."

"Everyone wears these?"

"Fleet soldiers get them as implants. Standard issue."

Chase kneaded his ear, trying to rub away the phantom tickling sensation, and held up the gray cloth with his other hand. Vidal took an identical one from her pocket and shook it out. It was a tube of cloth that she pulled over her head, letting it fall into folds around her neck. "It's a filter. Just in case you have any trouble with the atmosphere," she said, lifting it up over her mouth to demonstrate. Chase pulled his on, as did the others.

"Alright," said Vidal, passing out the silver return rings that they would need to get back to the *Kuyddestor.* "Our mission on Lumos is to track down an unknown acquaintance of the intergalactic weapons dealer Asa Kaplan, aka Jonah Masters, for information regarding his whereabouts. Is everyone clear?"

Derrick narrowed his eyes at Chase. "Why's the kid coming along?"

"That information's classified," said Maurus smugly. Derrick flashed him a hateful glare.

Vidal led the group on to the teleport circles stamped into the floor. "Corporal Lahey, if you would."

As he watched Lahey's hands fly over the console, Chase's heart began thumping wildly in his chest. The sensation of teleportation began, a burning tingle that ran up his back and down all his limbs. *Keep it together, keep it together,* he told himself. Suddenly the feeling ratcheted up a thousand degrees, and it felt like his entire body was stretched thin and set on fire, a pain more intense than anything he'd ever felt.

He heard himself start to scream, and the world went dark.

✳   ✳   ✳

Chase awoke lying atop a cot surrounded by curtains, in a white space he recognized as the medical bay. The pain was gone. So was everyone else. Confused, he sat up and reached for a curtain.

"Hello?" he called.

Soft footsteps approached, and Dr. Bishallany's shining head poked through the curtains. "There he is," he said with a smile. "Our hero resurfaces."

Chase dropped his arm. "What happened?"

Dr. Bishallany stepped inside the small space and sat on the edge of the cot. "What do you remember?"

"We were teleporting, and . . . it hurt. A lot. I blacked out."

Dr. Bishallany nodded. "And to your great fortune, you didn't go anywhere. According to the teleport officer, you faded out a little and snapped back together in a heap on the floor."

"Where's everyone else?"

"They've continued on the mission without you."

"What?" He looked down and saw that the return ring he'd worn was gone. The realization that he was missing the mission hit like a punch to the stomach. He couldn't believe Maurus had left him behind.

"Chase, you told me you'd used a teleport once before, yes? Can you tell me exactly what happened that time?"

Chase took a deep breath. "The first time was okay. I mean, it kinda burned, but I went where I was supposed to go. The second time . . ." He trailed off in embarrassment, realizing he should have told the doctor this story before. But they'd never discussed teleportation.

"Yes?"

"The second time I knew what was coming, and I think I flinched or something. And instead of teleporting to where I was supposed to go, I ended up outside the building." He left off the detail of the scaly Zinnjerha creatures that had swarmed over him, giving the first clue of his phasing ability when he escaped their claws unscathed.

Dr. Bishallany pursed his lips, deep in thought. "Chase, I

believe that in the time since you acquired your ability, your body has slowly developed a resistance to teleportation. In the same way that some people develop allergies, you felt only a small reaction the first time—the burning isn't normal, you know. The only side effect of teleportation, in a very small percentage of the population, is headaches. You had a stronger reaction the second time, and then when you were fired on with a disperser, which is basically the same technology, it was the straw that broke the camel's back. There's nothing you can do about it. It's a reflex you can't control."

Chase looked up with a stricken expression. "You mean I'll never be able to teleport?"

The doctor placed a reassuring hand on Chase's blanket-covered foot. "It's not the end of the world—space cruisers can still get you pretty much anywhere teleportation goes."

"So can I take a cruiser down to join up with Maurus and the others?"

Dr. Bishallany frowned. "The captain thinks it best you sit this one out. I'm sorry. If you're feeling okay, you're free to leave the medical bay whenever you like."

As the doctor stood and left, Chase stared at the blankets, reeling in defeat. Finally he'd been so close to making some real progress in his search, and thanks to his stupid freak body, now he was back to square one. Whoever had left the note probably wouldn't show themselves to Maurus, and he'd never know who it was or what they wanted to tell him. What an epic screw-up. He was so deep in his thoughts, he didn't notice anyone else around until a familiar sarcastic voice rang out.

"Doesn't feel good to get left behind, does it?"

Chase looked up, expecting to see only Parker standing by his bed. His gut hitched when he saw Analora at his friend's side, her brow creased with worry. The petty smirk on Parker's face faded. "Oh, man, I'm sorry. Are you okay?"

Chase's eyes flickered over to Analora. He couldn't tell Parker the whole story in front of her. "No teleportation for me today," he said in a tight voice.

Parker walked around the bed and punched him lightly on the shoulder. "You know, buddy, I've never been a big fan of the teleport." Of course, Parker had grown up with the knowledge that his parents were killed in a teleport accident. "At least you're okay."

"I lost my only chance to find that person," Chase said in a hoarse whisper. "To find your chip."

"It's okay. If this person wants to talk to you that badly, they'll come back. Making you go down to Storros was pretty shady anyway."

Analora finally spoke up. "So I still don't understand what happened. Someone stole something from your room and wanted to meet with Chase on Storros about it? Why?"

Parker shrugged. "It's . . . complicated. Not like you couldn't understand it," he added hurriedly as her eyes narrowed. "Just like . . . we can't tell you everything."

"I should be down there with Maurus," Chase mumbled, his mind still fixed on the huge opportunity he had missed.

Analora had gone very quiet, her brows knitting furiously. "We could still go," she said in a barely audible tone.

"Go where?" asked Parker. "Storros?"

She raised a finger to her lips. "Let's get out of here," she whispered.

Chase hopped off of the bed and followed Parker and Analora. Outside the curtained-off space, the medical bay was quiet, two long rows of empty beds. One nurse sat at a desk entering information at a console, but she only glanced up briefly as they left. Dr. Bishallany was nowhere in sight.

They slipped out the door and hurried down the metal corridor. Once they'd put some distance between themselves and the medical bay, Analora began talking. "When you came onboard, did anyone walk you through an emergency drill? Did they show you where the jump pods are?"

"Yeah," said Chase slowly. The jump pods were the escape shuttles for civilians and non-flight personnel. "But they only work when the emergency procedures are engaged."

"Well . . . there's a way around that."

Chase stopped in the middle of the hallway. "You're saying

we steal a jump pod to go to Storros?" Even Parker looked a little wary.

Analora stopped, tracing a finger along the wall of the corridor. "There are more than enough for everyone on the ship."

This was a crazy idea. She was clearly crazy. "I thought they just land on the nearest hospitable planet. Could we even make it come anywhere close to Lumos?"

"Oh. Well, no, you can't pilot a jump pod. There aren't any controls," said Analora.

Parker finally chimed in. "But there's got to be some sort of automated guidance system built in. I might be able to figure out how to override the automated part."

Chase burned a little at the admiring look Analora gave Parker. "We'd get in huge trouble," he said. "How do you know about this, anyway?"

Analora dropped her gaze to the floor, and her voice fell. "It's why Dany got sent to Fleet academy."

Parker arched an eyebrow. "Who's Dany?"

"He's my friend, Chief Kobes's son," she began softly. "We were orbiting Namat last year, and he really wanted to go see the Namatans, but he got in a big fight with his dad. As a punishment Chief Kobes forbid him to go, so instead he rigged a jump pod to take him down. A day later they found him there and brought him back, and Chief Kobes kicked him off the ship and sent him to Fleet academy."

"Sounds like the chief to me," said Parker, a bitter note in his voice.

"We can't do this," said Chase. "Parker and I have nowhere else to go."

Parker put a hand on his shoulder. "Hold on. It's not like Captain Lennard is going to kick us off the ship. Yeah, we'll get yelled at. Won't be the first time, either."

"He could send *us* to military school."

Parker rolled his eyes. "Yeah, right. He's going to send us to the Fleet academy for misbehaving orphans."

Chase flinched at the word *orphan*. But Parker was right, trouble or no, the captain wouldn't kick them off the ship, especially not to send them into the hands of the Fleet. But he would be angry. "What about you?" he asked Analora.

She bit her lip and shook her head a few times in thought before she answered. "I want to do it. Dany said it was worth every second. Worst case, my dad will just send me back to live with my mom. He's not like Chief Kobes—he won't send me off to the academy."

It was tempting, but Chase imagined Captain Lennard's reaction once he heard that Chase had stolen an escape pod to go off on his own. The captain thought of him as family, and had put himself and his crew in great danger to make sure Chase was safe. How could he betray him by doing something so reckless?

"I'm sorry," he said. "I can't. I'll wait for Maurus and the other expeds to come back and hear what they have to say." He kept his tone firm, but it was hard to watch the disappointed reactions on Parker's and Analora's faces.

"I'll go," said a scratchy voice on the other side of the hall.

Parker and Analora turned around, and behind them stood Lilli, a pale little apparition who'd materialized out of nowhere, as serious and unsmiling as ever. "I'll go down to Storros with you," she repeated. "Since Chase doesn't want to look for the person who contacted him."

"Hey, Lil," said Parker, glancing nervously at Analora. "You snuck up on us!"

"Where have you been?" asked Chase. "How long were you spying on us?"

Analora looked at Chase with a confused frown. "Is this . . . ?"

"She's my sister," he explained. "My *nosy* sister."

"I have as much right to go along with them as you do," Lilli flared, nodding her head at Parker and Analora. "You wouldn't have even given me the option."

"That's because I would have had to find you first," Chase snapped back. "You're a ghost."

Lilli raised an eyebrow. "*I'm* the ghost?"

"Hey, hey," Parker interrupted. "Save the sniping for the battlefield. Lilli, you want to take a jump pod down to Storros with us?"

"Yes," she said immediately.

All three of them looked at Chase, and for a brief second, he despised them. It would have been hard enough to watch Parker and Analora go, if they'd gone ahead without him, but there was no way he could refuse to join if Lilli was going.

"Great," he snarled.

Parker put an arm around his shoulders. "I knew you couldn't resist. Just had to get you out of your goody two shoes." He turned to Analora. "Look up the coordinates for Lumos, if you can. My computer's, um, on the fritz."

Analora high-fived him, grinning. "Let's meet at the starboard end of my hall in ten minutes. And dress warm."

CHAPTER NINE

"What's with the pretty scarf?" Parker asked Chase as they headed back to their room, flicking at the gray material around his neck.

Too furious to respond, Chase stalked beside him, eyes locked on the floor. As anxious as he was to find the writer of the letter, he felt sick about what they were about to do. He glared at Lilli, who trotted alongside him. "You're coming for real, not sending a copy with us. If we get in trouble, we're all getting in trouble. No disappearing."

Lilli gave an annoyed sigh. "Don't worry, I couldn't project that far even if I wanted to."

"So is this really you?"

"I'll go get myself," she said sarcastically, and vanished.

Chase looked around quickly to make sure there was no one else in the hall to have seen that. Back in their room, he grabbed a thin gray jacket—Fleet-issue with the symbols removed, just like the rest of the clothing the captain had provided for him and Parker.

Parker dug around in his drawer, pulling out something small. "I snagged an old translink from the engine room a while back, but I've only got the one." He tossed it once in his hand and held it out. "You can have it."

Chase shook his head, not looking up. "They gave me one already. You use it."

Analora was bouncing on her heels as she waited for them at the starboard end of her hall next to a nondescript door marked EGRESS. She was dressed like an explorer in pants with built-in kneepads and a canvas jacket with lots of pockets. Her long hair was tied back in a thick braid and a white tube scarf lay slouched around her neck.

"Wow, you don't mess around," said Parker.

She made a face. "This is what I wear when I'm helping my mom in the field. It's practical." Turning to Chase, she asked, "Where's your sister?"

"I don't know. She'll probably bail. We should just go." Suddenly Chase wanted to go as quickly as possible, to leave before Lilli could join. It was a terrible, horrible idea to let her come along.

Analora looked at Parker, who shrugged, and hit a red entry key on the door beside her. It slid open on a narrow hallway that was so dark and long that Chase couldn't see where it ended. Slim, evenly spaced doors, each one with a dark round porthole window, marked the escape pods that lined both sides of the hallway. Analora closed the main door again, and they hurried down the hall single file, past dozens of pods. Analora stopped in front of one. Her voice had grown nervous. "We'll just all cram in together, okay?"

Parker grabbed the door and opened, and the booth inside it lit up. "Let's do it."

The pod contained a very snug, bullet-shaped compartment. Analora stepped in first, pulling a screwdriver from her pocket that she used to pry open a tiny panel under the display, revealing a primitive little control console. "Hmm. Dany told me how to bypass the emergency protocol. . . ."

Parker leaned over her shoulder, giving directions. "Not that one. The other. Did you bring the coordinates? Here, just let me do it. I'll deactivate the comm system too, so no one can track us. It wouldn't do us much good if someone just teleported down to where we land and brought us right back."

"Oh, good idea," said Analora.

Chase closed the door behind them and watched over their shoulders, his back to the windows and vertical bars that lined the tiny capsule. His eyes kept going to how snugly they stood together, their shoulders just touching.

Analora took a deep, shaky breath. "Okay, I think that's everything. Now we just have to—"

A furious pounding on the outside door interrupted her. Lilli's livid face just barely topped the door window.

"She's too late, let's go," said Chase quickly. Analora gave him a strange look and leaned past him to hit the unlock tab.

Lilli squeezed into the capsule, glaring at everyone. She had put on a gray Fleet turtleneck sweater that was way too big and hung down almost to her knees. Parker opened his mouth like he was going to say something, and then thought better of it and just smiled at her.

"You made it," said Chase grimly. His pulse began to pick up as Lilli closed the capsule door. This had to be the stupidest idea anyone had ever had. What if the jump pod malfunctioned, and they ended up lost in space? What if they got stuck somewhere? Or blew up? He opened his mouth, about to suggest they call the whole thing off.

Parker pounded his fist against the capsule wall. "Let's do this."

"Okay," said Analora in a shaky voice. "Here we go." She reached over to the console and pressed a final key. For a second, nothing happened other than a few clicks around the inside of the escape capsule.

"Are you sure—" started Chase.

Before he could finish, the breath got sucked out of his lungs as the pod blasted upward, taking off like a rocket. They hurtled through the launch tube with a roar, and it was all

Chase could do to stay on his feet, gripping the bars inside the capsule with a terrified expression frozen on his face, unable to see anyone else's faces clearly because everything was vibrating so hard. A second later, the capsule went suddenly dark as they burst out of the *Kuyddestor* and into space.

"Crazy!" cried Parker. They were still tearing along at a dizzying speed, but the ride smoothed out and the vibrating lessened. Three portholes gave a glimpse of the dark, empty space outside the pod, and in one the sliver of a greenish orb.

"That's Rhima," shouted Analora, twisting around to look. "The moon." After a few minutes the moon was already gone from view, and beyond the thin wall of the capsule lay endless black parsecs of space. Chase looked over at his sister, who stared out the window, gripping the bars beside her so hard her knuckles were white.

"How does this thing land?" Chase asked over the roar of the capsule's thrusters.

"Um, I'm not sure!" Analora yelled back. "I never got to ask Dany about that."

There wasn't a gravity generator in the capsule, and as the capsule began to arc sideways, Chase had the sensation that he was falling from a very tall height. The four of them were packed tightly enough into the capsule that nobody could fly around and bang into anything, but whoever ended up on the bottom of the pile was going to get squashed. Soon the capsule was completely upside down, racing nose-first toward something they couldn't see yet, and Chase began to feel the blood rushing to his head.

Staring out the window as the faint glow of atmosphere began to creep into the surroundings, Chase became aware of fast, high-pitched breathing beside him. He looked over at Lilli again and saw that she was practically hyperventilating.

"Hey!" He nudged her with his elbow. "You okay?"

She looked at him with a frantic expression, her mouth hanging open. They locked eyes for a moment, and then she closed hers and pressed her forehead against her hand, grimacing. Chase realized that this was the first time she'd really gone out on her own. While he'd spent a week tearing around the galaxy trying to find his identity, she'd spent the entire time sedated in the hands of the Fleet.

"It's going to be okay!" he shouted, putting an arm around her skinny shoulders.

"You sure about that?" came Parker's voice from beside him.

Chase looked up and saw that the shuttle was racing over the surface of a planet, ripping through clouds as it screamed down toward what looked like a mountain range. This, presumably, was Storros. "Analora?" he asked with an unmistakable and embarrassing squeak of fear in his voice. She didn't answer, and as they neared the surface of the planet, Chase stared in frozen terror, watching what could only be their certain impending death.

When they got close enough that he could see individual trees and rocks, the capsule started to tilt again, swinging into a long arc that brought them parallel to the ground. The thrusters roared, and the capsule began to slow. Colors flashed by below, browns and reds and yellows, too quickly to tell what anything was. The capsule sank lower and lower toward the surface.

They hit hard and fast, but at the moment of impact, there was a flash of white, and suddenly the inside of the capsule was filled with protective foam that held them all perfectly in place—all except for Chase. In his panic, he couldn't stop his body's automatic reflex to phase, and the foam was not only around but inside him, packing the loose space between each of his phasing molecules. He was one with the foam, and it burned like fire.

"Parker," he tried to say as the capsule skidded and slowed, but only a panicky garbled sound came out. He couldn't let Analora see him like this.

The shuttle rolled to a stop, and not a moment too soon the door shot off, allowing Chase to swiftly grab the edges of the doorframe and pull himself free of the foam. He tumbled to the ground and started jumping and rubbing his skin, trying to make the tingling pain stop. Behind the shuttle was a long, deep gash in the earth, the broken limbs of trees swinging in their wake. They'd landed in some sort of forest full of short, uniformly spaced trees with gigantic yellow leaves, and a musty sweetness filled the air.

Lilli crawled out of the capsule, wide-eyed and silent with shock. Parker came next, digging himself free. "Holy suns of Taras, we're alive," he muttered, looking up at the bits of sky that peeked between the leaves.

Chase went back to the capsule to help Analora out. By the time he reached her, the foam was already starting to disintegrate. She smiled up at him, brushing a chunk of it from her sleeve, and took his hand to help pull herself out of the capsule. "Well," she said, blinking. "That was fun."

Lilli had sat down on a smooth brown rock. Her face was even paler than usual, and her dark eyes were locked on a point on the ground, deep in concentration. Parker and Analora were already talking and laughing, as though hurtling down to the middle of nowhere on a strange planet were no different than taking a jettaxi to a different part of a city. If Chase was feeling a little stunned, Lilli was probably in complete shock.

Chase crouched down at her side. "Are you okay?

"Just give me a minute," she said in a stiff voice.

Analora had plucked one of the yellow leaves from a tree. It was big enough to cover her entire face when she held it up. "I wonder what kind of trees these are," she said, folding the leaf carefully and sticking it in one of her pockets.

Parker took a deep breath of the sweet-smelling air and grinned. "We're on Storros!"

"Great, but we're not exactly in a city," said Chase. "How far are we from Lumos?"

"No idea," Parker said with a shrug. "Let's find a high point and see what's around us."

Shaking her head, Analora pulled a device from her jacket and flipped it open. After a moment, she pointed. "Lumos is that way."

Parker gave her an admiring smirk. "Of course, the great explorer Miss Bishallany would remember to bring a locator. What else have you got in there?"

"A distress beacon, a couple phoswhites, a tube of steam-gel, a utility knife, and a sandwich."

"A sandwich? Don't you eat scrappies?"

Analora gave a theatrical shudder. "Never. You know what those are made of, right?" Chatting like this, they walked off in the direction Analora had pointed, and Chase looked after them with a knot in his stomach. They were already making up their own inside jokes, and here he was stuck looking after his sister.

"Can you walk?" he asked Lilli.

She stared at him for a moment before answering in her solemn little voice. "Yes." She made no move to rise.

He stood and held out his hand. "Come on." When she

still didn't take it, he sighed impatiently. "You can't just sit here all day."

Lilli scowled at him. "I'm just orienting myself, calm down. That jump pod..."

She was obviously still shaken. "I've never done anything like that before either," Chase told her. "I thought I was going to throw up on myself."

She tipped her choppy blond head back and looked up at the sky. "How are we going to get back?"

"Didn't that problem occur to you before you agreed to come along?" Chase paused, making an effort to filter the irritation back out of his voice. "They'll probably come looking for us before we have to hunt for a way back."

"They're hosting the peace talks today. Is anyone even going to miss us?"

"Dr. Bishallany will. Now get up, please." He held his hand out again.

She allowed him to pull her off the stone, letting go of his hand immediately after, and plodded along behind him. Ahead of them, he could hear Parker's and Analora's voices. They had gone ahead, but the trees grew extremely dense and Chase couldn't see where they were.

"Parker! Hey, Park! Slow down!" Chase hurried through the brush, irritated that the two of them had just wandered ahead together without waiting. Glancing back to make sure Lilli was still behind him, he pushed onward, shouting Parker's name again.

A high-pitched scream echoed through the trees.

"Analora!" Chase took off running through the forest, following the sound of her voice. He burst into a small clearing, where she and Parker stood huddled on top of a rock. Sitting on the ground before them was a small creature covered in shaggy violet-gray fur. Chase couldn't see its face, but it had hunched shoulders and long, stringy arms.

"Go! Get away!" Parker shouted at the creature, kicking at it. The creature snatched his foot with both arms, and Parker nearly fell backward off the rock, grabbing Analora's shoulder for balance.

Without thinking, Chase raced forward and yanked the furry animal back by the scruff. The first thought that crossed his mind when he touched it was that underneath the violet fluff, its body felt as hard as armor. The second thought, when it turned to face him, was less of a thought and more an incoherent blare of terror. Instead of the monkey head he half-expected, the creature had a withered, wrinkly face, with oily black eyes and a puckered hole for a mouth. It hissed when it saw him, a pair of rubbery black lips pulling back from a mouthful of needle-thin teeth.

He'd successfully diverted the creature's attention away from Parker and Analora—now it pivoted around, reaching for him with long arms that ended in a cluster of flat, wriggly feelers. He tried to bat the arms away, but in his fear he phased right through them. A sane voice in the back of his head tried to tell him that this thing couldn't hurt him, but he couldn't stop his adrenaline from spiking, making it impossible for him to stop phasing long enough to push the creature away.

He turned to run, and in one corner of his eye saw his sister trying to scale the bendy limbs of a tree. At least a dozen more of the same creatures were emerging from the woods, pulling themselves on their long arms. He felt a tingling sensation at his ankles and realized the first creature was trying—and failing—to grab him by the legs. He glanced back to see if Analora was seeing this, but she had somehow gotten hold of a dead tree branch and was swinging it at the approaching creatures.

A rough plan was forming in his head to lure the creatures away and let everyone else escape, when a soaring screech exploded behind him. Suddenly the entire clearing was filled with fat sparks of light that drifted lazily through the air. Squinting and batting them away, Chase realized that the sparks were only light, not fire, and that they were making the creatures back off. He ran to the tree to help Lilli down, but she was staring past him, eyes wide and frantic. He turned around to see what she was looking at.

At the edge of the clearing, a yellow single-rider hovercart hung above the ground. Its driver stood over the seat, holding a long rifle-like object that must have been the source of the spark explosion. A gauzy mask covered most of the person's face, but by the long torso and stumpy legs it was obvious that this was not an Earthan.

The Storrian pushed back the gauze mask, revealing a coral-colored head sporting only a few fine wisps of hair, with tiny black eyes, a soft, flat nose, and drooping turtle-like mouth. He said something in a rounded, soupy language. A millisecond later, Chase's translink kicked in, and in his right ear he heard, "What are you doing on my property? How did you get here?"

"We . . . crash-landed," said Parker, still standing atop the rock.

Two rows of short stalks oozed out of the Storrian's forehead, right above his eyes, and arched in a way that made him look confused. He shook his head and gestured for them to come forward. "Earthans?" He mumbled something that the translink interpreted as "Gerp, gerp gerp."

"What?"

"Get in. I'll take you back to the hive with me," came his translated voice.

Parker looked back at Chase, eyebrows raised. Going with an alien stranger to his hive—his *hive*—didn't seem like the smartest plan, but letting him leave them in the forest full of little sharp-teethed monsters sounded worse. And this Storrian seemed, well, if not friendly, then at least not unfriendly. Chase nodded, first at Parker, and then at the stranger.

The alien hooked the light-rifle back onto the side of his hovercart and drove the vehicle farther into the clearing, where Chase saw that he was pulling a sort of hovertrailer behind. He hopped down and walked to the back, moving things around in the trailer, then waved the children over.

Chase took a step forward, but Lilli grabbed his arm and pulled him back. Her face was frightened and confused. "What are you doing?" she hissed.

Chase shook his head. "It's fine. He's just taking us back to his, um . . ." Suddenly he realized why she looked so confused—Lilli hadn't received a translink. "Don't worry. He's going to help us." He looked back at Analora. "He's a Storrian, right?"

Analora nodded. "Yup. Oh hey, I forgot—I brought extras." As they were heading toward the hovercart trailer, she handed something to Lilli. "Put this in your ear."

The Storrian stood beside the trailer as they all climbed in, a good foot taller than any of them, with broad shoulders and that impossibly long torso. Chase and Parker squeezed in among the cylindrical containers sticky with a black substance. "Sorry about the mess," said the Storrian. "I was collecting havarnox sap."

"Oh, great," muttered Analora.

He climbed back on his hovercraft, and soon they were

soaring through the trees. Parker tipped his head back and looked up at the leaf-dappled sky. "Well, this isn't turning out so bad."

"Other than almost getting eaten by those monsters," said Chase.

Parker shrugged. "'Almost' doesn't count." He rubbed his finger along some of the black sap on the container before him and sniffed it. "Smells good. I wonder if—"

He lowered his sap-covered finger to his mouth, when Analora snatched his hand away from his face. *"Don't put that in your mouth."* Her eyes were huge. "Don't *ever* put a raw foreign substance in your mouth until you *know* it's not poisonous."

Parker blanched a little. "Why? Is this—?"

She pulled her scarf from around her neck and used it to vigorously wipe the sap from Parker's finger. "Storrians process havarnox sap into a syrup. If you had some of the syrup, you'd get an upset stomach. When you distill the syrup more, you get a drink called Noxosot that's really popular with certain types of humanoids. But the sap itself is really toxic for Earthans. You'd be dead in five minutes."

Looking disturbed, Parker rubbed his finger. "Good lords. I'm glad you were here."

"I still can't believe you almost ate that. *Never* eat before you know. It's one of the first lessons my mom taught me."

"Yeah, well, my childhood didn't include a lot of inter-planetary travel." Parker's eyes flickered to Chase—was that embarrassment on his face? After getting over his shock of Parker's low-key near-death experience, Chase found himself surprised and even a little pleased that there was something Parker didn't know. Not that he could say he wouldn't have tried the same thing himself.

"When we get to this guy's hive we can figure out where we are," said Chase. "And the fastest way to get to Lumos."

"If we can get him to understand us," said Parker, looking out at the trees as they whipped past. "What are the odds a Storrian tree farmer has a Fleet-quality translink at home?"

"Did you say you have some extras?" Chase asked Analora.

She shook her head. "It won't work. Storrians don't have ear canals like we do."

When they emerged from the forest, the land spilled into a wide plain covered in yellowy-green grass that smelled sharp and spicy. The sky that stretched over them was the soft coral pink of a cabbage rose, and far away in the dis-tance, a towering cluster of conical buildings rose from the ground.

"That must be Lumos," said Analora.

Parker whistled. "We landed pretty close."

"This is close?" asked Chase. The city had to be at least half a day's walk away.

Parker gave him a condescending look. "You realize this planet has seventy million square miles of land, right?"

Lilli's scratchy voice rose from the back of the cart. "Is that a train line?"

Everyone turned around to catch a glimpse of what appeared to be an elevated train platform that emerged from the forest and vanished quickly behind a hill. "Good job, Lil," said Parker. "I bet that goes to the city. Look, you can see it down below too."

They soared over a hillock, and on the other side lay a few conical buildings made of a woven material that gleamed gold in the rose-hued sunshine. As they pulled up alongside the lowest one, another Storrian came waddling out of the building.

"What have you got here?" This one's voice was higher, feminine, although she had the same wispy, almost nonexistent hair on her own head.

"Crash-landed in our orchard," said the farmer gruffly.

The female Storrian tilted her forehead stalks in the same confused gesture and went back inside, while the farmer came back around to help the children down from the trailer.

He started unloading some of the havarnox sap containers, but seeing all the children take a step back, he stopped suddenly. "Oh, I'm sorry. I forgot. You're the first Earthans we've ever had here." He rubbed his fleshy hands on his roughspun pants and left the containers where they stood. "Come inside."

They followed him into the building, down a warm honey-colored hallway, and into an open central area ringed with several stories of large cubbies. One of these held a table and chairs, where he gestured for them to take a seat.

"We're trying to get to Lumos," said Parker in an excessively slow, loud voice, as if speaking more clearly would help the Storrian understand their foreign language. The Storrian shook his head. "Lumos," Parker repeated loudly. "Lumos. Lumos."

Still the Storrian looked at him with a blank expression.

Parker frowned at Chase. "I'm saying it right. Why doesn't he understand? Lumos!"

The female Storrian came back into the room, and Parker tried shouting the name of the city at her, but she ignored him, gesturing for the farmer to leave the room with her. Something about the way they were acting struck Chase oddly. He stood from the table, holding a finger to his lips and putting out a hand to tell the others that they should stay put. Silently he crept down the hall, sidestepping into another room to listen.

The farmer muttered to her in a low tone. "Earthan children crashing into my orchard and destroying half my trees. War breaking out on the moon, Federation ships invading our orbit. All these foreigners—it'll come to nothing good!"

"Don't worry," she said. "The border security hover's already on its way. They'll be off our hands in a few minutes."

Chase cursed under his breath and slipped into the hall to hurry back out to the others. "We've got to go. Now. They've called the border security to come get us."

Hissing angrily, Parker jumped up and made a break for the door, Analora hot on his heels. Chase pushed Lilli in front of himself, just in case the farmer came after them and tried to grab someone.

Chase could hear the roar outside before they even made it out the door. An enormous black hovercraft hung overhead, darkening the yard as it descended toward the property. A handful of Storrian border guards in thick-plated gear hung halfway out of the vehicle with annirad blasters slung from their shoulders.

A voice boomed through the air, so loud it made Chase's ears hum and nearly drowned out the interpretation from his translink. "You have illegally entered Storrian borders. Do not resist capture—your rights are forfeit and any attempt to flee will authorize use of force."

CHAPTER TEN

Panic roared through Chase's head as he watched the black border security hovercraft landing outside the Storrian farmer's house. For the first time, it dawned on him that by taking that jump pod to Storros, they hadn't just broken a rule on the *Kuyddestor*—they'd broken the immigration laws of this planet. And now they were in very deep trouble with an authority that wouldn't be nearly as kind to them as Captain Lennard.

The first Storrian border guard jumped down from the vehicle, his boots kicking up a puff of dust. Something clicked, and Chase pivoted on his heel. "Run!"

Parker was closest to the farmer's hovercart and took a running jump onto the seat, powering up the vehicle so quickly that Chase had no time to wonder how he'd figured out the controls. "Come on!" he shouted as Chase and the girls rushed after him.

The stumpy-legged border guard ran toward them in inexplicably long galloping strides, as two more of his comrades dropped to the ground behind him. Chase stood at the rear of the hovercart's trailer while Analora and Lilli scrambled onboard, prepared to distract the soldier by letting him try to grab him. But the guard stopped a few meters away and pointed his blaster at Chase's chest.

Behind him came a garbled scream from Analora. He steeled himself against the blast, but before it came, he was lifted up from behind as the girls grabbed his arms and pulled him onto the back of the trailer. Parker took off just as the guard fired, and the blast hit Chase in the foot instead. The vehicle lurched forward so hard he nearly tumbled back out of the trailer before he caught himself. His whole leg tingled with numbness, but he somehow managed to scuttle inside.

Two more guards came loping after them, one of them fast enough to catch up and leap, grabbing onto the edge of the trailer. The hovercart strained against his extra weight dragging on the ground. Chase tried kicking at the guard's hands, but it was the same as with the creatures in the forest—in his panic, he couldn't stop himself from phasing through the man's long fingers.

Suddenly the Storrian was struggling, fighting against something clinging to his back. Something small and pale and ferocious . . . and Lilli-shaped. With a gasp Chase looked over his shoulder, but there in the back of the trailer Lilli hunched, staring at the floor with a focused, intent expression. The traveling copy she'd projected was a wild animal, tearing at the border guard's clothes and hair. At the moment he lost his grip on the trailer and went skidding to the ground, her copy vanished and she sat up.

Analora clutched Chase's arm with an iron grip of panic. "What's going on?" she screamed.

Chase twisted out of her hold before he could start to phase out of it. "Help me!" he shouted, rolling the remaining barrels of havarnox syrup out of the moving cart with Lilli's help. The barrels split and splattered their black contents across the spicy-smelling grass. Behind the fallen border guards, the looming shape of the hovercraft rose and started after them. A second later it vanished behind dense yellow foliage as the hovercart passed into the havarnox forest.

Parker steered as well as he could through the thick tree growth, but the hovercart was unwieldy with its awkward trailer, and more than once he had to make a sharp turn, crashing the side of the trailer into a tree and throwing all his passengers into one another.

Chase was phasing out of control—every time his shoulder slammed Analora's, he couldn't stop from sliding through her a little bit. If she noticed this, she wasn't giving any sign. "Could you be a little more careful?" he shouted up at Parker.

"Are you kidding me?" yelled Parker. "Do you want to try this?"

Lilli sat silently, gripping the edge of the trailer as she tried not to fly around. Analora looked worse, her face a cold mask of shock. She kept glancing over at Lilli, but didn't say anything.

A high-pitched, wheedling sound echoed through the trees behind them. Lilli bowed her head for a second and looked up. "Someone's coming after us. On a hoverbike."

"We'll do better on foot," said Parker over his shoulder. Quickly he pulled to a stop and rolled off the side of the hovercart, and everyone scrambled down from the trailer. The high-pitched purr of the hoverbike echoed between the trees.

Analora looked around. "Follow me." She led them away from the cart and trailer, into an area where the trees grew more closely together. Brush underneath tangled and caught at their feet, but Chase slid right through it. Analora charged ahead, weaving between trees and warning the others about uneven spots in the ground. Soon they found themselves in the middle of a dense cluster of saplings. "He'll have to get off the bike if he wants to come after us," she said.

"Genius!" whispered Parker. "I'll run around behind him, and—"

"Guys?" said Lilli in a high-pitched voice. She was looking past them, and when Chase turned around, he saw one of those rubber-lipped, needle-toothed creatures slinking through the underbrush toward them.

"Give me a phoswhite!" he said to Analora. With a wide-eyed nod of understanding, she pulled two sticks from her jacket, keeping one for herself. They struck them as softly as possible against the trees, and a bright white glow filled the area. Chase tried to use his body to block the light and focus it only on one area. It worked almost too well—the creature had turned and was moving away from them, but the glow was strong enough to shine through half the forest.

The whirr of the hoverbike grew louder and suddenly stopped.

Chase made a face at Analora and threw his phoswhite stick as hard as he could into the forest, where it landed and continued to glow through the underbrush. Shaking her head, Analora tucked hers inside her jacket to hide the light. All four of them stood still, barely daring to breathe as they listened to the Storrian border guard moving through the forest.

The sounds came closer. The click of a blaster rifle setting being changed. The soft crunch of boots treading on under-brush. Heart pounding, Chase turned to the others and made a hand motion to fall back. Parker shook his head, holding up a finger for patience.

"I know you're there, come out," the border guard called. "You've broken the law and you can't stay here."

Chase looked down at Lilli. Her face was drawn and she was breathing quickly. He took her hand and gestured for her to slip away with him.

One more soft crunch sounded, this time far too close.

A hand shot from between the trees as the Storrian jumped at them, grabbing Lilli's arm. She screamed, and Chase grabbed the guard's arm, yanking on it to no avail. The Storrian tried to grab him with his other arm, letting his blaster fall loose on its strap, but Chase slipped free. Analora dashed away between the trees. Parker was already long gone.

Somehow Lilli was suddenly free and running after Analora, with, of all things, a smile on her face. Chase stayed behind with the Storrian, now facing him alone. The guard swiped at him, passing through Chase's shoulder.

"Try again," Chase said, jogging backward a few steps. The Storrian kicked at the underbrush and hiked his blaster back up on his shoulder.

Chase took another step. The Storrian aimed at his feet, but before he even fired a shot, Chase's legs were already tingling. Looking down, he saw that he'd walked right into another one of those hideous forest creatures. It was trying to bite at his legs and getting nothing. The Storrian cocked his head in confusion and fired, hitting Chase's legs first and then the creature, who went flying.

Chase turned and bolted through the trees on numb, tingling feet, not waiting for the Storrian to take another shot.

"Chase! Chase!" came Parker's frantic voice. Chase followed it, trying to zigzag between the trees. Blaster fire echoed through the forest, and splintery explosions of bark showered him from both sides as he ran.

Finally he came upon the clearing where the soldier had left his hoverbike. Parker, Analora, and Lilli already sat astride it, bobbing above the ground. Thanks to the wide bottom halves of the Storrians, there was enough room on the saddle for Chase to squeeze on behind Lilli.

"Go!" he yelled.

The hoverbike was lighter, faster, and much more maneuverable than the cart had been, and Parker wove through the trees, zipping deeper into the forest before the border guard could catch up or try to stop them. Chase strained to listen if any other vehicles were coming after them, but he couldn't hear anything over the purr of their stolen bike.

For a moment he just tried to catch his breath as the trees flew past in a blur. Any relief he felt about escaping the border security was canceled out by the fact that they'd now added stealing a hoverbike to their list of offenses. He craned his head around to look at Lilli's face, but her eyes were closed. Some of Analora's hair had come loose from her braid, fluttering back in the wind. Chase brushed the strands away a few times and finally gave up, letting them tickle his face.

Just as Chase was preparing to shout up to Parker to ask if he had any idea where they were headed, the bike slowed down. Chase peered around his sister's head and spotted a gigantic metal pylon ahead of them that rose high into the trees.

"It's the train line!" said Analora. "We can follow the tracks to Lumos." Parker was already urging the bike up higher, through the leaves and into the air above, where they could see how the elevated tracks stretched on for miles. He brought them right up under the track, where a metal lip came down and blocked their view of the horizon—also making them essentially invisible to anyone who might be looking for them as long as they stayed behind it.

They hurtled along underneath the tracks, a good twenty meters aboveground. Chase held tight to Lilli, not daring to look down again after the first glimpse of how high they were. Lilli in turn held on to Analora, whose arms were nestled snugly around Parker's waist. Chase gritted his teeth and watched the pylons whip past.

With no warning, a gravity train blasted by overhead like an explosion. The shock wave sent the bike careening down a few feet, tilting them hard to the left for a few breathless seconds. Chase dug his fingers into Lilli's side so hard she squeaked, staring down at the distant ground and wondering what would happen if he fell. Dr. Bishallany had tested his phasing enough to know that it was an adrenaline-linked involuntary reaction, but they never had a chance to test his reaction to falling onto solid ground. Would he phase right into the ground and be okay, or would he shatter every bone in his body like a normal person? Before he slipped off and found out the answer, Parker was able to right the bike, and they hurtled onward.

Before long the view below began to change from brush and fields to pavement as they reached the outskirts of the city. Chase couldn't see much more below than an occasional pedestrian or a dartlike vehicle zipping beneath the tracks, but it wouldn't take more than one person noticing the four Earthan children on a Storrian border patrol hoverbike to set off some alarms.

He tried to lean around Lilli. "We need to ditch this bike!" The wind snatched the words right out of his mouth, but enough must have gotten through, because Parker nodded and began steering them down toward the ground.

They sailed to a stop alongside the base of a pylon. As she climbed down from the bike, Analora already had her locator out and was frowning as she poked at the screen.

"Here, let me see it," said Parker, reaching for the locator.

Analora pulled it out of his reach with an irritated sigh. "I can do it."

Chase peeked around the pylon at the city. The tall, conical buildings around them were made of the same curious woven material as the farmer's house, rosy gold in the afternoon sunshine. Other buildings were smaller, bullet-shaped, and made of a chalky white material, with wide windows that stretched halfway around. Storrians in groups of two or three strolled down wide sidewalks of black marble in clothes of loose, gauzy material, while in the streets light, open carriages pulled by furry cow-like animals moved passengers at a tranquil pace beneath the shadows of the hovercars that flew overhead.

"Rostanna is both a square and a hotel," Analora said, scrolling and zooming on the locator. "And it looks like maybe their capitol building as well? Which were you supposed to go to?"

Chase frowned. "I don't know. The person just said the Rostanna."

"Well, they're all at the same place. How we find this person when we get there is up to you." She looked up. "Oh man, we're going to get spotted in a heartbeat. Chase, pull your scarf up and cover your face." She helped him adjust the silky gray tube scarf Vidal had given him so that only his eyes were showing.

Parker snickered. "That's cute."

"You get one too, pal," she said, shaking out her white scarf, which was nearly big enough to double as a thin blanket. Dark splotches marred it where she'd used it to wipe the havarnox sap from Parker's finger.

Parker looked alarmed. "You can't use that. It's got poison on it."

She grabbed the middle of the scarf with both hands and ripped it unevenly in two, handing him one half. "Don't chew on it and you'll be fine. Wrap up. Lilli, can you unroll the neck of your sweater and pull it over your head?"

"These are terrible disguises," said Chase.

"We'll use back streets and keep close to the buildings," Analora said. "Unless you have a better idea?"

They looked like a band of ridiculous nomad hobos with their scarf- and sweater-covered heads as they scurried out from behind the train pylon. Analora pointed at a smaller street that branched off from the main boulevard, her locator still in her other hand. Even on the smaller street there were Storrians on the sidewalks, and Chase knew they were attracting attention.

As they walked, looking up only in quick glances, something stood out to Chase: The only people on the street, besides them, were Storrians. The last planet he'd been on, the Federation colony Qesaris, had a mixed population from all kinds of civilizations at the Alpha, Epsilon, and Iota levels. The streets had been divided into blue and gray sectors determining what kinds of species could go where, but he'd spent most of his time there in the all-encompassing gray sector, surrounded by Ambessitari and Shartese and a variety of other unusual creatures. There were none of those here.

The streets led around the circular buildings in meandering paths, never going straight for very long. Analora and Parker argued over the route on the locator, but the one thing they agreed on was that it was best they walk quickly. The closer they got to the Rostanna, the more Storrians they encountered on the sidewalks, and nearly everyone flared their eyebrow stalks curiously when they looked over at the strange little group.

Lilli was the first one to hear the whine of the hoverbike, and she tugged urgently at Chase's sleeve, pointing back at the dark, armor-clad Storrians atop it as it came flying around a white building. "Border guard!" she squeaked.

Parker cursed and dashed toward the nearest building, one of the taller woven ones, and they all ducked through the rounded door. Golden shade seeping through the woven exterior provided light inside, and it took Chase's eyes a moment to adjust. Like the farmer's house, the center of the building was empty all the way to the top, and the walls were lined with hundreds of small cubby spaces connected by winding paths that jutted out like balconies with no railings. Storrians trundled along these precarious pathways, their stumpy legs and low center of gravity keeping them steady, and they hummed as they went, the sound blending and echoing up through the enclosed structure to make a beautiful, gentle harmony.

He only caught a few seconds of the music as they rushed around the base of the interior, unnoticed by the Storrians above, and exited onto a different street. The hoverbike was nowhere in sight, but knowing it was somewhere nearby kept them all looking up nervously as they walked.

"We're pretty close now," said Analora. "Four more, um, blocks."

The sun wasn't even at its peak in the sky yet. Chase's steps grew faster. Despite all they'd had to do, he was proud that they'd made it all the way here on their own. Who would they find there waiting for them? What he learned here could change everything.

As they neared the square, a faint roaring noise started to come from down the street, echoing off the high woven walls of the buildings. Chase glanced at Parker, who frowned, shaking his head. "I don't know," Parker muttered. "Let's all stay close together."

The noise made itself out to be some sort of chant, but the collective roar of voices was too muddled for the translink to decipher what was being said. As they rounded the corner, hundreds of Storrians appeared, crowding side by side in the square, pumping both arms over their heads as they chanted.

With a shock, Chase finally understood what it was they were saying: *"Blast them out, send them back."*

"Are they talking about . . . ?" he shouted, barely making his words heard over the chants.

"The Werikosa occupation," answered Parker. "They're protesting."

The soft coral faces of the Storrian protesters were twisted into harsh scowls, their tiny eyes pinched with anger, in sharp contrast with the leisurely, harmonious lifestyle he'd seen in the rest of the city. Chase wondered why they were so enraged over the occupation of a moon thousands of miles above them. Obviously none of these people lived on the moon they were so worked up about—what difference did it make in their lives if another species wanted to share it with them?

Over a thousand wispy Storrian heads, Chase saw a flash of blond. It grew closer, bouncing among the crowd, and finally came close enough that he could see that it was Parri Dietz. A wave of protesters crushed toward him, pushed out by some force deep in the crowd he couldn't see, and he had to adjust his footing or risk phasing through one of them. When he looked back up again, the reporter had somehow clambered up on a chalky ledge, touching her temple and looking out over the fracas as her lips moved, probably reporting on the scene.

Another crush of Storrians, this time almost a stampede, rushed toward them. "Link hands!" yelled Parker. He took Chase's hand, but a large Storrian pushed between them, and Chase slipped away. On his other side, Analora shrieked, grabbing Lilli and pulling her backward in a hug. Soon Chase couldn't see any of them, just a horde of protesters streaming by on either side. The chanting was loud, but threading between the protests was a singular high-pitched scream.

"Lilli!" he shouted. Struggling to stay on his feet, he began to push through the crowd in the direction he'd seen her and Analora go, trying to move around the protesters by letting himself phase through arms and hips to move more quickly. The Storrian bodies were so wide that he couldn't see more than one person past himself, so he dropped to a crouch to see if he could spot anyone's feet, but all he saw was a shuffling forest of thick Storrian legs.

A hand—an Earthan hand—reached down toward him, and he took it. To his surprise, it was Parri Dietz. "Are you okay?" she shouted, pulling him to his feet. His face scarf, he realized, had long since collapsed around his neck. "I saw you go down. Come with me."

Chase shook his head, resisting. "I have to find my friends!"

Parri Dietz pointed in the direction she was heading. "They went into a building over there. Just follow me."

Getting through the crowd was tougher when he couldn't let himself phase anymore, but Chase let Parri Dietz lead him to a white building at the end of the square. To his immense relief, the others were already inside. Analora crouched in front of a table where she was tending to a shaken Lilli. Parker grinned at him, although Chase guessed most of the grin was for Parri Dietz. "Glad you could join us."

A Storrian woman came down a steep ramp with a pile of tablecloths in her arms, and Chase prepared himself for a scolding and ejection from the building. "You poor children!" she cried. "I saw the little girl fall—are you alright, child? Come up to a dining room where it's safer. Ms. Dietz! So nice to see you here again."

With a wary look, Chase nodded at the others to follow the woman up the ramp. The crush outside the door was getting worse, and they were clearly trapped for the time being.

The chalky white building was lined with cubbies just like the woven ones, and here each cubby contained a table, making Chase guess that this was a restaurant. They went all the way to an upper cubby with a long viewing window from which they could look out onto the square. Parri Dietz lifted her ever-present camera to film the waves of Storrians shouting and pushing at one another.

The square—actually more a circle—was ringed by both the woven gold and chalky white structures, but standing out among them was a pale blue building with elegantly wrought silver frames covering each of its round windows. Watching, Chase realized that the stream of people going in and out of the blue building, though mostly Storrian, included the occasional Earthan. He peered closely to see if he could spot anybody who seemed to be looking for someone.

The Storrian woman had gone through a high doorway into another cubby and a minute later brought them each a steaming bowl of some kind of milky drink. Chase sipped it to be polite, silently gagging at the creamy, intense floral flavor. The woman looked out at the protest with them and folded her arms. "The police won't put a stop to these protests because they want those Werikosa off our moon just as much as any of us. But it's been destroying my business for weeks."

"Why do you want them gone?" asked Chase. "It wouldn't affect you if they just stayed up there, would it?"

The woman gave him a strange look. "Yes, because they would be *closer*. They're fine where they are, back on Werikos."

"Werikos is a wasteland," said Parri Dietz, still looking out the window. "Their seasons grow more and more severe, killing thousands each year."

"That's not our problem," said the Storrian woman. "If they

took better care of their resources, maybe it wouldn't be such a miserable place." Abruptly she returned to the back room.

"The Werikosa can't win anyway," said Parker. "Federation laws give a planet ownership over its own moon. They're squatting on land that doesn't belong to them."

"If that's the case, then Storros owns Werikos too," said Parri Dietz, looking back from the window. When Chase frowned at her, she continued. "Werikos is, technically speaking, another moon of Storros, even though they have completely separate civilizations. It's farther away than Rhima, and their orbit has been degrading for millennia. That's the reason why their environment is worsening, not mismanagement of resources. Without a new homeworld, the Werikosa civilization will eventually vanish."

"And since they don't have the giant rhenium deposits that Storros does, nobody's going to fall over themselves trying to help them," added Parker. Parri Dietz nodded at him with a wry smile.

Chase looked back out the window. Time was ticking away, and anxiety had started building up under his skin. "Where do you think we were supposed to meet this person?" he asked Parker in a low voice.

Parker shook his head, staring at the crowds. "No idea. This might be a bust. Whoever picked this place to meet was not using their thinking brain."

Parri Dietz put her camera in a jacket pocket. "Where were you kids trying to go?"

"Um, the Rostanna," said Chase.

"Which Rostanna, the capitol building or the hotel?" she asked. "You'll have a hard time getting to either. This square has been the focus of all the protesting after the occupation began. Until the Fleet showed up, early negotiations were being held at the capital building." She gestured out at the arching blue walls. "Do you need help getting somewhere? My driver's docked right outside the city—we can give you a lift."

"No thanks," said Chase quickly. As cool as it was to be talking with an intergalactic newscaster, he was still wary of her camera and the trillions of people it reached. Chase looked over at Analora and Lilli, who had both sat down on the floor. "Do you two want to stay here while I go out and look around?"

"No, we'll come," said Analora, getting to her feet. "We should stick together."

Chase glanced out the window one last time. A dark movement caught his attention: a black-haired Earthan slipping out a side door of the capital building and into the crowd of protesters. He had to lean forward and squint to make sure, but it was definitely Ksenia.

"It was nice to meet you," he said quickly to Parri Dietz. "We have to go now. Come on!" He rushed down the ramp and out into the street, the others close behind him. The top of Ksenia's dark head was visible over the crowds—she was much taller than the Storrians. "Hey!" he shouted. "Over here!"

Just in time Ksenia's face came into full view. Her eyes locked onto him with frightful intensity, and swiftly she began to work her way over toward him.

A Storrian stepped between them, blocking his view. Chase looked up in annoyance as he moved to step around, but then he realized who it was.

Border patrol.

They were surrounded.

CHAPTER ELEVEN

Rigid with frustration, Chase looked out into the crowd as a Storrian border guard placed an electrocuff on his left wrist with the warning that he would be stunned if he tried to escape. Ksenia had vanished. If he had been on his own, he could easily have slipped away into the crowd of protesters and gone after her. These guards couldn't hold him. But looking over at Lilli's wide, frightened eyes as the guard cuffed her, he shook his head and stood there with the sinking feeling that once again he had missed the opportunity to find some answers.

The woman who owned the restaurant they'd been at stood outside its doors, her eyebrow stalks cocked suspiciously as she watched them get taken away. The protesters, once they realized that the guards weren't going to disturb their activities, mostly ignored them. Parri Dietz was there too—filming them, of all things.

Chase turned away, raising his hands to shield his face from the camera. "We came down from the *Kuyddestor*," Parker called out. "Can you let someone know what's happened?"

Chase didn't hear if Parri Dietz replied. The guards led them in a tight group out of the square and down a gleaming boulevard to where their black hovercraft was parked.

Analora and Lilli climbed into the boxlike rear compartment of the hovercraft, taking seats on benches facing each other. Parker slid in next to Analora. One solitary guard sat in the back with them, his blaster resting on his knees.

They didn't speak a word on the short ride. Chase looked at everyone's drawn faces, knowing he wore the same frightened expression. Alternating waves of dread and anger washed over him: dread, because he didn't know what happened to children who were arrested by an alien government, and anger, once again, at Parker, Analora, and Lilli for wanting to take this risky trip in the first place. And along with that came frustration with himself, of course, for not having the guts to stop them rather than going along. Nothing good had come of the journey, and now the captain was going to be interrupted in the middle of the peace negotiations and forced to deal with the mess they'd created.

The hovercraft came to a gliding stop, and the guards hustled them into an immense steel and glass structure that looked entirely different from the rest of the buildings in Lumos.

Almost immediately inside the building they were taken into a large holding cell with no windows and stale air. A thick metal door slid closed behind them.

The cell was full of benches, but when Chase went to sit on one, he realized that the seat was stained with oily patches of a blue-greenish substance. He leaned over and examined it, frowning.

"Werikosa have been here," said Analora, crossing her arms. "A lot of them, by the looks of it. Their skin secretes this oil that protects them from high UV rays and a bunch of other harsh climate factors. I guess it gets everywhere too."

Lilli stood before one of the stained benches in her over-long sweater, looking it over as if she were seeking the cleanest place to sit. She glanced at Chase, and he saw violet crescents of exhaustion under her eyes like he hadn't seen in months.

"Are you okay?" he asked.

"I'm just really tired."

"Take a nap. Who knows how long we'll be here."

She shook her choppy blond head and looked at an open door in the corner of the cell. "Is that a bathroom?" Excusing herself, she crossed the room and went inside.

Analora gave him a funny look. "What *is* she?" she whispered, once Lilli was no longer in the room.

"What do you mean?"

"I saw what happened. When that guard was chasing us,

there were two of her for a few seconds. How did she do that?"

Chase froze, uncertain how to proceed.

Parker snorted. "That's crazy. Whatever you think you saw, it must have been a hallucination. Lilli's just a normal kid."

"Don't treat me like I'm stupid," said Analora sharply. "I know what I saw." She turned back to Chase. "That's why you're on the *Kuyddestor,* isn't it? Because of her. Is she some kind of science experiment?"

"No." Lilli stood on the side of the holding cell, glaring at Analora. Chase hadn't even heard her come out of the bathroom. "I'm just a normal kid, like Parker said." She sat down hard on one of the benches, right in the middle of a grease spot.

Analora frowned at Chase, and he knew she wasn't convinced. It was silly to feel jealous, but despite all the effort Chase had made to seem normal around Analora, he had a sudden urge to show her that Lilli wasn't the only special one. He squashed the foolish thought immediately. What she'd seen was how Lilli used her ability to get the guard off their cart. But what she'd missed was how Chase's phasing had hampered him from being able to kick the guard's hands, or stop the forest creatures, or do just about anything when it really mattered.

He motioned for Parker to join him on the other side of the cell. "Did you see Ksenia at the protest?" he asked.

"See who? The tall Earthan lady with the dark hair?"

"That was Ksenia. She came over with the ambassador yesterday. I saw her on the soldiers' level right before we realized your chip was stolen—she must be the one who took it and left the note."

Parker raised his eyebrows. "Why would she make you come all the way down here to talk? She could have told you this stuff on the ship."

"And she could have asked you permission to take your microchip, but she didn't. Maybe she's worried about eavesdroppers, or maybe she thinks the ship is bugged."

"There are ways to get around a bug other than traveling all the way to the next available planet," said Parker. "Like a jammer."

Chase huffed impatiently. "I don't know what her reasons are!"

Parker raised his hands. "Lords, I'm not saying it wasn't her! Right now I agree—it sounds like it was. I just wonder why she wanted to get you so far away from the captain if it was only to talk."

Chase ran his fist along the edge of a bench. "I guess we'll never know. By the time we get out of here, everything will be over."

The door to the holding room slid open, and an officer stepped inside. "Time for processing." He looked around the room, his gaze falling on Chase, who stood closest to him. "You first."

Taking a deep breath and glancing back at the others, Chase stepped into the hall. The officer waddled beside him, indicating where he should turn. There were signs on the wall, but they were all written in a round script he couldn't read. Eventually they came out to a big open area sectioned off into little round cubbies, where dozens of Storrian workers sat at consoles. The Storrian beside Chase gestured toward the rear of the room. "My colleague is waiting for you back there."

As they crossed the open space, Chase glanced over at a long counter, behind which sat a Storrian arguing with, or rather being argued at by, a human. A human in a gray Fleet uniform.

Chase stopped in his tracks. "Hey!" The soldier turned, and to Chase's surprise, it was the sharp face of Lieutenant Vidal. She blanched when she saw Chase, and her mouth fell open.

"Keep moving," said the officer beside Chase.

"Wait!" Vidal rushed toward him, dodging around cubicles. "What are you doing here?"

Flushing with both embarrassment and relief, Chase told her, "We, uh, got picked up for entering the planet illegally."

"What do you mean?"

The Storrian on his left had placed a hand on his arm, and so his words came out in a rush. "I came down with Parker and my sister and Analora Bishallany. We were following you."

Vidal's face creased with confusion. "But how did you even *get* here?" Before Chase could reply, the Storrian officer began pulling him away, and he had to step along with him to keep himself from phasing. Vidal reached out toward him with one hand. "Just sit tight! I'll get you all out once I get Maurus free!"

Get Maurus free? Chase didn't have much time to question this information, because he found himself in one of the cubbies, being offered a chair opposite another Storrian immigration officer. She scarcely glanced at him, using one long finger to pick something from her soft, droopy mouth, and placed her hands on her console.

"Name and origin," she droned.

"Um, Corbin Mason," he said, using the fake name Parker had chosen for him months ago. "I'm, uh, Earthan."

"Mr. Mason, what was your purpose in illegally entering the borders of Storros?"

Should he explain everything that had led him to this point? "Somebody left a note in my room—I live on the *Kuyddestor*, the Fleet ship orbiting around here. And in the note, the person told me to meet her on Lumos, and I tried to come down with some Fleet officers, but when I tried to teleport . . ." He trailed off, trying to think of a way to explain his inability to teleport.

The officer slowly raised her eyes from the console. "A short answer will suffice, Mr. Mason."

He froze a moment, racking his brain for a simpler explanation. "I came to meet a friend."

The officer typed his response. "Did you come to Storros intending to take up illegal residence on this planet?"

"No. I just told you why I came here."

"Were you planning to bring assistance to any illegal aliens currently residing on Storros?"

Chase stared at her. Was she for real? "No."

"Do you know the location of any illegal aliens currently residing on Storros?"

"Of course not," he snapped.

The Storrian smoothed back her eyebrow stalks and placed her hands on her lap. "Mr. Mason, are you aware that illegally entering Storros is punishable by up to ten years in prison and a five-million intercurrency fine?"

His irritation quickly gave way to a racing pulse. "I'm just a kid," he said in a weak voice. "You can't put me in prison."

The Storrian pushed herself away from her desk and motioned for him to rise. "Don't be so sure about that. We're done. Please accompany Officer Squoda back to the holding room."

＊　　＊　　＊

Chase had been staring for what felt like hours at an unintelligible script carved into the back of one of the holding room benches, nerves twisting his stomach. Parker and Analora were both convinced that the captain would be able to get them free, and Chase agreed that that made the most sense. They were dumb kids who'd made a mistake, not refugees or criminals. But still, until they were safe and sound back on the *Kuyddestor*, ten years in a Storrian prison seemed like a very real possibility.

The door to the holding cell opened, and Lieutenant Vidal stepped inside. The stress and surprise was gone from her face, and in its place was blazing fury. "*You stole a jump pod? What on Taras were you kids thinking?*"

"We're so sorry, Lieutenant," blurted Analora.

"Captain Lennard has been informed and has claimed responsibility for your actions, including the *astronomical* fine. The Storrians are releasing you into my custody. Analora, this is for you." Vidal twisted the teleport return ring from her own finger and handed it over. "Your father wants you back immediately."

"Like, right now?" asked Analora in a voice so timid Chase barely recognized it.

"Like right now. I wouldn't want to be in your boots. Go. The rest of us have to wait for the *Kuyddestor* to send down a transport vehicle."

Analora ducked her head in shame as she put on the ring. She glanced at Chase and Parker. "Good luck. See you when you get back . . . I hope." Vidal punched something into her communicator, and a moment later, Analora faded out of the room.

"The rest of you come with me," said Vidal brusquely, leading them out of the holding cell.

Chase rushed ahead to talk to her. "What did the captain say?"

Vidal shook her head as they walked. "He's not happy. People get kicked off the ship for what you kids did. I have no idea what you thought was so important down here that you had to go and do something like that." Chase began to turn back toward the central processing area, but she stopped him. "No, go this way. We have to pick up Lieutenant Maurus from a different holding area."

"What happened to him?"

Vidal gave a short, irritated sigh. "Someone alerted Storrian authorities that the former alleged Trucon plotter was walking around on their planet. They picked us up not long after we arrived and accused the Fleet of deceiving them because we didn't state his species in our entry request."

It had been a long time since Chase had heard Maurus referred to as the alleged engineer of the Trucon disaster. "Who would have done that?"

"Maurus has his enemies," said Vidal dryly.

And I can name one of them, thought Chase. "Where's Lieutenant Seto?"

"Our entry visa was revoked. I had to send him back to the ship already."

They followed Vidal up a long ramp that spiraled around to another level. "Are the high-security holding cells this way?" she asked a passing officer. They continued to a desk, where she provided a chip scan and badge swipe.

Maurus came from deep down the hall, flanked by two of the largest Storrians Chase had seen yet. His cheeks were flushed, and his eyes dark with anger. When he saw the four children standing behind Vidal, a confused scowl etched itself into his face. The officer at the desk stopped him and pressed a boxy, gunlike device against his wrist.

"Ouch!" Maurus jerked his hand away. On his wrist, a spidery pattern glowed orange under his skin.

"The tracer under your skin will dissolve as soon as you clear our orbital borders. If you're not off the planet within one hour, you'll be picked up again and sentenced for illegal attempt at residence."

"Like I'd stay on your stinking heap of a planet," Maurus spat, rubbing his wrist. "I'll have my blaster back now."

"Your weapon has been confiscated and destroyed, along with any other devices you were carrying."

"My communicator? My return ring? Those items are the property of the Federal Fleet. If I'm supposed to get off your cursed planet in such a blasted hurry, then why did you destroy the one item I needed to leave?"

"We've got a transport coming to get us at the Beman port," said Vidal, flashing Maurus a warning look. "We'll be off-planet shortly."

"You will be escorted to the port," said the stony-faced Storrian. The two huge guards flanking Maurus stepped forward.

As they exited the building with their escort, Maurus turned to Chase. "What on Hesta's seven suns are you doing here?"

"It's a long story," Chase faltered.

"They took a page from the chief's son and stole a jump pod," said Vidal in a clipped tone.

"They *what*?" Maurus's voice grew dangerously loud.

"Keep your voice down. They crash-landed outside Lumos and got picked up by immigration, just like you."

"I can't believe you!" Maurus turned on Chase, his dark eyes flashing. "I'm incredibly disappointed. This was Parker's idea, wasn't it?"

Feeling miserable, Chase began to apologize, but behind him Parker made a loud noise of disbelief. "Oh, so he's the one who needed to come here, but I'm the troublemaker, huh?"

"Enough." Vidal's voice was steely. "No more talking until we're back on the *Kuyddestor.*"

They were escorted by hovercraft to the port, where a Fleet transport was already docked and waiting. Maurus quickened his pace toward the sleek silver vehicle. "Seto, is that you?" he called out.

"Keep your temper," Vidal warned, putting a hand on his arm.

Maurus arched an eyebrow. "Why?"

Bootsteps rang out as someone descended from the cockpit, and Lieutenant Derrick jumped down beside the vehicle, smiling like a satisfied cat. "I insisted they let me come to your rescue, Maurus. What a shame that someone with your level of infamy can't even visit a cesspool like Storros without attracting attention."

"I knew it was you, you—" Maurus broke into a string of foul Lyolian curses, but because of the translink, Chase understood every word. He grimaced at Parker, who mouthed the word *Wow.*

Vidal ushered them all up into the transport ship. Lilli sat down quickly, not talking. Chase slid into the seat next to her and leaned forward. "Everything okay?" he asked. She nodded, but looked pale and worried.

"Scared about the universe of trouble we're going to be in, in"— Parker checked an imaginary watch—"ten minutes?"

"Cool it," said Chase.

In the cockpit, voices were escalating. "The assigned pilot of the mission," said Maurus hotly.

"Until you got yourself arrested by immigration authorities, at which point you are automatically suspended from duty," said Derrick.

"And whose fault was that?"

"I have no idea what you're referring to, and I don't like your tone."

"You just wait until—"

"*Knock it off.*" Vidal's voice cut sharply through. "Derrick, take the yoke. Maurus, go take a seat in the back."

His face livid, Maurus stormed into the rear cabin and dropped into a seat. "I'd feel safer letting Parker pilot," he muttered.

Parker grinned. "Happily!"

"Buckle in," growled Derrick from the pilot's seat. Vidal took the navigator's place beside him.

They lifted gently off the ground and soared out of the port, accelerating sharply once they'd cleared the final towers of the city. Maurus pulled up his sleeve and looked at the radiant tracer on his arm. As the sky outside the windows darkened, the orange glow faded and vanished. He rubbed the spot and pulled his sleeve back down, frowning over at Chase.

They traveled through space in silence for a while. Chase looked at Lilli, but as usual she sat quietly, focusing on the ground in front of her. He started to turn away when she gave a small gasp.

"Everything okay?" he whispered.

It took her a moment to react before she looked up at him, blinking. "I don't think so," she said solemnly. A bad feeling lodged in his gut.

"Home sweet home," said Derrick at the console. "*Kuyddestor* flight deck, this is Lieutenant Karsten Derrick on approach, requesting entry."

They waited in silence as the ship filled the window.

"Flight deck, requesting entry," Derrick repeated, a trace of irritation creeping into his voice. "Hello?"

A hiss sounded from the console. "Entry denied," said a curt, raspy voice.

"What?" Derrick glanced over at Vidal. "You've got to be kidding me."

Frowning, Vidal started scrolling on one of the console screens. "Try again."

Before Derrick could make the request again, another transmission came through. "Transport, do not approach the ship."

Maurus sat up straighter in his seat and leaned forward, suddenly alert.

"Flight deck, you'd better explain yourself," Derrick snapped, veering toward the ship.

A jumbled sound came over the console, as if someone were running fingers over the microphone on the other end. The voice broke through again, breathless and urgent.

"Transport, get out of here! The ship is under attack!"

CHAPTER TWELVE

The *Kuyddestor* loomed before them, filling the whole window with its smooth metal curves. Like a massive building floating in space, it looked immense, impervious.

"The ship is not under attack," said Derrick in an irritated voice. "Look at it!"

Vidal had taken over communications at the console. "*Kuyddestor* bridge, this is Lieutenant Vidal, please respond. We've received an unusual communication from the flight deck." She paused, and when no one responded, she tried again. "*Kuyddestor*, please confirm your status."

Chase stared out the window, feeling as confused as Vidal sounded. "Oh no," said a small, desperate voice beside him. He turned his head to glance at Lilli, but a flash in the window diverted his attention.

On the tail section of the *Kuyddestor*, a flat orange sheet of fire exploded outward, taking out a chunk of the ship at least two levels high. Shouts of shock filled the tiny transport shuttle.

"Fall back!" commanded Vidal.

The *Kuyddestor* receded slightly as Derrick pulled away. "What was that? Did they just get fired on?"

"From where?" asked Maurus. "The *Falconer* is the only other ship nearby."

Parker shook his head. "It looked like an internal explosion."

Vidal kept trying to contact the *Kuyddestor* to no avail. Maurus shifted as far forward as possible, his eyes glued to the scene.

Something must have gone wrong at the peace talks. Was this why Ksenia had wanted him to get off the ship? Had she known something might happen? Guilt rushed over Chase as he realized that they had sent Analora back to the ship just in time for this. Would she be okay? Would everyone else?

The wisp of dread that had stuck with Chase since they'd left the *Kuyddestor* twisted into a thick coil that squeezed his stomach. If someone really was attacking the ship, the first person they would go after was the captain. Chase glanced over at Lilli again. Her eyes were closed, face waxy, as if she were trying to send a copy somewhere—like to the ship.

"Hey, stop it!" he said, grabbing her shoulder and giving her a shake. If something happened to the ship when her copy was on it . . . he couldn't finish the thought. "Cut it out!"

Parker and Maurus both turned to them, watching as her eyes snapped open, wide and frightened.

"Don't do that!" said Chase.

Lilli took a deep breath. "Soldiers have taken over the ship."

In a flash, Maurus was crouched beside her. "What happened? What did you see?"

Her voice was shaky. "There was another power failure, a big one. This time it lasted longer, and when the power came back on a whole bunch of soldiers teleported onboard."

"I told you someone was hacking the power systems!" said Parker, his eyes bright and fierce.

"What kind of soldiers?" Maurus asked. "Storrian? Werikosa?"

"Fleet soldiers?" asked Chase.

She squinted, trying to remember what she'd seen. "They were kind of like Storrians, but not really. They were a funny color, kind of blue."

"Werikosa," said Maurus quickly. "What was the explosion?"

"I'm not sure. They're making everybody go to the flight deck right now."

"You said you couldn't travel that far," said Chase.

Lilli looked at him with a stony expression. "I lied."

At the front of the shuttle, Vidal had turned around in her seat. "How does she know this?"

Maurus looked up at Vidal. "Did you try to contact the *Falconer?*"

"No," she said, eyes locked on Lilli.

"Tell them the Werikosa have hijacked the *Kuyddestor*. We need to inform the Storrian defense minister as well."

Vidal's eyes flickered to Maurus. "How do we know that's what's really happening?"

"Just trust me, okay?" Maurus put his hand on Lilli's wrist. "Trust her."

Vidal paused, just long enough for Derrick to jump in. "This is crazy," he said. "You'd have us believe the Werikosa, who can barely run their own planet, have commandeered our starship based on the word of a very imaginative seven-year-old?"

"I'm not seven," Lilli squeaked with barely contained rage.

"You're also not aboard the *Kuyddestor* right now, so it isn't exactly possible for you to know what's going on there, is it?"

"She knows." The stern authority in Chase's voice caught Vidal's attention, and he returned her stare without blinking, trying to convince her with his expression. He wouldn't give up their secrets unless he absolutely had to.

"Maurus," Vidal said in a voice sharp enough to cut carbonite. "Is there something I need to know about these children?"

Maurus looked intently at Lilli's wrist in his hand. He gave her tiny paw a squeeze and looked up. "You'll have to ask the captain about that, Lieutenant . . . but yes."

Vidal looked closely at each of them, and without a

comment sat back down at the console. "I'm sending out a star system–wide alert on the hijacking of the *Kuyddestor.*"

"Are there any other ships besides the *Falconer* in the vicinity?"

"The main shipping lane has been more or less abandoned because of the Rhima dispute." She paused. "Wait, there is something—a commercial vessel, it looks like—stationary on the far edge of the star system. They don't have any call letters."

"Tell them to stay clear of the area," said Maurus. "And send—"

"The *Falconer* is requesting we dock with them," interrupted Derrick.

"Do it," said Maurus. "Any demands the Werikosa have will probably be sent to them."

Chase could see the signs of a scowl on Derrick's face as they zoomed high above the surface of Rhima, leaving the *Kuyddestor* stationary on the other side. On the greenish sunny side of the moon, the sleek *Falconer* was already waiting. Minutes later they were docking alongside the embassy ship, and opening their doors on an extended portal.

Two Federation guards in dark blue waited on the other side of the door, along with Ksenia. Her tall, lithe frame was draped in a deep burgundy suit, and her dark hair was now knotted up on top of her head. She surveyed their small group. "Which of you is the lead officer?"

Vidal confirmed and introduced her crew, vaguely referring to the children as "civilian passengers of the starship." Chase stared intently at Ksenia, hoping to catch her eye, but she didn't even glance at him. Was she pretending not to know who he was, or had he guessed wrongly that she did?

"I'm Ksenia Oriolo, the Federation plenipotentiary for the Rhima terraforming project. Come with me." She ushered them into the ship, down the hallway, walking with sure, determined strides. The *Falconer* was a completely different kind of ship—where the *Kuyddestor* was all functional metal and hard edges, the walls of the embassy ship were paneled in rich, dark wood, and thick blue carpet muffled their steps as they walked.

"How much information do you have?" Vidal asked.

"We only confirmed what you said in your alert. The Werikosa have taken control of the *Kuyddestor.*" She was smooth, confident, and almost too calm.

Vidal continued without hesitation. "Is Ambassador Corinthe . . . ?"

"On the *Kuyddestor* attending the peace talks. I should have been there as well, but I had urgent business on Storros. Until his safety is secured, I'm the primary representative of the Federation and will run the details of this mission."

Lieutenant Thandiway, do you take your orders from the Federation? The captain's words echoed in Chase's mind. Would Ksenia be giving orders to the few remaining Fleet soldiers? Vidal didn't say a word, and Chase wondered if roles were different in an emergency.

A Federation Guard approached them in the hallway. "Madame Advisor, the hijackers have initiated contact. How would you like to proceed?"

Ksenia didn't break step. "Send the feed to the Condor conference room, and tell my secretary to join us." Swiftly she led the group into a long, elegant room dominated by a lacquered table. Everyone quickly took their places in the deceptively heavy-looking seats around the table. Chase hesitated at the door before entering, unsure if they would be allowed to join, but Parker blew past and sat down like he belonged there, so Chase followed, making sure to keep Lilli by his side. No one said a word about them being there, but they were all staring expectantly at the silvery blue adamantine screen at the front of the room.

Ksenia looked around the table, lingering a bit on Chase's face. She tipped her head in the tiniest acknowledgment, and a rush of jittery joy filled him. It *was* Ksenia who'd tried to contact him. "Start the feed," she said.

Chase's first thought after the screen illuminated was, *I thought we were talking to a Werikosa?* The face that filled the screen looked remarkably Storrian—same drooping beak of a nose, same tiny eyes and turtle-like mouth. Only after a few seconds did he start to see the differences: The Werikosa's features were a little broader, a touch coarser. And of course there was a light blue-green sheen to his skin, the protective oily secretions Analora had told them about.

"Greetings, Madame Advisor," the Werikosa said. Beneath the translink version, Chase could hear that his native language was full of raspy sharp edges, unlike the slushy language of Storros. "We are in the process of sending over a list of demands."

"You've done something very foolish, Petrod," said Ksenia, in a tone that suggested she'd spoken with this particular Werikosa before. "I won't listen to another word until you confirm that no one aboard the *Kuyddestor* has been hurt."

The Werikosa swayed his head. "Hurt is . . . open to interpretation. No one is dead. Yet." Chase closed his eyes briefly, relieved that everyone was still alive.

"Don't make that mistake. You're in enough trouble as it is." Ksenia shook her head incredulously. "Did you really think doing this would improve your situation? The Federation won't allow you to stay on Rhima after this."

"You think it matters to us what the Federation allows? We already know what the Federation allows—it allows our wealthy Storrian brothers to ignore our pleas for help, to close their borders to our people, it allows us to work our-selves dead terraforming a paradise that we won't be allowed to stay in.

"Our planet is dying, our people are helpless. We are doing this for all the Werikosa children who didn't make it to their first year because they starved, for all the villages that have been destroyed by sun flares during the Seasons of Fire. No one wants to help the Werikosa, so now we must help ourselves."

"You *had* a stake in the moon before you did this. Now I can't help you."

"Currently the Storrian officials are not accepting our transmissions—"

"Because they do not bargain with criminals," Ksenia interrupted.

"And so we are counting on you to ensure that our de-mands are met. If Storros doesn't agree to grant us complete use of Rhima, we will use the full force of this starship to at-tack their planet."

"You won't live that long, Petrod. There's no way your pal-try band of misfits can hold against an entire starship full of Fleet-trained soldiers."

"No? Well, maybe we should just kill them all." Petrod stepped out of the frame, revealing the bridge behind him with all its officers crowded into the middle tier, Lennard and Forquera, the navigators and communications officers, pale but defiant. Behind them lurked three Werikosa strapped with heavy blaster rifles. Chase broke out in a sweat at the sight, knowing any of their lives could end in a heartbeat, at the whim of this lunatic.

"Don't worry," came Petrod's voice. "We prefer to keep them all alive. We don't want to hurt anyone, not even one wretched Storrian." He stepped back in front of the camera. "But we want our moon."

The transmission ended abruptly. The entire conference room seemed to take a collective deep breath as everyone leaned back in their seats. Ksenia issued orders to her staff, who quickly dispersed, leaving just her and the transport arrivals in the conference room.

Parker leaned back in his seat. "I say just give them the moon and be done with it."

The corner of Ksenia's mouth tilted up. "Were it only that easy. Storros already went into these negotiations intending to send the Werikosa back to their own planet. After this they won't cede one inch."

"Can't the Federation just tell them to?" asked Chase.

Maurus shook his head. "The extent of the Federation's power over its members ends more at suggestions than commands. In the end, each planet still gets to make its own decisions." He looked at Ksenia. "You know this Petrod individual?"

"I've been supervising the terraforming of Rhima for the Federation for the past two years. I've had my share of dealings with him. A hothead, and not a particularly smart one. I don't think he's the worst of your worries."

"The power outage," said Parker immediately.

Ksenia nodded. "Someone on your ship must have been working with the Werikosa to time the disturbance and arrange a way to teleport all those soldiers onboard. You have a traitor in your midst."

Parker slapped his hand on the table, vindicated, and Chase looked over at Maurus and saw his own dread reflected in the Lyolian's eyes. His first guess at the traitor might have been Lieutenant Derrick, just based on what a jerk he was, but Derrick looked completely stunned.

"What are our next steps?" asked Vidal. "Has Fleet high command responded yet?"

"They have," said Ksenia. "The nearest starship that can help us is the *Destrier.*"

"Sinjan Devore's ship?" The sudden alarm in Maurus's voice made Chase's skin crawl. What was wrong with Sinjan Devore?

Ksenia nodded again. "The *Destrier* has been dispatched from the Ichis star system, but it won't get here for three days. That's how much time we have."

"Time for what?" blurted Chase.

She turned her dark eyes on him. "Time to get the Werikosa to abandon this madness. The *Kuyddestor* has enough weaponry onboard to wipe out half the population of Storros. If we fail, and the Werikosa begin their attack, the Fleet will have no choice but to destroy the *Kuyddestor* and everyone on it."

CHAPTER THIRTEEN

Chase leaned his forehead against the window, looking out at the flat green terrain of Rhima hundreds of miles below. A few patchy clouds were scattered over the moon's surface, but there was little else to break the monotony of its landscape. It didn't really look like much worth fighting for. And it definitely didn't look like anything worth losing the entire *Kuyddestor* over.

He turned around to face the velveteen-paneled sitting room where he, Parker, and Lilli had been taken after everyone else left the conference room. Ksenia had been the first to leave when she was called up to the bridge, so Chase never had an opportunity to ask her any of the million questions piling up in his mind. It didn't look like he would get a chance anytime soon, either.

Seated in the corner by a tall china cabinet, Parker stared hard at the floor, chewing on his lip and tapping his foot. He glanced at the window. "Anything good out there?"

"I can't see the *Kuyddestor* anywhere," said Chase.

"I'm sure the pilot is trying to make sure we keep the moon between us and them. Not that it'll help. If they want to fire on us, we're toast."

Frowning, Chase flopped down in a plush burgundy armchair. Beside him, Lilli was very quiet. He glanced over often to make sure she wasn't trying to send a copy back onto the *Kuyddestor* again. Kneading his fists into the armrests, he tried to reason with the panicky voice in his mind. The Fleet wouldn't destroy one of its few starships, would it? *It would, if this were the plan to get rid of Lennard and Maurus and any other loose threads left over from the Trucon plot.* But that was a crazy thought—the Fleet couldn't have known that the Werikosa were going to hijack the ship.

He needed to talk to Ksenia and find out what she knew. Was it really just an accident that they were all off the ship when it was attacked?

The door to the sitting room slid open, and Maurus entered. "I need your help." He went straight to Lilli and crouched beside her chair. "Can you get back onto the ship to see what's happening?"

"Yes," said Lilli quickly, sitting up straight.

"No." Chase looked at Maurus. "Please, don't make her do this. If she gets hurt there, she'll get hurt here too."

Lilli shot him a scornful look. "Do you realize how fast I can disappear? Nobody can hurt me."

Those words were familiar—Chase himself had said them before. He was the one who should be taking these risks, the one who couldn't get hurt even if he tried. "Get me onto the ship instead. Shoot me like a missile. I'll go right through the walls."

Maurus made a face and shook his head, his attention still on Lilli. "Can you get a message to the captain?"

"No," she said. "They've moved the entire command crew into the flight deck, and there are a ton of guards there. I couldn't do it without being seen."

Parker spoke up. "I still don't understand how they were Able to take over the ship so quickly. The *Kuyddestor* has enough crew and guns to stop an army."

"Most of the guns are locked in the armory, and the locks don't work anymore," said Lilli.

"What do you mean?" asked Maurus. "Did you see something else?"

"I eavesdropped on some conversations. Once the Werikosa got onboard, I guess the controls went crazy. Some things still worked, like communications and lights, but others just stopped responding. Weapons, locks, piloting controls."

Parker smacked himself on the forehead. "It was a trojan."

"A what?" asked Chase.

"It must have been the blackout that happened a week ago. I bet somebody used it as a cover to install a trojan horse into the ship's mainframe—a back door to access all the controls. Now whoever has control is making it impossible for the crew to fight back." He leaned forward. "Is there any way to sneak back onto the ship? If I can get access to the mainframe, I might be able to figure out a way to override the trojan."

"You'll still need someone to help you fight off the hijackers," said Chase. "I should go too."

Maurus held up his hands. "Slow down, guys. I don't really see how we could get back on the ship right now, and nobody's going to want to send children to do the fighting."

"Ksenia might," said Chase.

"Why do you say that?" Maurus asked with a frown.

"Because I think she's the one who took Parker's chip and left me the note. I saw her in Lumos, where we were supposed to meet."

"Really? Are you sure?"

"I didn't get a chance to talk with her, but I know she saw me there."

He held Maurus's gaze for a long time, and for a second it seemed like he might have convinced him. Then Maurus shook his head. "Even if it she was the one who contacted you, what does that mean? That she's working for Asa? That she has Fleet connections? Do you think she even knows about your—" Maurus waved a hand up and down at Chase, leaving his ability unspoken. "You don't know what her intentions are."

"That's why I need to talk to her."

Leaning back, Maurus rested his elbows on his thighs. "We need to be very cautious about this until we know more about her, and about what's happening aboard the *Kuyddestor.*"

The door slid open again, and Vidal stood in the doorway. "What's going on?" She walked toward them, her eyes on Lilli. "How do you know what's going on aboard the *Kuyddestor*? Are you psychic?"

"No," said Lilli, drawing out the word. She glanced at Maurus.

Maurus chose his words carefully. "Lilli's an . . . exceptional child. We were just talking about a way to get Parker access to—"

"So that whole story about them being stranded orphans that we're prepping for the cadet program?" Vidal interrupted. "That was all bogus?"

"Oh, we're totally stranded orphans," said Parker. "That part's right on the money."

Vidal crossed her arms. "If there's something I should know,

now is the time. Don't leave me in the dark when the entire ship is at stake."

With an exasperated sigh, Lilli closed her eyes. A second Lilli appeared behind Vidal, tapping her on the shoulder. Startled, the lieutenant turned and uttered a surprised "Ooh!" as the copy vanished again. When she turned back to the real Lilli, her eyes were round. It took her a moment to find her voice. "Can . . . can all of you do that?"

"No," said Chase bluntly.

"They each have different skills. Parker is an exceptional hacker." Maurus glanced over at Chase, his dark eyebrows knitting, and said nothing about Chase's phasing. "They can help us—it's our biggest advantage in this situation. They're not just normal kids."

Vidal blinked. Her eyes kept going back to Lilli. "Can she contact the captain—?"

Maurus shook his head. "We just established that the entire command crew is unreachable."

"What about the engine room?"

"I can check there." Lilli closed her eyes for a moment, and Chase gritted his teeth until she reopened them again. "There's no one in the engine room. From the Fleet, I mean. Lots of Werikosa."

Maurus shook his head again. "That won't work then."

"If you can get me on the ship, I can get disable the trojan." Everyone turned to look at Parker as he spoke. "For now, just get me a networked computer. I'll try to see if there's any kind of tiny chink in the *Kuyddestor*'s firewall that will get me access from outside the ship. No promises though."

As Maurus and Vidal discussed options for getting Parker a computer, Chase leaned toward his sister and spoke softly. "You said they were taking everyone to the flight deck. Did you see Analora there?"

Lilli glared at him, eyes flashing. "I thought you didn't approve of me traveling to the ship?" Chase looked away, and her tone softened. "I didn't see her. Maybe she's hiding."

Inside the walls of the ship. Chase could picture her there, hiding out from the Werikosa. He hoped that was where she was. "If you do see her, tell her help is on the way. Everything's going to be fine."

"Is it?" For a second, her tough façade fell, and she was just his little sister, looking to him for reassurance.

"Of course. Nobody's going to blow up the ship. No one's going to get hurt." A tiny bit of relief crept into her expression when he said this, but he wasn't nearly as confident in those words as he sounded. "I need to go find Ksenia and ask her some questions."

"She's on the control deck, just down the hall from the

conference room we were in." Lilli closed her eyes for a second. "If you jump left in front of the door and step forward, there's a closet where you can hide and listen in."

Chase stared at her. "Did you just send a copy up to scope things out?"

A tiny, proud smile appeared on her face. "Instead of really 'traveling,' I can send out a flash, just to be there long enough to get a quick look. It's so fast no one sees—usually. I slipped up a few times on the ship, but I'm getting better at it."

Was this why she'd been disappearing in public on the *Kuyddestor*? "You've been practicing?"

"Of course. I practice all kinds of things. You know, 'Anything worth doing takes elbow grease and time.'" She paused, and her mouth twisted in a funny way. "That's something Dad used to say."

"Oh." It sounded like good advice, even if knowing the source felt like pins sticking in his heart. In all his tests with Dr. Bishallany, they'd never spoken of Chase actually trying to practice or improve his phasing. It was just something that he did. Was this something he should have been working on? With these thoughts in mind, Chase left the sitting room to look for Ksenia.

The *Falconer* was tiny compared to the *Kuyddestor*—only three levels, and the back portion all devoted to the engine core. Chase wandered through the middle level, where the conference room and control deck were located. He stopped in front of the door to the control deck, and before anyone could open the door, he jumped into the wall on the left like Lilli had told him to do.

The space he landed in was pitch dark and tight—the inside of the wall, but not an open crawl space like on the *Kuyddestor*. By the burning sensation in his torso, he could tell there had to be some sort of beam that ran through the middle of the space, dividing him in half and forcing him to continuously phase around it. Hissing quietly through his teeth, he took a big step forward and emerged into a slightly less dark and more open area. This must have been the closet Lilli meant—there were jackets hanging behind him and a row of shelves to his left filled with binders and neatly stacked containers.

The voices on the other side of the door were quiet. There were vents cut into the bottom of the door, so Chase crouched down to be closer. A man's voice came through, giving what sounded like a list of updates.

"Storrian fleet has taken position around its borders. Their coverage is spotty at best."

"They'll get slaughtered," came Ksenia's voice. "They've never had to fight off more than a few ragtag border jumpers—never an all-out war."

"We've also got a request for comment from that reporter from the UNN."

A long, irritated sigh. "That pesky woman. Tell her due to the sensitive nature of the situation, we're unable to comment at the time. If she persists, have Mallory give her some sort of blow-off remarks."

"Very well."

"If that's all, I'm going to head back to the ambassador's chamber to prepare for further negotiations with Petrod."

"Just one more thing. The Fleet soldiers onboard have requested network access."

"Oh? Did they say what for?"

"I think they want to try to make contact with the crew being held hostage. At least that was my impression."

"Good luck with that. Petrod's got the ship locked down tight. Go ahead and set them up with a console, though." Ksenia paused, and in a lower voice asked, "Did you disable their transport like I asked you?"

In the darkness, Chase's eyes widened. Why on Taras was Ksenia trying to trap them on her ship?

"Of course, Madam Advisor."

"Excellent. It's for their own protection. I don't want them to get any foolhardy notions about heroics. We're shorthanded enough as it is."

"I understand."

There were footsteps, and the sound of a door zipping open and closed. Chase sat in silence for a moment, absorbing what he'd learned. He would have to tell Maurus about their transport. Ksenia's words about disabling their vehicle to protect them rang false—she wanted to make sure they didn't leave her ship. He started to rise, but stopped when voices from the piloting crew started up again.

"Keep a close eye on those heat sensors. We won't have time to prep for a jump if those slugs decide to come for us after all."

"Understood."

"What a Hesta-horking disaster this is," muttered the first speaker. "Never thought *she'd* end up in command of the mission."

"She's a little high-strung, I guess."

"More than that. I heard she got shipped out here two years ago as a punishment for some Federation scandal. It's probably driven her over the edge working with slugs and those wacko Storrians for that long."

The second crewman made a noise of agreement, and they settled into silence again. As quietly as possible, Chase slipped out the back of the closet, through the wall, and, after a cautious peek, into the hallway, where he hurried back to tell the others what he had learned.

CHAPTER FOURTEEN

When Chase got back to the sitting room, everyone had left but Parker. A staffer was already setting up a computer at a mahogany coffee table. Parker looked over the man's shoulder, hands twitching as if he wanted to do it all himself.

"Alright, that's good, I can take it from here." He prodded the disgruntled staffer from the seat and sank before the console. His expression immediately settled into what Chase recognized as fully immersed mode, eyes bright and alert on the screen while the rest of his face went slack and his hands flew over the keyboard.

"Parker, we need to talk." Chase waited to continue until the staffer had left them alone. "I went to the control deck and heard some weird stuff."

Parker didn't turn his head away from the screen. "Yeah, that's cool," he muttered.

"Ksenia had her crew disable our transport," Chase said as

loudly as he dared. Parker nodded, still typing. Chase waved his hand between Parker and the screen. "Hello, will you listen to me? We're trapped here."

With visible effort, Parker pulled his eyes away from the computer. "I heard you," he said dryly. "And wow, that's weird. But I'm trying to hack through the multiple firewalls of a Titan-class starship, which is kind of impossible, so that our friends don't all die. Please don't be mad if I place more priority on what I'm doing than what you're talking about. Tell this to someone who can actually do something about it, like Maurus."

Chase gaped, speechless. Half of him wanted to punch Parker in his know-it-all face, but the other half of him knew he was right. Parker gave him a long, sober look without a speck of his usual flippancy and turned back to what he was doing. Feeling weirdly chastised, Chase left the room and went to look for Maurus.

He found all three Fleet officers and Lilli in the dining room a level below, sitting at an elegant table with china plates of creamy pasta in front of them. Vidal was the only one eating, while Lilli stared stonily at her untouched plate and Maurus and Derrick engaged in a heated discussion.

"What you're saying is patently untrue. The velocity forces alone would crush you in a millisecond," said Maurus, smashing his pasta with a fork in demonstration.

Derrick made a scornful face. "It is possible, if you do it with the right degree of torque."

Vidal smiled at Chase and waved him over to the seat beside her. "We were all starving. It's going to be a long day—you should have something to eat, too. Keep your energy up." She flagged an attendant who waited in the corner of the room, and leaned toward Chase to gesture at the two arguing. "This is so old. They've been fighting about the same thing, in one form or another, since the first day Maurus came aboard the ship."

"Lieutenant Derrick doesn't like Lyolians?"

She sighed. "Karsten . . . has a tradition to uphold. He comes from a long line of jerks."

The attendant set a plate of the same short, creamy pasta on the table. When Chase looked up to thank him, he saw blank, glassy eyes and realized the man was actually an android. His stomach growled. It had been ages since he'd scarfed down a synth croissant from the canteen, and he started shoveling pasta into his mouth. "This is really good," he mumbled.

Lilli glared at him. "It's gross."

Vidal smiled, shaking her head. "These Federation bigwigs get served real food every day, no synth. We should have a plate sent up to Parker, too."

"He won't eat right now. Not while he's working." Realizing he'd been distracted by the food, Chase set down his fork.

"Um, I need to tell you something. I overheard Ksenia tell someone from her crew to disable the transport we came in."

"What?" Vidal raised a hand to get Maurus's and Derrick's attention. "Guys, stop your bickering and listen to this. Say it again, Chase."

Uncomfortable with the sudden attention, Chase locked onto Maurus's eyes and repeated the information. "She said something about how she didn't want us to run off and try to do something heroic."

"You're joking," said Derrick. "Where did you hear this and in what context?"

Maurus was already on his feet. "That's madness. I'll go to the flight deck and check it—"

Suddenly the room was spinning, and everyone and everything went flying as an earsplitting *BOOM* shook the entire *Falconer*. All the china plates were dashed from the table, splattering the carpet with cream sauce. Chase landed on the floor, dazed. He'd flown right through the back of his chair.

Vidal groaned and rubbed her forehead. "What on Taras was that?"

Maurus grabbed the edge of the table and pulled himself up. "Get to the control deck!" he barked, running out the door with Derrick.

For a panicked moment, Chase couldn't see his sister anywhere. "Lilli?"

"Here," she said in a shaky voice, crawling out from behind an overturned chair.

Shaking off her bruised head, Vidal climbed to her feet and followed Maurus, turning to Chase and Lilli in the doorway. "You kids stay in here!"

Were they under attack from the *Kuyddestor*, or was this some kind of horrible accident? Chase itched to run after the soldiers and see what he could learn, but beside him Lilli looked pale and terrified as she stood. He couldn't leave her alone. At the far end of the room, the serving android stood up and began methodically gathering the broken dishware. Chase leaned against a chair to catch his breath.

"What are you doing?" Lilli asked impatiently. "Let's go after them!"

The hallway was empty, but at the other end of the hall Chase could hear shouting from behind the closed door of the control deck. "Meet you inside?" he asked Lilli. She nodded, and without a word Chase jumped through the wall and stepped into the coat closet. Lilli was already there, standing off to the side.

"Have you lost your mind, Petrod?" came Ksenia's voice from the other side of the door. She sounded furious, but also shaken. "We're trying to work with you to resolve this in a peaceful manner. No one on the ship has been trying to break down your defenses, I promise you that."

The voice that answered was a loud, angry blare, and Chase clutched his ear as the translink boomed a translation. "Someone on your ship is launching a hacker attack on our firewalls as we speak. The first one was a warning shot to get your attention. You have one minute to make it stop or we will annihilate your vessel."

Parker. Chase looked at Lilli, eyes wide, and with a nod she vanished.

"Get the boy," Ksenia growled in a low tone. In a louder voice, she said, "Be reasonable. You *know* me. We've worked together. We'll investigate your concerns—"

"Fifty seconds!"

Footsteps were running out of the control cabin already. Chase turned and leapt at the back of the closet, racing through the inside of the walls until he burst through the velveteen panels of the sitting room.

Lilli was already there, pulling on one side of the computer. "You have to stop!" she shouted. "They're going to kill us!"

"Just let me do this!" yelled Parker. "I'm already through the first firewall!"

Chase reached between the two of them, phasing between their arms, and tried to grab the computer. His hands phased uselessly through it. *Focus!* he screamed at himself, and just like that, his hands latched onto the metal frame.

Parker glared at him from the other side of the computer,

trembling and white with a rage that Chase had never seen before. He yanked it toward himself again just as a handful of Federation Guards came through the door. Lilli moved away, but Chase and Parker stood frozen as a Guard raised his hand-blaster and fired a short blast at their hands.

"Ouch!" roared Parker as the computer crashed to the floor. Chase stumbled back, rubbing his numb hands.

"What are you doing?" Maurus pushed past the Guards. "Did you just fire at *children*?" He pulled his own weapon and pointed it at the computer.

Before he could fire, a monstrous roar tore through the ship, and everything and everyone was flying, falling, the ship around them shaking like the rage of an angry giant. The first thing Chase saw once the room had stopped spinning was Lilli, staring down at him and crying. He peeled himself off the floor and put his arm around her. Maurus was already beside them, helping Parker to his feet.

They hurried past the dazed, groaning Guards sprawled across the sitting room floor and ran down the hallway. Maurus waved them toward another doorway and into a room filled with rows of passenger-style seating. "Don't look out the window," he commanded.

Of course it was impossible not to look after he'd said that, but Chase immediately regretted it. The green horizon of Rhima stood sideways as the ship hurtled in an uncontrolled fall toward the moon's surface. Because the ship's gravity generator was still working, they couldn't feel a thing, but the sight made Chase instantly dizzy.

"I said don't look," snapped Maurus. He pushed Parker into a seat and hit a lever beside it, and a five-point harness popped out around him. As he helped Parker fasten the straps around his chest, Chase made Lilli sit down and did the same for her. He pushed Maurus away when he tried to help. "I'll be fine. Go save the ship."

Maurus hesitated a moment. "Stay with them," he commanded. Another explosion hit as he turned around, throwing him to his knees and filling the room briefly with light from a brilliant white fire outside the windows. Smoke poured in from the hall as Maurus stumbled from the room.

"Please buckle in, Chase," said Lilli, tears streaming down her face. It was a futile action—he would be thrown right through the harness when they crashed. Still, he sank into the seat beside her and fumbled with the straps.

A deep shudder ran through the ship. Outside the window, the horizon slowly tipped back to a level plane, but they were still plummeting toward the moon. An unsteady rocking motion tipped the entire ship back and forth, and the engines screamed in deceleration.

"I'm sorry," came Parker's choked voice over the roar of the engines. He gripped the straps of his harness with white knuckles. "This is my fault."

The engines whined even higher, creating a vibration that rattled the walls, but they seemed to be slowing as the ship neared the surface. Squeezing Lilli's hand, Chase couldn't stop himself from watching out the window as it came closer and closer, holding his breath for the second when they would make contact. It came with a deafening crunch of metal, and they all went lunging forward in their seats. Chase popped right out of his harness like he'd expected and fell to the floor, rolling through several rows of chairs with a series of grunts as Lilli's screams—and possibly Parker's?—rang out. The *Falconer* skidded across the landscape, sliding around out of control but gradually slowing down. Finally the entire vehicle lurched up on one side slightly before falling flat with a final crash.

For a moment, no one said anything.

"I cannot. Believe. We're alive." Parker dropped his head forward, still clutching the harness.

Chase sat up, his head still spinning, and started to crawl back toward the others.

The door slid open, and Vidal and Derrick rushed in. "Oh, thank the stars, he put you in here," wheezed Vidal. "Come on, we have to go. Petrod's going to fire again."

Before Chase could argue, the officers hustled them from their seats and ran with them down the hallway, while all around staffers and crew frantically gathered what they could. At the exit, the door was locked.

"Unlock the door!" shouted Vidal. No one was listening. Derrick pulled a blaster from his belt and fired at the lock mechanism, kicking between each blast. Vidal did the same, timing with him, and after half a dozen blasts, the door began to come loose. They pushed it out far enough to almost squeeze through, but not enough.

"There's a brace bar on the outside blocking it!" shouted Vidal. She hurled herself at the crack, but even her tiny frame couldn't fit. She looked to Lilli, but before she could ask, Chase grabbed the blaster from her hand and leapt at the crack, his skin tingling where he had to phase through the metal.

He landed on pebbly ground and wheeled around. A thick metal bar held the door tight to the vehicle, but it took only one shot with the blaster to knock it away and the door fell away onto the ground.

Derrick swept Lilli into his arms and jumped down, Parker right beside him. Vidal still stood inside the ship, looking down at them. "Run!" she shouted, motioning away from the *Falconer*. She looked back inside the vehicle, and an anxious look crossed her face.

"Come on!" yelled Derrick.

She turned back, eyebrows scrunched. "I can't—"

The missile hit so fast, Chase didn't even hear it coming. It struck somewhere on the other side of the ship, filling the air with an earsplitting thunder. The shock wave tore through him, strong enough that he fell back onto the ground. Struggling to sit up, he saw Lilli, Parker, and Derrick all lying dazed. Vidal had been thrown past them, and lay in a groaning heap on the ground. Derrick was at her side immediately.

"Maurus!" she screamed, fighting to get back to her feet.

Federal Guards and staff came stumbling out of the ship, shocked and bleeding. Ksenia appeared, confused, her dark hair half undone and tumbling into her face.

But no Maurus.

Before anyone could stop him, Chase took a running leap back into the *Falconer*, sprinting down the hallway. Smoke hung thick in the air, and so, eyes burning, he ran at a crouch, covering his mouth with his sleeve. Another missile might not hurt him, but if he dropped dead of smoke inhalation, he wouldn't do anyone any good.

He came upon Maurus so suddenly that he nearly tripped on him. He was lying on the floor outside the control deck, one shoulder of his uniform burned away. Chase dropped to Maurus's side, shaking his good shoulder.

Groggily Maurus responded, pushing himself to his knees

to crawl down the hall inch by painful inch with Chase's help. By the time they made it back to the exit, Chase was dizzy from smoke and had no idea how Maurus was even still going. They fell out of the ship and into the waiting hands of Derrick and several Federation Guards, who held them up as they hobbled away from the smoking wreck.

Two more missiles hit, right on top of the other, and the *Falconer* exploded behind them. Most people hit the ground automatically, but the Guard on Chase's right was still standing, and took a chunk of debris in the back of his leg. He fell with a grunt. Ears ringing, Chase looked around the chaotic, smoky scene, frantic until he saw Parker and Lilli huddled together. Vidal scrabbled across the ground, ash and tears streaking her face, and nearly tackled Maurus, sobbing into his chest. Maurus pressed his face into her hair, holding her tightly with his one good arm.

Feeling like he was intruding on something private, Chase looked away. Across the way, Ksenia sat, stunned, while one of her staffers mopped blood off her forehead with a torn-up jacket.

"They can't do this," she said faintly, staring at the flames licking the smoldering ruins of the *Falconer*. "I have diplomatic immunity."

"I don't think that counts for much here," muttered Maurus

as he plucked up the burned edge of his jacket, hissing at the long burn that ran down his arm, pink layers of skin already peeling back.

"We need to try to contact the Fleet," said Vidal, wiping at her face and straightening up.

"With what?" Derrick gestured at the *Falconer*. "We're stranded with no comms."

As they debated, Chase crossed the area and knelt beside his sister. "Are you okay?"

She gave him a somber look. "I'm not hurt, but I'm pretty much reading your lips right now."

"My ears are ringing too." Chase looked around at the flat, green landscape—all low rocks and pebbles covered in something like moss. Terraforming had made it possible for them to stand on the surface of the moon and breathe its air, but from what he could see it was nothing more than a barren wasteland. Just above the far horizon, a long, ghostly sliver of massive Storros hung suspended in a sky the gray of twilight.

"We're totally stranded," said Parker. He looked at Lilli. "I don't suppose you can find us a ride out of here?"

She arched a thin eyebrow at him. "It's not like calling a jettaxi."

"I guess we just wait until we all starve, or the Werikosa come back to kill us."

"They're not going to come after us anymore," said Chase. "They just wanted to wreck our ship."

"You're right," said Parker in a flat voice. He picked up a pebble and threw it hard, almost hitting the smoking hulk of the crashed ship. "I'm sure they'll keep us around long enough to watch the Fleet blow the *Kuyddestor* out of the sky."

CHAPTER FIFTEEN

A thick column of black smoke rose from the wreckage of the *Falconer*. They were sitting a good hundred meters away, but Chase could still feel waves of heat coming off its twisted, fire-licked frame. A few people spoke quietly in small groups, while others sat staring at the horizon, obviously still in shock. Maurus lay on his side on the rocky terrain, grimacing as Vidal and Derrick examined his wounded shoulder.

Vidal got to her feet, looking around the group of stunned survivors. "Is everyone accounted for?"

Ksenia nodded as she joined their group. "Yes. Most of the *Falconer*'s crew were androids, fortunately." She had walked over to the crest of a low hill to look at the horizon. Pushing her hair back from her blood-crusted forehead, she said, "I have a rough idea where we are. There's a gravity mineworks that we should be able to walk to. We'll be able to find food and water and communications there. It's . . ." She paused and frowned before waving her arm vaguely toward the darkening horizon. "It's somewhere in that direction."

Parker gave a half-laugh. "I don't suppose you thought to grab a locator off the ship before it blew up."

"*You.*" Narrowing her eyes, Ksenia towered over him in her torn maroon suit. "I don't want to hear a word from you. The *Kuyddestor* wouldn't have attacked us if it weren't for you. This is all your fault."

Parker scowled up at her. "I was getting past the firewalls. I was doing more than anyone else."

"You were deliberately provoking the hijackers. *I* was running the mission. It was my decision to make whether we took offensive action or not."

"We asked your permission to get on a networked computer," hissed Maurus from where he lay on the ground. "You just didn't think Parker would be capable of breaching their security."

"Of course not!" cried Ksenia.

Vidal jumped in. "The Werikosa would have attacked us eventually. They were looking for any excuse."

"No they weren't," insisted Ksenia, pushing her hair back in an agitated manner. "They wouldn't have attacked us if they hadn't felt threatened." She turned back to Parker. "You brought that attack on us. You did that to him." She pointed at Maurus's raw, red shoulder.

Parker stared at the ugly wound, momentarily lost for words. For a moment Chase was torn between wanting to defend him, and not wanting to anger Ksenia before he even got a chance to talk to her.

"Leave him alone," growled a scratchy voice. Lilli crouched on the outskirts of the group, glaring at Ksenia through narrowed eyes. "It happened, and it's over, and finger pointing isn't going to change anything. At least we're alive."

One of the *Falconer*'s pilots, whose broken arm hung in a sling, asked, "But for how much longer?"

No one answered, and the only sound was the flickering of flames and metallic creaks as the remains of the *Falconer* fell apart. Maurus pushed himself up on one elbow, stifling a gasp. "For now let's focus on getting to the mineworks. Are we talking about far as in a day's walk, or more than that?"

Ksenia pursed her mouth. "I saw it through the window as the ship was coming down. It's walking distance."

It took a while to gather themselves up and scavenge what little supplies they could find. The Guard who'd taken shrapnel in his leg couldn't walk, and two other crewmembers stayed behind with him. The rest of them set off slowly across the endless mossy rocks of the Rhima landscape. Ksenia marched ahead with her few remaining staffers, her dark eyes wide and watchful. The crew of the *Kuyddestor* followed silently, casting occasional glances into the sky, as if they might see their starship somewhere up there. Derrick had torn up his own jacket to fashion a sling for Maurus's wounded arm, frowning as Chase watched him lower it carefully over Maurus's head.

Maurus kept up with the rest of them, but he walked stiffly, his face tense, eyes fixed straight ahead. The sling seemed to help stabilize his arm, but clear liquid seeped from his burned shoulder and soaked the gray fabric. "We need to find a place to keep warm," Chase said to Parker in a low voice. "The sun's going to set soon."

"No it won't," said Parker. "It looks like dusk because we're at the terminator. The line between light and dark."

"Right." Chase nodded. "And soon it'll be completely dark."

"No," corrected Parker. "Rhima is tidally locked to Storros— the same side always faces the planet. It revolves around the planet, so all sides see the sun at some point, but it doesn't rotate on its own. I think I read it takes thirty-nine days to make a full revolution, so we've got a good day or two before the darkness gets this far."

"Lords, Parker." Lilli gave him a sideways look. "Spending time with you is like hanging out with an encyclopedia."

Chase stifled a laugh and gave Lilli a thumbs-up as she tried to hide the smile creeping over her face. Scowling, Parker stomped away to walk in a different part of the group.

As long as they walked, the landscape never changed— gray tinged with mossy green and mostly flat, with some low rolling hills and dull skies. The twisted hulk of the *Falconer* soon lay far behind, with only a thin plume of smoke to mark where they'd left it. Chase's clothes smelled burnt, and he felt filthy. He ran his hands through his hair and looked at the sky, worrying about what was happening to the crew on the *Kuyddestor* and how Analora was doing.

"Why hasn't anyone come to look for us?" he asked. "The Storrian defense fleet probably saw what happened, didn't they?"

Vidal, walking ahead of them, glanced back. "I'm certain they did. But what do you think would happen if a Storrian ship comes anywhere near Rhima, let alone tries to land on it?"

"Oh," said Chase, as understanding dawned on him. Regardless of whether or not they knew that there were *Falconer* survivors, the *Kuyddestor* hijackers would ensure that nobody came anywhere near their coveted moon.

Derrick spit on the ground. "We're trapped down here like rabbits in a cage."

They stopped after an hour of walking over the monotonous land to take a short rest. Maurus sat on the ground, holding his shoulder at a funny angle. Vidal crouched beside him, talking in a low voice. When Chase approached, he saw that Maurus was shivering. "Chase, can you look around and see if anyone has any water?" she asked softly.

He went straight to Ksenia to ask. She was sitting on a

boulder with her staffers gathered around her. They appeared to be arguing about something, but before he could overhear what they were talking about, the staffers left.

"No, there's no water," she told Chase when he asked. "My staff thought to take all their personal items and electronics, but nobody took any survival equipment."

Analora would have known what to take, Chase thought. It was a perfect opportunity to ask Ksenia about everything—the microchip, the note, the meeting on Lumos—but suddenly he wasn't sure how to begin. Should he just ask her outright if she'd left the note? What if she said no? A musty, mossy smell blew by on a breeze, and without thinking he wrinkled his nose.

"Stinks here, doesn't it?'" Ksenia gestured at the green horizon. "Part of the oxygen production program was a surface-wide distribution of lichen spores. That's what you're smelling. Along with a blend of factory-generated gasses and liquids." She poked at the thick, spongy lichen covering the boulder she sat on and frowned. Chase glanced at the lichen and looked up, about to ask what she'd been doing in Lumos, but he found her giving him the peculiar, intense gaze he'd seen before.

"What?" he asked.

She spoke quietly. "Chase, if the *Kuyddestor* doesn't survive this . . . situation, would you like to come with me? I can find you a new home. One where you belong."

Chase took a step closer. "Are you the one who left me the note?"

She paused before giving him a tiny nod. "Yes, I am."

Excitement started to rush up, but he dampened it with caution. "Why did you want me to meet you in Lumos?"

"I wanted to meet with you in private." She looked over her shoulder. "We shouldn't even be talking about this now."

But he needed more confirmation from her. "So you know who I am." She nodded. "Did you know the ship was going to be hijacked?"

She flinched in surprise. "If you're suggesting that I somehow had a hand in this . . ."

"No, no," Chase said hastily. "I just thought maybe, because it happened when . . ." Fearing that she might cut the conversation off, he went straight for the big questions. "What do you know about my parents? Did you work for Asa Kaplan?"

"We can't talk about that here." Ksenia stood. "Come with me when this is over, no matter what happens to the *Kuyddestor.* I'll have all the answers for you then. I'll find you a new home."

The reaction Chase felt to the idea of leaving the ship was so powerful it surprised him. "The *Kuyddestor* is my home. I can't leave it."

"You don't belong there," she said firmly, turning away to end the conversation. "We'll talk about this later."

When Chase returned to the other side of the group, Maurus was hunched over, taking tiny sips from a flask that Parker had somehow wheedled out of one of the staffers. He managed a wink when he saw Chase's worried face. "Don't worry, I'll live. What does this put you up to now, three times you've saved my life? Soon I won't want to leave your side, Chase Garrety."

Vidal was talking to the Federation staffers, who stood in a tight unified group. She came over and crouched next to Maurus. "The staffers have decided to go back to the ship."

"What ship?" asked Maurus. "There was nothing left."

"They think they'll have a better chance of getting rescued if they stay there. They're scared about getting lost."

"We'll find the gravity mines, right?" asked Chase.

"We will." Vidal smiled at him, but her eyes showed enough doubt to make Chase worry. She put a hand on Maurus's leg. "If this is too strenuous for you, you can go back with them."

Maurus shook his head. "It's not as bad as it looks," he grunted, struggling to his feet.

Vidal sighed, making a face at Chase. "Well, that's good, because it looks like raw meat."

If Ksenia was disturbed by her staff's lack of faith in her leadership, she didn't show it. The staffers set back the way they'd come—easy enough to follow, by the path of crushed and bruised lichen they'd left in their wake. The rest of them continued on, guided only by Ksenia's promise that they were going the right way.

After two more hours of walking, they were all starting to cast dubious glances at one another behind Ksenia's back. The same endless terrain rolled out ahead of them, with no mineworks in sight. "We're just walking with no direction," muttered Parker, his face drawn and pale under the smears of ash. "We've gone maybe ten miles, with a viewing radius of four miles at best, so we've covered about a hundred and thirty square miles of, oh, about thirteen *million* square miles total on the moon. I hope this lichen is edible, because we're going to be doing this for a while." He spoke loudly enough for Ksenia to hear, but she didn't respond. Chase kept his eyes on the ground, ignoring Parker like everyone else.

Not one minute later, the frame of the gravity mines appeared on the horizon, a tiny blip on the flat plain. Ksenia whipped around, flashing them all a fiercely triumphant expression. It was around that time that Chase first noticed the wind—not the tepid mushroomy breeze from before, but a thin cold draft that raised the hairs on his arms. It picked up quickly, swirling through the group in chilly bursts. He shivered, rubbing his arms.

Parker looked over his shoulder. "Oh, that is not good."

Chase turned in the same direction Parker faced, and his stomach dropped. A smudge rising off the ground had replaced the normal horizon of endless lichen, like someone had run their thumb over the edge and blurred it until there was nothing but an ominous dark grayness. "What is that?"

"Windstorm!" shouted Vidal.

Chase looked around to find his sister, panic shooting through him. His first instinct was to run, but where? There was nothing that could offer shelter on the flat moon, and they'd never make it to the mineworks in time.

"Let's move!" Derrick motioned to the left, toward a slight crest in the landscape, and everyone broke into a run. Chase checked to make sure both Lilli and Parker were there, and Maurus as well, who ran in a loping jog, his burned arm held tight to his chest.

The windstorm moved faster than they could run, and soon the air around them was swirling in fierce currents. A distant whistling roar behind them grew louder and louder. The winds came on them in full force, ripping through their ranks and tearing at their clothes. Worse were the tiny bits of debris that blew in their faces with the strength of a sandblaster—even phasing couldn't stop Chase from getting a mouthful of grit when he tried to tell Lilli to pull the back of her sweater up over her head. They jogged onward, jostling against one another as the gales alternately pushed and slowed them.

Chase tried to keep pace alongside his sister, but she stopped to wipe lichen from her eyes and then ran with one sweatered arm held over her face. They fell back to the rear, and slowly a gap started to grow between them and the rest of the group, the swirling winds blotting them out of view little by little. Suddenly Derrick appeared in front of them, squinting, and he dropped to one knee, gesturing for Lilli to climb up on his back. Once she was on, he stood, and he and Chase sprinted to rejoin everyone else.

When they reached the crest, the ground rose before them in a short incline. Derrick, who had returned to the lead with Lilli clinging to his back, paused at the top. They were at the lip of an enormous crater. The walls of the crater went sharply downhill, leading to a round, flattened bottom, like a shallow bowl. In the center of that bowl was a cluster of buildings.

Vidal gave a whoop, but the sound was snatched away by the fierce winds at their backs, and without another word everyone started running down the pebbly slope. As soon as they'd gone a few meters, the winds began to die down, and the sound of their ragged panting could be heard.

Jogging sideways, Maurus slipped and fell on his good shoulder. Chase ran to him, but Vidal was already there, helping him back up. Little bits of lichen and dirt were stuck to his wounded arm, and his face was rigid. He got to his knees and waved them both soundlessly on toward the settlement.

In the gray twilight, a motley collection of cargo trailers and smaller dome-like structures lay clumped together like a growth on the dismal soil. A few spiraling antennae sprouted up among the structures. Lichen grew alongside the buildings and up the walls in thick curly patches. There were vehicles too: a small, rusted hovercraft parked by a shed, a few dented hoverbikes leaning against a random piece of corrugated fence.

"Hello?" called Ksenia. No answer. She called again, but this time made an unintelligible noise that might have been a Werikosa dialect but sounded more like she was choking on a mouthful of nails. The translink interpreted it as "Greetings!" There was no reply, no movement.

They split up and moved among the structures, looking for any sign of life. Derrick put Lilli down and started walking up to each building and throwing the makeshift doors open with a shout. Chase followed with Lilli and Parker at his sides, peering down the streets. There had to be at least twenty structures erected more or less haphazardly in the tiny village.

Maurus hobbled down one of the bigger streets, his teeth clenched. "It's deserted. Your terraformers have left the settlement."

Ksenia stood in between two rows of structures, arms crossed. Her voice was tight with irritation. "This isn't the settlement we built for them. We never would have put one at the bottom of a crater; they're all scheduled to be lakes in the next phase. These aren't even buildings. They're scrap material. That's a shipping container. And that's a piece of wall from the biodome garden we put in. What did they do?"

"Looks like they colonized," said Parker simply.

Chase saw an open barrel and went over to see what was inside. It was too dark to be completely certain, but it looked like it was filled with water. Rainwater? He stepped back, looking at a long metal crate punched full of ventilation holes. He very nearly missed it, but at the last second he saw a tiny bit of movement, and his gaze zeroed in on something shiny in two of the ventilation holes. Eyes.

"Hey!" he yelled in alarm, stumbling backward. "I found somebody!"

Maurus was at his side in an instant, blaster drawn with his good arm. "Come out!" he shouted.

A harsh strange cry cut through the air, and suddenly there were Werikosa everywhere: spying down from the tops of buildings, sliding out from under structures that looked fully planted in the ground. They were shorter than Chase would have guessed—much shorter than the Storrians.

They were friendlier too, approaching him and Maurus with open curiosity. One reached out and touched Chase's arm, leaving a shiny blue-green spot on his skin. Another moved in on Maurus's burned arm, sniffing the raw skin and burbling something that the translink didn't pick up.

Maurus moved back cautiously, raising his blaster. "Stay back."

"Put down your weapon, Lieutenant," said Ksenia in a hard voice. She looked around at the Werikosa, shaking her head. "You won't need it right now. These are children."

CHAPTER SIXTEEN

Once the crew had lowered their weapons, a few adult Werikosa began to emerge, melting out of the scenery like ghosts. They were more cautious than the children and hung back, muttering among themselves. One especially lean and leathery older male stepped out ahead of the group, dressed in ragged black attire and bare feet, with a blaster rifle slung loosely around his back.

The adults were bigger than the Storrians, but as Chase had noticed when they spoke to the hijacker Petrod, their features were similar to those of the other civilization with tiny, wide-set eyes, flat nose, and drooping upper lip that curled over the rest of their mouths. But where the Storrians had eyebrow stalks that oozed in and out of their foreheads, the Werikosa had a hard-looking ridge of skin there that didn't seem to move as much. There was something unrefined about their expressions and movements, and it was unsettling to

Chase because he couldn't read them and didn't know what to expect.

"Who are you?" Ksenia barked. "Where is Mathid? What is this place?"

The Werikosa's face darkened. "How do you know Mathid?"

"He was the head of the mineworks, last I knew. My name is Ksenia Oriolo. I'm the Federal plenipotentiary for the Rhima terraforming project. We were just attacked by your leader Petrod—I assume you're aware he's hijacked a Federation starship?"

The Werikosa simply stared at her, giving no sign whether he knew about it or not.

"He shot down our ship; we crashed some distance from here. Some of our people were injured."

"We know about your ship." He took a step back and signaled to a few of his people. "Come with us."

Another Werikosa, this one younger and wearing only a loose vest and baggy trousers, charged out of the crowd and pointed angrily at the Earthans.

"These ship dwellers are the enemy, Bawran," he said, eyeing them with his eyebrow ridges pressed back flat against his forehead. "If Petrod meant to destroy them, we should finish his task, not offer them aid."

Hands went to the waists of everyone carrying a weapon. Chase grabbed his sister by the arm, pulling her behind him.

Bawran faced the group of survivors. "Do not draw your arms. We have no intention of fighting with you, but we do have the means." To the younger Werikosa, he said, "Go clear out the central trailer. We will put them there."

The younger Werikosa got in his face, pushing against his chest. "These are our prisoners! Do not treat them with hospitality!"

"Enough!" shouted Bawran, pushing the youngster roughly away. For a second, it looked like they might break into a fight, but Bawran took a long step forward, lips slightly curled back, and after a few tense moments the young Werikosa backed down and stormed away.

As Bawran led them through the murky twilight paths of the settlement, more faces peeked out from behind cracked doors and window holes. He sent several others running ahead, and by the time the group reached the center of the community, they had emptied out a long cargo trailer that was open on one end and dark as a cave inside.

Glancing back at the rest of the group, Ksenia led the way up into the cargo trailer. Maurus marched beside Chase, his burned arm held tight against his stomach, and grabbed him with his other arm for support. Chase checked to make sure that Parker and Lilli were nearby and found them sandwiched between Vidal and Derrick.

The inside of the trailer was lit only with a few dim LED

lights plugged into the ceiling. Thick rugs and rough blankets lay in tangled piles against the wall, making Chase wonder if they had forced someone from their home.

Ksenia stalked through the dingy space and whirled around to face Bawran. "What is this place? What happened to the settlement the Federation constructed for you by the Yoder mineworks?"

"Mining operations have ceased," said Bawran, standing calmly in the middle of the room as the rest of their group entered. "A few of our people still hold the location, but the windstorms tore up the biodome and damaged some of the buildings. The craters are safer and mostly free of windstorms."

As Chase helped Maurus settle down onto a blanket, he noticed the back of the trailer was filled with jumbled heaps of broken electronics and other junk. Parker walked toward it, his eyes traveling over the items with a cool, almost android-like, analytical gaze.

"You realize that these craters are destined to become lakes, don't you?" Ksenia told the Werikosa leader. "They'll fill with water and all these homes will be lost. The windstorms will decrease as vegetation expands and the atmosphere balances out."

"That is a question for the future. For now, this is better than worrying if a house will fall in on our children." Bawran stepped toward the exit as if to leave.

Ksenia did not relent, pushing on with her questions. "How did all these women and children get here? We didn't arrange for families to accompany the terraformers to Rhima. Did you smuggle them over?" Bawran said nothing, and Ksenia continued. "Do you realize what a bad idea this is? This moon is not ready for settling. It doesn't have the resources to sustain a population."

"Our people are not dying of the sun illness here," Bawran said. "That is already better."

"You'd rather watch them starve?" she asked.

A scowl formed on Bawran's face, but before he could answer, a breathless, stocky Werikosa lugging a large composite chest entered the trailer. "The injured?" he asked, making a beeline for Maurus before anyone could answer him and providing enough distraction for Bawran to leave.

Deftly the medic cut away an entire half of Maurus's jacket, shaking his head as he turned to paw through items in his chest, a strange collection of junk, tubes, and loose wires that didn't look particularly sanitary.

"Do you have steamgel in there?" Maurus asked.

The medic waved a hand at him. "No use talking—I won't understand a word. Just sit still. This will hurt." He grabbed Maurus's wrist and lifted his arm away from his body, while with the other he poured a bottle of watery liquid over Maurus's shoulder, rinsing away the sand and lichen stuck to it.

Maurus closed his eyes and slammed his head backward into the wall behind him, yelling through his teeth. The medic pulled a jar from his chest and shoved it at Chase. "Put this on him while I locate some bandaging."

Cautiously Chase popped open the lid and peered at the jiggly yellow cream inside. It smelled pungent and weirdly appetizing. He glanced up at Maurus.

"Do it. Please." Maurus had cracked his eyes open, but closed them again, breathing in short gasps. The raw, red skin on his shoulder was visibly tightening and contracting. Feeling anxious, Chase dipped his hand into the cream and scooped out a slippery handful. Immediately his hand began to burn, and a large splat of cream hit the floor below him.

"Careful, Chase," said Vidal, poised at his side to take over.

Shaking his head, Chase smeared the cream as delicately as possible down Maurus's raw arm before he could lose any more of it. For a moment, Maurus seized up, but then he sank back against the wall, his mouth hanging open in a slack grin. He turned to Vidal. "Hey there, pretty," he slurred.

The medic was back at their side, shaking out a fraying piece of material that had seen better days. Glancing at Chase, he frowned. "Why didn't you use the spreader?"

Chase looked down at the jar and noticed a plastic spoon-like piece snapped onto the lid. He started to shrug, but the medic had snatched up Chase's hand to scrub off the excess cream. He peered into Chase's eyes. "Why aren't you affected?"

It must have been one of those involuntary self-preservation reflexes Dr. Bishallany had tested for, the molecules in his hand letting the powerful cream phase through. But what if he had needed the cream himself? "I don't . . . I'm not . . ." Chase began haltingly. But the medic, not understanding anything without a translink, turned back to Maurus, his question only rhetorical. He hoisted Maurus back off the wall and began wrapping his shoulder tightly, while the Lyolian leaned against him, a vacant, drugged smile on his face.

As the medic finished up with the wounded, Bawran returned to the trailer. He wore a grim expression. "I've alerted Petrod of your arrival. He's ordered us to keep you here, Madame Oriolo, until the dispute has come to a satisfactory conclusion."

"As a hostage?" she asked sharply.

"As an esteemed guest. The young ones can stay with you, but I'm afraid the soldiers in your company must leave their weapons and come with me."

"I won't allow it. We're not a threat to you. Some of them can barely walk."

Bawran looked over at Maurus, who was absently picking at a loose thread on the edge of his bandage. "They're to be quartered somewhere else. The ones who can't walk will be carried."

Several Werikosa carrying weapons, led by the young hothead in the vest, marched into the trailer and began rounding up the soldiers. Derrick, who sat on a blanket beside Lilli, gestured angrily. "We'll stay with the children. I'm not leaving them alone here."

The hothead Werikosa approached Maurus, pointing his blaster at him with an aggressiveness that made Chase freeze. "Stand up," he growled. Maurus stared at the ground, mumbling to himself. A lock of dark hair had fallen across his face. The Werikosa nudged him gently with the nozzle of his blaster rifle, and with his lightning-fast Lyolian reflexes, Maurus reached out and snatched the weapon, pulling it down toward himself. His eyes were bright and alert again—the cream's narcotic effect had already worn off. How long had he been faking it?

Chase could see what was going to happen. "Let go!" he cried. But the Werikosa moved quicker than he had expected, and before Maurus could react, he whirled around and slammed the butt of his rifle into Maurus's bandaged shoulder. Maurus fell back with an agonized scream.

"Hey!" Looking outraged, Derrick sprang to his feet, blocking the Werikosa from swinging at Maurus again. He grabbed at the blaster, and for a moment the two of them wrestled for control before Bawran slid up behind Derrick and grabbed his ear, yanking him away shouting. The younger Werikosa raised his blaster and hauled back as if to smash Derrick in the face with it.

"Hotha!" shouted Bawran. "That's enough!"

Eyeing his superior with obvious malice, Hotha threw the blaster over his shoulder and yanked Maurus to his feet, shoving both him and Derrick toward the exit. Maurus stumbled and fell to his knees, and Vidal rushed to his side, glancing back with a face full of worry.

"Just go," said Ksenia. "I'll take care of the children."

Cold fear settled into Chase's stomach as he watched the three soldiers leave with Hotha's blaster rifle aimed at their backs. If the young Werikosa really wanted to prove his loyalty to the cause, this could be the last time Chase would see them alive. He looked up at Bawran. "Don't let him hurt them."

Bawran gave him a flat stare that he couldn't interpret, and walked toward the exit. "I have no way to lock you in here, but know that if you try to run, you won't get far."

Once they were alone in the dim trailer, Ksenia sank onto a pile of blankets, running her hands over her face. "How did this happen?" she groaned, shaking her head.

Chase crouched down beside her, leaden hopelessness seeping through him, making him feel like he weighed a million pounds. He had barely allowed himself to think about what would happen if the *Kuyddestor* were lost, but the idea of anything happening to Maurus and the other soldiers on top of this was paralyzing. He, Parker, and Lilli could be stranded on the moon for ages, or rescued by exactly the part of the Fleet they'd been avoiding. The only thing coming to their aid anytime soon was this approaching Fleet starship, the *Destrier*—the very name of which had made Maurus visibly blanch when he heard it. And that "aid" sounded less like assistance and more like annihilation. But there was one possible resource that they hadn't yet discussed.

"If we can get to the mineworks, maybe we can still call for help," he began.

Ksenia arched an eyebrow and sighed. "The *Destrier* won't be here for days, and I highly doubt the Storrians will risk any of their defense to attempt a rescue mission. We'd be better off trying to negotiate with our captors. Bawran seems better acquainted with the humanoid mind-set than most Werikosa I've worked with."

But the *Destrier* wasn't what Chase was thinking of, and neither were the Storrians. If Ksenia knew Asa like she said, maybe she knew a way to reach him. He'd helped them out once before, and even though Chase still didn't really trust him, there weren't a lot of options left. "What about Asa?"

Ksenia leaned forward, giving him an unusual look. "What about him?"

"Maybe, if he's close enough . . . do you know how to contact him? Do you think he might be able to help us?"

She stared at him for a moment before resting back against the wall again. "I wish he would," she said. "But I wouldn't put a lot of hope in that avenue."

Before Chase could ask what she meant, a few Werikosa children slipped back into the trailer, coming over to crouch beside them. The children didn't speak much, but when they did it seemed like they were using some sort of baby talk, because the translink never interpreted it. One took Parker's hand and placed it within her own, making a raspy noise like a giggle as she squeezed it.

"Nice," said Parker sarcastically when he drew his hand away, blue-green with the Werikosa's skin oil. He wiped it on a blanket. Another played with Lilli's hair, leaving punkish streaks of colored oil in the blond as she sat frozen and grimacing.

Two adult Werikosa entered, carrying four large and misshapen metal bowls that looked like they had been beaten out of pieces of tin siding, and distributed the bowls to their guests. Inside was a thin, gray gruel. Chase inhaled the steam rising from his bowl, but it smelled like hot granite.

"What is this?" asked Lilli in a disgusted voice.

"I believe," said Ksenia dryly, "that this is a lichen stew." One of the Werikosa was trying to demonstrate to her how to tip the bowl at her mouth. "Yes, thank you, I get it."

Chase was being encouraged to do the same, so he reluctantly lifted the bowl and slurped a tiny bit of the stew. It had an earthy flavor, much like he imagined dirt would taste, and although it didn't make him gag, he certainly had no desire to eat any more. He tried to set the bowl down, but all the Werikosa were staring at him, and it seemed rude to turn down their offering.

Parker was trying to hand his own bowl back. "I'm so full, thank you, no, no more mud stew for me." Lilli had shoved hers away untouched, and they looked at the bowl, and then at her, their beady eyes round and inexpressive, making it impossible to tell if their feelings had been hurt. Could they even get hurt feelings?

A deafening metallic crunching noise cut through the air from outside, startling them all. It sounded almost as if a vehicle were crash-landing somewhere in the village. Immediately Ksenia stood and exited the trailer, striding right past the Werikosa and their gruel. Chase looked at their hosts and shrugged apologetically, and ran after her with Parker and Lilli to see what was going on.

They had to circle around to the outside of the settlement until they found what had happened. A hoverbike had landed just outside the structures and appeared to have dragged along several enormous pieces of warped metal sheeting and a tattered, once plush crimson chair.

"Is that—?" Chase began to ask.

"Did you steal that from my ship?" shouted Ksenia, her face turning red with anger.

Bawran walked out from around the back of the hovercraft. He was bare-chested, and although he was definitely older, his build was still muscular and powerful. A dark blue-green sheen covered his face, until he pulled a rag from his pocket and wiped away the thick layer of oil.

"What is this madness?" Ksenia cried. "What do you mean by gutting our ship for salvage not six hours after we were shot down by your colleague?"

Bawran shrugged. "I apologize. It didn't appear that you would be using the ship again, and good metal is in short supply here. As are most things."

"Other than lichen," said Parker under his breath.

He unhooked the chair and set it on the ground. "I found some of your people with the ship. I'll send Hotha over to the mineworks for a bigger hover so we can bring them here to you."

"We need to contact the Federation," said Ksenia. "I'll go with him to the mineworks so I can send a message out."

As he untied the bindings on a sheet of metal, Bawran gave her a look and simply shook his head.

"This is unconscionable!" shouted Ksenia. "Do you people not understand loyalty? I was on *your* side. I sympathized with the Werikosa plight."

"Would you like any of these items back?" Bawran asked as he unloaded a gilded chest from the back of the bike. "You may have them."

"It's not about the ship, you fool." She walked up and got in his face. "Petrod *tried to kill me.*"

Bawran look impassively at her. "He must have had a good reason."

Ksenia glanced at Parker, who ducked his head and looked away. She was trembling with rage. "This won't end well for you. I promise you that. Your people will be dragged scream-ing from this moon and dumped back on Werikos where you belong."

Bawran had stopped unloading his trailer, and his expres-sion was grim. "They'll find we put up a fight. We have women and children here, yes, but we also have weapons. We have an army."

"Your army is a joke. You have no concept of the Federa-tion's strength, and no idea what you're facing." Whirling around in her tattered suit, Ksenia stormed off, and Bawran started dragging his new metal pieces over to stack against one of the sheds, humming a tune and never sparing a glance for Chase, Parker, or Lilli.

CHAPTER SEVENTEEN

Parker pawed through the piles of junk at the back of the trailer, pulling out a cracked screen and tossing it to the side. Chase sat back on a pile of rugs next to Lilli, watching the curious Werikosa hanging around the front of the trailer, although they hadn't offered them any more food. Ksenia had not returned since her confrontation with Bawran. He glanced over at his sister, whose eyes were wide but glazed with exhaustion.

"You okay?" he asked softly.

She looked up at him with uncharacteristic openness, and he saw the depth of worry in her expression. "What's going to happen to us? If they take out the ship, if Uncle Lionel is gone . . . where will we go?"

"That's not going to happen," he assured her. "They'll figure this out before anything bad happens. We'll be fine."

Lilli answered this with an unconvinced look, and the best

he could give her was a smile and a hopeful shrug. They both knew he was just trying to make her feel better, but somehow this made him feel closer to her than he had in ages.

After leaving Bawran they'd wandered around the settlement until they figured out where the soldiers were being held, in a cargo container on the other side of the settlement. The container was guarded by a handful of young Werikosa, including Hotha. They were too far away for the translink to interpret what the Werikosa talked about, but their strutting and aggressive postures made Chase nervous.

Something Parker was tugging at snapped, and he cursed, wiping his hand on his jacket.

Chase looked back at the mound of broken electronics. "You okay over there?"

"Yeah," Parker muttered. "Just trying to get at the insides of this enclosure."

"Are you building us a ride off this place?"

"A news feed. We need to find out what's going on up there." Parker pointed skyward. "There's enough random junk here to build a fully automated house if I had the time. They've got all these huge antennae here in the settlement—there's one attached to this trailer. There must be a way to tap into a feed."

Intrigued and more hopeful than he'd felt since they'd crashed, Chase joined Parker's scavenging hunt. They sorted through boxes of cables and piles of broken or discarded pieces of equipment, clothes, and utensils. Parker hooted when he finally pried open a ruined chassis and found a fully intact radio circuit board inside. "This looks good," he said, peering at the silvery surface of the board.

Within minutes he had wired up the cracked screen to the board. "Now to tap into the antennae outside." He untangled more cable, jumpered a few pieces together to make it longer, and fed the end of it through a hole near the base of the wall before standing to leave. "When I knock, keep feeding that coax cable through."

A few seconds later, his knock came on the back of the trailer. Chase tried to push the cable into the hole, but it started to bunch up in his hand. Parker's muffled voice shouted something unintelligible outside the trailer. Chase glanced at Lilli. "Keep an eye on those guys," he said, nodding at the Werikosa, who were busy playing with strings in the carpets. Then he plunged his head through the back wall.

"Whoa," said Parker, jumping back as Chase's face came through the trailer.

A quick glance confirmed that no one was around to see. "What did you say?" Chase whispered, his neck already tingling fiercely where he was phasing through the wall.

"I said that the cable must have caught on something. It's not coming out."

"Hold on a second." Chase's arm came through the trailer next, and he reached back into the wall, fishing around until his numb fingers came upon the bunched-up cable. It took a minute of concentration to get his fingertips to grab onto the cable while the rest of his hand was phasing.

"This is so weird," said Parker, watching him. "What does it feel like?"

"It's not awesome," said Chase through gritted teeth. "It burns."

"I bet it does." Parker took the cable from him, once Chase had managed to weave the entire thing around the blockage and through the hole. "Thanks. You can put your head back inside now."

Chase rolled his eyes and ducked back through. Lilli glanced at him, but the Werikosa were still playing with their strings. Parker jogged back inside. "Okay, we're all hooked up. Let's see."

He moved a bit of wire from the screen up and down a row of knobby bits on the circuit board, watching the flickering screen carefully. A tinny voice came from the minuscule speaker holes on the sides of the screen, and a second later a blurry video feed lit up the screen.

"The hijacking occurred at approximately fourteen hundred local Earthtime. Few details are available as to how the Werikosa were able to pull off such a highly orchestrated attack, but here with more information is our reporter on the scene, Parri Dietz."

At the sound of the video feed, several curious Werikosa crept to the back of the trailer and crowded in, watching the screen in awe. Parri Dietz's calm, professional face filled the screen, but Chase could barely hear her speak over the Werikosa's delighted squeals.

"The standoff between the hijacked starship and Storrian defense fleet continues. Officials have not been able to determine if there were any survivors in the Federal embassy ship that was shot down late yesterday, as the moon is still being closely guarded by the hijackers, but they say that there may have been—"

The image cut out. Fearing that they'd been discovered, Chase looked up in alarm. Instead he saw that two of the Werikosa kids had followed the cable back to the hole and yanked it, disconnecting the middle cables to twist them into bracelets.

"Hey, knock that off!" shouted Parker, trying to snatch the cables back from them. "I need that!" The ones who had been watching the news feed took the screen from his hands, turning it around and poking at it. "Let go! I was using that!" He grabbed for it, and the Werikosa made a high-pitched noise of delight and scampered out of the trailer.

Parker roared with frustration. "They're like a pack of

animals!" Chase shrugged, exasperated. These kids thought it was all a game, and short of roughing them up or making a loud fuss, he couldn't see a way to stop them. Parker snatched up the circuit board and what cables he could get away from the Werikosa. "Come on, let's get out of here."

They went out into the dusty street. "Well, at least we learned that nobody's looking for us," said Chase grimly. "Now what? Is there a way to contact someone? Lilli, can you maybe travel to Parri Dietz?"

Lilli shook her head. "That would take ages—I have no idea where she is."

Parker looked at the circuit board in his hands and sighed. "At the very least, maybe I can send out a super primitive SOS signal on a public distress band to let them know someone's here." He lifted his head and looked around. "Let's see if we can use that big yagi antenna over there."

They had to slide past a few stacks of crates and a pair of Werikosa women who barely glanced at them to get to the building where the antenna in question was attached. Parker used a pocketknife to pry open a panel at the base of the antenna, and plugged the loose cable in the box onto the circuit board.

"I'm not sure this will work," he said with a frown. Parker fiddled with some switches on the circuit board until he seemed satisfied. With another wire, he started to short two spots on the circuit board, muttering to himself as he did. "Stranded on moon. S-O-S. Crash survivors. Please send help."

"What's going on here?" came a translinked voice behind them.

Filled with dread, Chase looked back to see Bawran standing behind them. A handblaster hung at his waist.

"We were playing a game," he said quickly, stepping toward Bawran so he wouldn't notice Parker untwisting wires behind him. "Hide-and-seek. With the other kids here."

"Hide and what?" Bawran asked. "We don't know that game."

"That's why we're teaching it to them," said Lilli.

"And we're about to lose!" Parker barked, dashing right past Bawran, the circuit board stashed in his jacket. Running after him, Chase paused once they were back in the street, but Bawran didn't appear to be coming after them. The Werikosa children were all there, cheering and ready for play, and Parker swiftly handed over the circuit board, which one of them took as if it were a precious gift and ran off.

They wandered back down the street, surrounded by their new friends. Chase looked up at the sky. He wondered what was happening aboard the *Kuyddestor* at that moment, and if they'd ever get onboard again. How long had they been on Rhima now? Half a day? More? Parker had been right about the tidal-locking—the sky never changed, and it just looked like dusk the whole time.

"They're all okay right now," said Lilli beside him, as if she'd read his mind. When he looked over at her, she said, "I've been checking. Sending quick flashes up to the ship. Everyone's fine so far."

"I can't believe you can travel that far," he said.

"Practice," she told him simply. He looked over at her pale face, her tired eyes, and for a moment a preposterous possibility occurred to him—one that he quickly pushed out of his mind.

On the far side of the settlement, shouts arose, Maurus's clear baritone rising above the rest.

"What on Taras—" Chase began. They ran toward the commotion just as a hovercraft lifted off the ground, stirring up dust and lichen. The only person remaining was Ksenia, shouting in the vehicle's wake. The door of the container where the soldiers had been kept swung on its hinges.

"What happened?" asked Chase. "Where did everyone go?"

She whirled around, livid. "He took them."

"Who?" asked Parker.

"Hotha. He rounded up the soldiers and took them away to the gravity mines."

A bad feeling started to grow in Chase's stomach. "Why?"

Ksenia gave him a flat look. "Why do you think? To hurl them into the center of the moon, most likely, and prove his loyalty to the cause."

This couldn't be happening. Not so soon. Chase began to back away from the building. "Where is Bawran? We have to stop them!"

Ksenia scowled. "I just saw him leave on a hover, off to raid my ship again, I'm sure. They waited until he was gone to do this. By the time we catch up with them, it will be all over."

Parker was already off and running down the street, skidding to a stop at the row of hoverbikes. He fiddled with one for a moment, and with a sigh of disgust moved on to the next before standing. "These are a mess. It's going to take me hours to fix either of them." He looked over to the side, where a third hoverbike frame rested, but it had already been raided for parts, and the handlebar and entire seat segment were missing. Parker leaned over and did something to the controls, and immediately it powered up, lifting off the ground. "And this is the one that works. Great."

Ten minutes later, they had hauled the plush crimson chair around from the junk pile and lashed it to the hoverbike frame with loose cabling. Parker had jerry-rigged a handlebar out of some piping. "It's way out of balance so we're probably going to wear out the bearings really quickly, but as long as it doesn't leave us stranded in the middle of the moon, this should do."

"As long as we don't hit another windstorm," muttered Lilli.

"Well, that too, Miss Sunshine," said Parker. "Get on." He stood at the controls, his feet balancing the two main slats of the hovers. Lilli climbed into the armchair, and Chase hopped on the back, hugging the back of the seat.

"What are you doing?" Ksenia's voice cut through the air. She stood at the edge of the building, looking over their rigged-up hoverbike.

"We're going to help Maurus and the others," said Parker.

"You don't need to go," she said quickly. "I've contacted Asa. He's on his way."

Was she telling the truth? Chase's heart leapt at the possibility. "You contacted Asa? How?"

Ksenia nodded. "Bawran is hiding a comm station in his trailer. I just found it."

"You just found it," said Parker sarcastically. "How convenient. And what did Asa say?"

She was lying. She had to be. But her answer came immediately. "He's on his way here right now. If you leave, you'll miss him."

This made Chase pause. "But they're in trouble now. If we wait for Asa, it might be too late."

"They're just Fleet soldiers. Stay here with me, where it's safe." If Chase had doubted her connection to Asa before, now she even sounded like him, placing their safety over the safety of their friends in the Fleet.

"Nope," said Parker. He hit the drive gear and they went sailing down the street, trailed by cheerfully screaming Werikosa children. The chair rocked back hard against its ties, causing one heart-stopping moment when Chase thought they were all going to go flying, but it stayed put. Soon they were speeding across the floor of the crater.

The steep crater walls loomed ahead. "Either we're going to fly up this thing, or we're going to smash into a million bits!" shouted Parker, cranking up to full speed. As they came closer, Chase's heart pounded harder and harder. Then they hit . . . and shot straight up the hill. They weren't even halfway up when the bike began to strain, and the smell of bitter, hot plastic wafted up from below.

"Come on!" Chase roared, pounding his fist against the back of the chair. The hoverbike slowed to a crawl. They weren't going to make it. The engine started to make high-pitched broken sounds, and the bike sank to a stop, grinding against gravel.

"No!" cried Chase. He leapt off and pushed the back of the chair. It felt like he was trying to push a starship, not a hoverbike.

Muttering under his breath, Parker leaned down and fiddled with the controls, yelping when he touched something hot. He wrapped his hand in the hem of his shirt to pry open the console. "We must have already eaten down on the bearings and put too much friction on the forward rotor," he said. "Looks like it just tripped a fuse. I can jumper across it—it's not like this bike has more than one ride left in it. But I need a small piece of metal for the jumper."

Chase felt around in his empty pockets, looked around at the barren soil, but saw nothing useful. Then he glanced down, and spotted a tag at the rear of the hovercraft, attached with a thick piece of twisted metal wire. "Hang on," he said, kneeling to a crouch to untwist the wire. The metal was stiff and bit into his fingers, making it harder to untwist when his hands started to automatically phase through it. Gritting his teeth, he eventually pulled it free and passed it up to Parker.

"That'll work." Parker went to work on the controls, cursing under his breath, and they waited nervously for a minute to see whether their rescue mission had already come to an end.

"Should we—" Chase started to ask.

"Here we go!" yelled Parker. The bike roared back to life and shot upward, soaring over the crest of the rim. They sped onward across the featureless surface of the moon, cheering like they'd won the lottery.

In the distance, the shadowy outline of the gravity mines rose against the horizon. They hurtled toward it, but it was so far away they barely seemed to make any progress. Clutching the armrest with one hand, Lilli tried to pull her sweater over her face to block herself from the lichen and dust they were stirring up. Chase clung to the back of the chair, his arms and hands beginning to cramp and ache.

Finally, after what felt like at least an hour of travel, the mineworks loomed before them. A gigantic metal frame held up drills that soared into the sky, the lowest section covered with metal panels—probably, Chase guessed, to protect against the windstorms. A long, lichen-covered warehouse was located right beside it, and a menagerie of dormant heavy machinery lay between the two. The lower buildings of a settlement were grouped farther in the distance.

Parker drew to a stop alongside the outer building, parking the hoverbike beside the metal panels on the frame. As soon as he turned the whirring engine off, they could hear shouting from somewhere inside.

Lilli closed her eyes for a moment. "They are right inside, by the mine shaft," she said, heading for a gap in the panels.

Chase's feet felt like jelly after standing on the vibrating base of the hoverbike for so long, but he rushed after her. They ran down a short hallway that opened onto a giant outdoor area of a monstrous open framework, like they were standing inside the bottom of a half-built skyscraper. In the center, a drill as wide around as a transport shuttle hung suspended above a massive, ragged hole in the ground.

Shouts echoed from across the way, joined by the terrible sound of blaster fire, but the drill blocked their view of what was happening. Chase grabbed Parker and Lilli, pulling them to slow down. If blasters were being used, he didn't want them anywhere near the fight. "Stay back here! Don't go any closer!"

Parker shouted something, but Chase didn't hear it. He sprinted as hard as he could toward the gigantic drill, coming around the side to see what was happening.

Hotha stood near the edge of the mine shaft, with two more Werikosa standing behind him. All three carried heavy blasters. Hotha was shouting at someone, waving his weapon around.

As he drew a little closer, with a plummeting feeling in his gut Chase saw that Maurus, Vidal, and Derrick were lined up right at the edge of the chasm. Hotha raised his blaster to point it at Derrick, but with his quick Lyolian reflexes, Maurus reached out with his good arm and knocked it upward, so the blast flew harmlessly over their heads.

In response, Hotha kicked Maurus in the knee and swung the nozzle of his weapon into Maurus's burned shoulder. With a yell, Maurus buckled at the waist. All Hotha had to do was shove a bare foot in his chest.

And just like that Maurus toppled backward, vanishing into the mine shaft.

CHAPTER EIGHTEEN

For a moment, the universe froze. Chase slowed to a stop, staring at the empty space where Maurus had disappeared into the mine shaft, unable to believe what he'd just seen. His mouth fell open, and all the air rushed out of him. Was that it? Was he too late? The rumblings of a terrible noise began to grow in his chest.

A scream sliced through the air. Vidal threw herself at the edge of the chasm, scrambling forward to look down into it. Her shrieks went up an octave in an unintelligible garble of words. Behind her, one of Hotha's colleagues raised a foot as if to kick her in after Maurus. Derrick threw himself at the man, wrestling him backward.

This shook Chase out of his stupor. He started running toward them again, and as he did, the words of Vidal's cries became clear.

"Hold on! Just hold on!" Was she calling out to Maurus?

With a surge of hope, Chase raced toward her side, but before he could get there, Hotha stepped forward and pointed his weapon at her back.

"NO!" roared Chase. His cry caught everyone's attention, and immediately Hotha swiveled around, aiming directly at Chase's chest. Blaster fire erupted from the nozzle.

Both Derrick and Vidal cried out, but Chase braced himself in time, and the blaster fire only made him stagger one step back, scowling at the numb sensation it left in his chest as it passed through him. Hotha lowered the weapon and cocked his head. Even Hotha's companions paused to stare at Chase, and Derrick was looking at him in a way he never had on the ship. "What on Taras—?"

Hotha raised his blaster again to fire, but Chase dodged him this time, trying to lead him away from Vidal, who still crouched at the edge of the mine shaft. As he jogged backward, in the corner of his eye he saw her climb over the edge and down into the hole. Hotha jogged toward him, pointing his blaster again.

"Hey you!" Lilli stood off to the left, and her cry caught Hotha's attention. When he turned, she blinked out and reappeared a few feet to her right, then blinked out again and appeared diagonally behind that, and then again, and again. Chase wanted to strangle her for not staying out of it like he'd told her, but he saw his opportunity to grab a long, heavy pick off the ground and swing it at Hotha's head. The Werikosa fell flat on his face, and Lilli grinned at Chase.

"We'll talk about this," he said, pointing at her in what he hoped was an authoritative way.

Derrick had managed to pin down one of the two other Werikosa, but the second was coming up behind him, blaster raised as if to club the soldier with it.

A loud rumble shook the air, and a monstrous mechanical digger rolled toward the mine shaft on thick tank treads, a gigantic scoop on a long metal arm poised over the cabin. Behind the controls, Parker's pale face was fixed on the fight before him. As the shovel of the machine swung down, Derrick tore free and rolled out of the way, and the shovel clamped over both of the Werikosa, trapping them against the ground.

Climbing to his feet and wiping his brow, Derrick gave Parker a thumbs-up. He jogged over to the edge of the chasm and squinted down. Then he jumped.

Chase raced to the edge of the pit. The top of the mine shaft was even bigger than he had realized—the entire *Falconer* could have fit from end to end across its width, though it narrowed farther below. The walls were steep but not smooth, and a thousand ledges of broken moon rock jutted out to create handholds. Derrick had landed on a wide ledge just below the lip.

Chase sucked in his breath when he saw Maurus farther

down, clinging to an overhang. The rock he'd caught hold of to stop his fall jutted too far out for him to reach any other location, so he hung uselessly, unable to climb or swing to another spot. Vidal had climbed down to a ledge nearby, but she couldn't find an angle with enough leverage to offer him her hand.

Derrick scrambled down the wall to a wide, flat shelf of rock and positioned himself on a ledge just to the left of Maurus. He dropped to his stomach and wriggled off the edge of the overhang, extending his right leg toward Maurus. "Here!" he shouted. "Grab my foot!"

Maurus pushed sideways off the rock wall and seized Derrick's ankle, using his momentum to swing to a small ledge nearby, but the motion must have been more than Derrick expected, and it yanked him right to the edge of his platform. Maurus let go to grab onto the next outcropping of rock, but Derrick slipped from his handhold and slid down the wall with a shout, grabbing desperately at anything to stop himself.

Chase looked up for rope, for tools, for anything to help. "Parker, get that machine over here!" he yelled. The shovel wasn't nearly long enough to reach, but it was all they had. He heard an anguished cry, and what he saw when he looked down again made his heart stop. Far below in the canyon, Vidal had scrambled down to a ledge where Derrick lay facedown and very still. She kneeled by his head, while Maurus's anguished shout echoed up the rocky walls.

"Chase, look out!" came Parker's panicked voice behind him.

A jumble of images and movement came at him when he looked over his shoulder—Hotha, bleeding and furious, sprinting at him, and a flash of Lilli, sending a copy in to trip him before he reached Chase.

Alone, Chase could have braced himself against Hotha and let him blast through and into the void. But some instinctive, irrational part of himself automatically reached out to grab Lilli, even though she vanished as soon as he touched her arm. But it was enough to tip him over and sent him careening into the pit along with Hotha.

For a split second, there was nothing but air and the tangled limbs of the Werikosa. Chase reached out instinctively, catching the edge of a brown rock, and he grabbed it. Hotha plummeted past him.

Before Parker's white face appeared at the edge of the canyon, Lilli was already there, crouched on the very rock he was holding on to. Her face was fierce, but tears were streaming down her cheeks. "Here!" she shouted, extending her hand toward him. "Take my hand!"

If he hadn't been so close to falling to his imminent demise, Chase would have laughed. "You can't lift me," he gasped. "Thanks for the offer though."

He could feel his hands slipping through the rocks, burning as his body tried to phase away from the sharp edges. *Stop it, stop it!* He focused every bit of energy into keeping himself solid so that he wouldn't tumble down the steep shaft after Maurus and the others.

If he could just angle the jump right, he might land on the tiny ledge nearby. But if he missed . . .

Parker's head appeared over the top of the canyon, followed by a length of cable. "Grab this!" But it was impossible—even with Parker stretching down as far as he dared, the end of the cable was still a good arm's length away from Chase.

His arms burned with the effort of holding on. Chase glanced around, looking to see if there was something else he could safely drop onto. The giant drill was possibly within reach, but what would he do if he landed on the curved surface of the drill bit? Shoot down it like a curly slide?

"Don't do it!" yelled Parker, reading his movements. "I'll get another rope!"

But there was no time left—Chase's stamina was giving out. He used his feet to push off from the stony wall, barely catching the edge of the drill bit with his hands and swinging his body to land on the curved surface below. Immediately he started to slide, picking up speed as he whipped around the bit. The metal was smooth from wearing against hard moon rock, too smooth to leave anywhere to grab onto.

A bright light flashed in his eyes as he scrabbled and slid down, again and again as he whipped around the curves. Was something floating in the mine beside him, or was he halluci-nating? He tried to turn himself sideways, to wedge his body into the curves, but all he managed to do was turn himself around so that he was sliding backward. Any second he was going to shoot out into the mine shaft like a greased egg.

This had been a terrible idea.

The end of the drill bit came without warning, and for a moment Chase was weightless, flailing through the air before the inevitable plummet down toward his doom. But instead, three walls appeared around him, swallowing him up as he hit a hard metal floor. The canyon still swam before his eyes in a dizzying swirl, and it wasn't until he started to roll across the floor that he realized he'd landed in the back cargo area of some kind of small cruiser, the entire back hatch of which was wide open. He turned to see who was piloting, but the back of the cargo hold was just a blank wall with a door.

With a gut-wrenching turn, the cruiser whipped around to show the surface above the canyon, and standing right out-side the hatch was Parker. Seeing Chase, Parker leapt into the cargo area beside him with a relieved grin.

"Who's piloting this?" Chase yelled. He looked around for any clues as to whose cruiser this was, but the inside of the cargo hold was blank and sterile.

"Who cares?" Parker grabbed hold of the wall as the vehi-cle shot across the mine, coming level to where Lilli was on the other side of the mine shaft. Chase reached out to help her aboard, and as soon as they were all inside, the rear hatch of the cargo hold closed, encasing them in the cruiser.

Chase dashed to the window on the back hatch, looking down as the canyon shrunk away below them. "No, we have to get Maurus!" he shouted, pounding on the window. "Go back!"

Parker was trying unsuccessfully to open the door into the rest of the vehicle. "Hey!" he shouted. "Whoever you are, let us out of here! We need to go back for someone!"

Without warning, the room simultaneously shrank and expanded, with the accompanying brain-compressing feeling that Chase recognized as a fold. The back window went immediately dark—whoever had picked them up had leapt right off the surface of Rhima into deep space.

"No!" he screamed, beating against the blackened windows. They'd left Maurus and Vidal there, stranded at the bottom of the canyon. And Derrick . . .

Lilli sat hunched on the floor, her cheeks still stained with tears.

"Hang on," Chase said to Parker, gearing up to jump through the locked door and rush the pilot's deck.

"Be careful," warned Parker. "You don't—"

But before he could finish, the cargo door zipped open, and Chase stumbled backward, stunned into silence. Because the person who walked through the door was someone Chase hadn't seen in months, someone he hadn't expected to see ever again.

Mina fixed him with her piercing blue eyes and smiled. "Hello there. It's nice to see you again."

CHAPTER NINETEEN

When Chase saw Mina in the cargo hold of that transport vehicle, the first feeling that flooded through him was relief. Dependable, reliable Mina—he'd never been so happy to see her placid face, and for the first few seconds, it didn't matter how she'd found them, or what kind of conclusions that led to about Ksenia. He just wanted to hug her.

He gestured out the window, although the green sphere of the moon wasn't visible. "We have to go back. Maurus is still down there with two others."

Dependable, reliable Mina's brown hair swung around her heart-shaped face as she shook her head. "I'm sorry. Maurus is on his own now."

It took a moment to register her answer. Was she really refusing to help? This wasn't some random stranger who'd picked them up—this was Mina, their friend. As soon as the thought entered his mind, Parker's judgment echoed behind it: *She's not your friend. She's an android. She doesn't have friends.* But she *knew* Maurus. They had all traveled across the galaxy together, as a team. Why wouldn't she want to help him? "Are you kidding? We can't leave him stranded. One of his crewmembers is hurt really bad—maybe dead."

Her tone was unyielding. "We're not taking him with us."

"This is Asa's order, isn't it?" said Parker in an acid voice. "Where is he? Let me talk to him."

"Soon. We're heading back to his ship right now."

"You're taking us to Asa?" A jolt of surprise ran through Chase like an electric shock. Of course that was where Mina would take them, he knew that, but still . . . After all these months of waiting, after the dramatic events of the past twenty-four hours, he was finally going to see Asa very soon.

Parker gave an angry laugh. "Of course. He didn't send her to save us. He sent her to capture us." He crossed his arms, narrowing his eyes at Mina. "Did Ksenia really contact Asa? Or did you hear my SOS? How did you know it was me?"

Mina ignored Parker and looked at Lilli huddled against the wall. "Are you alright?"

Chase shook off his shock, his frustration with Mina returning. "She's going to be, because you got her off that moon. Maurus and Vidal and Derrick are not, because you—"

"That's not going to work, Chase," said Parker. "She doesn't care. They're on their own now."

But Chase couldn't forget the last image he'd seen of Derrick, lying broken and still on the hard moon rock. Maybe he'd been a complete jerk to Maurus on the ship, but at the mine shaft he'd fought alongside them, and he'd always been good to Lilli. And if he hadn't survived, would Maurus and Vidal be able to climb out of the mine shaft anyway? Even if they could, more vicious Werikosa—Hotha, if he was still alive, or others like him—would find them, and they no longer had any weapons to defend themselves with.

Chase placed himself in front of Mina. If her orders from Asa were not to take any Fleet soldiers onboard, she wouldn't break them. But there had to be a way around her android logic. "Please, do *something*. Tell the Fleet they're there. Or if you don't want to talk with the Fleet, tell a news reporter. Or anyone. Just, please. They're trapped and hurt."

Mina arched a perfect eyebrow, analyzing him for a minute. "I can do that. I'll put the word out." Chase tipped his head back with a loud sigh of relief. At least it was something. Mina turned to head back into the front of the shuttle.

"I'm coming with you," Parker told her.

"Not right now. Stay back here with the others. I'll let you out once we're docked on the ship." The door closed behind her before he could protest.

Parker slammed a hand on the wall and leaned forward. "That's it," he said, shaking his head. "We're done. Asa's not going to let us go back for Maurus, and he's definitely not going to help the *Kuyddestor*, much less let us go back ourselves. Ever."

Lilli looked up at Chase, panicked. "We have to go back," she said. "We have to help them. There's not much time left."

Chase didn't know if he wanted to explode from the pressure or just sit down and cry at how hopelessly things were turning out. It was too much, all of it. As often as he had dreamed of the day he would confront Asa with all his questions, this wasn't the way he'd imagined it would play out. Their last interaction replayed itself in his memory on a nauseating loop. Asa had been furious with Chase for trying to save Maurus's life, and coldly indifferent when the warlord Rezer Bennin had threatened them. Sure, he'd leapt in front of blaster fire to protect Parker at the end, but otherwise he'd been completely detached. If Chase was going to meet Asa again, he would have preferred to meet on his own terms, not as a captive. And not with the fate of the *Kuyddestor* and everyone they knew hanging over their heads.

Parker looked around the cargo hold, his face tight with suspicious anger, reminding Chase that he wasn't the only one with a million questions saved up for Asa. Beside him Lilli seemed to draw further inside herself. Chase peered closer at her, but he couldn't tell if she was traveling or not. "Hey? You there?"

She looked up at him, blinking as if she'd just awoken.

"Did you travel to the *Kuyddestor*?" he asked. She nodded. "What's going on?"

"I found Analora. She's hiding in the walls. She's really upset because her dad's with everyone else on the flight deck."

Chase frowned. "He'll be fine as long as—"

"No." She shook her head violently. "He won't be fine. They've told everyone that if the *Kuyddestor* comes under attack, they're going to vent the flight deck. Everyone will get sucked out into space."

Chase tried to keep the horror from his face as he kneeled beside her. "We'll tell Asa. We can still ask him to help."

Parker scoffed behind him. "Yeah, he's got a great track record of helping others out of the good of his heart. And he loves the Fleet." He slid down the wall to a squat. "No, he's going to stick us all in some remote prison compound again, where no one will ever find us. Not that anyone will look for us, because everyone we know will be dead by then."

"Way to think like a winner," Chase snapped over his shoulder.

"You think I'm not as upset as you? I've never had the feeling like I was *home* before we started living on the *Kuyddestor*. But he's got us. We're trapped."

Chase realized he'd never gotten past his annoyance at how easily Parker had settled on the ship to understand what it actually meant to Parker to have a home with friends and freedom, with no android monitoring his every move. "He can't keep us. I can get away."

"Of course *you* can escape." Parker tipped his head at Lilli. "She'll figure out something too, because she's special like you, but I'll be stuck, just like I was before."

Chase turned around fully and locked eyes with Parker. "We'd never leave you behind. I promise. And anyway, he's not going to lock us up in some remote compound. We'll convince him he has to help us."

Parker shook his head. "It'll never happen. Did you really think we were going to get back on the *Kuyddestor* anyway? Even Maurus knew it was impossible. We can't go back."

"We can," said Lilli, with a sudden finality that made them both look at her. She lowered her head and said nothing else.

Parker looked around suddenly and headed over to the window. "We're slowing down."

"Do you see a ship?" asked Chase.

Parker craned his neck as far as he could both ways. "Nope. We must be approaching head-on."

Chase joined him at the window to look out as the frame of a spaceway came together around them and the stars receded, and the shuttle came to a smooth stop in a docking bay. A pair of massive outer doors slid shut at the end of the spaceway, enclosing them in the larger ship.

Chase's heart slammed in his chest as they waited in the cargo hold. An impatient part of him wanted to phase out into the docking bay to start getting a look at where they were, but fear of losing track of Lilli and Parker made him stay. Finally the rear hatch opened onto the bay. Mina stood just outside the cargo hold, joined by a slender man with receding blond hair.

"Hello," he said, bowing slightly at the waist. He looked somewhat familiar to Chase, but he couldn't place where from.

"This is Jericho," said Mina. She motioned for them to exit the shuttle. "Come along."

Chase put his hand on Lilli's shoulder to reassure her as they stepped into the ship. The walls of the docking bay were pristine white, but more strangely, the massive chamber was empty and dead silent.

"Where is everyone?" asked Chase, who had grown accustomed to the daily churn of activity aboard the *Kuyddestor*. He didn't spend a lot of time on the flight deck, but when he did there were always at least a dozen people hard at work.

Mina led them across the room and opened a door at the back of the docking bay. "There is no everyone. The ship mostly runs itself."

Their footsteps echoed off the walls as they walked from the docking bay into a spacious white hallway with wide blue floors. Parker turned to Mina. "So this is the mother ship I never got to see. How long were you guys tracking us?"

"Since you sent the SOS," she said.

"No." Parker's angry voice echoed down the empty hall. *"How long* have you been tracking us?"

"Oh." She shrugged. "Since you boarded the *Kuyddestor.* More or less. You never destroyed your chip."

"But I firewalled it."

"And checked the signal a hundred times a day. That's basically cutting off communications with someone and then strolling past their house every day thinking they won't notice you because you're wearing a different colored shirt." She looked Parker up and down. "You seem well. You've gotten taller."

"That's what growing humans do," he replied crisply.

They hadn't seen what kind of ship they'd arrived at, but going by the time it took them to walk down what felt like endless empty hallways, Chase guessed it was a large one. Most of the doors they passed were closed, although they got an occasional glance into a sterile meeting room or a darkened lab. How many people did it even take to run this ship, he wondered, and were any of them besides Asa humans?

Finally Mina led them into an elevator, and they descended several floors. The elevator doors drew open, and standing in the hallway right before them was Asa Kaplan. His tall, lean frame, all wide shoulders and narrow waist, took Chase by surprise again—he'd forgotten what an intimidating figure Asa cut in person. His dark hair, slicked back severely, framed his pale face, which was a study in controlled intensity, as if he were holding back an explosion of glee or rage or some other gigantic emotion.

"You're here." His tone was darkly triumphant. "Well done, Mina." They crossed over to a door opposite the elevator, which opened on a large sitting room with a console-topped desk at one end and a black leather seating arrangement at the other. Asa led them to the chairs and bade them sit while he stood and looked them over with his hard blue eyes. Chase stared back at him, his heart racing. There was so much he wanted to say, to ask, but he found himself afraid to open his mouth.

Fortunately, Parker had no such fears. "Don't you have anything better to do than stalk and kidnap a group of kids?"

Asa raised an eyebrow. "It's nice to see you again too, Parker."

"It's not nice to see you at all," Parker spat. "Did you order Mina to leave our friends behind on Rhima? They were in trouble, and one of them—"

"I told her to only bring the three of you onto my ship," Asa interrupted. "And those aren't your friends. They're Fleet soldiers."

Anger finally loosened Chase's tongue. "You don't get to

say who's our friend. Maurus is one of the best friends we have."

Asa gave Chase a glare that made the words dry up on his tongue, and continued. "Mina will give you a tour of our ship and show you which areas are off-limits. Once you've settled in—"

"You can't do this," said Parker angrily. "We're not staying here."

Asa raised his eyebrows. "You think you have a choice? I'm still your guardian, Parker." He gestured at Chase and Lilli. "I'm their guardian, too."

"According to who?" cried Chase in frustration. "How do you know us?" He glanced over at Lilli, who was leaning back against her seat and looking paler by the minute.

"Some guardian you are," sneered Parker. "I'd take you more seriously if you hadn't run off and ditched us on Qesaris. After the first time you ditched us, on the *Kuyddestor.*"

Asa's face remained expressionless at these accusations, and he responded calmly. "If you'll recall, on Qesaris I'd been blasted in the chest. I couldn't fight. And Mina was no match for that many Fleet soldiers. Leaving was the only tactical decision."

"You sound like an android," said Parker.

This, of all things, made Asa flinch. After a pause, he said,

"Well, it was easy enough to find you again. You couldn't stop toying with that chip. Every time you tweaked your chip's signal, I knew exactly where you were. I stayed just outside the *Kuyddestor's* range, waiting for the right time."

Like a spider, thought Chase. *Waiting for us to fall into your web.* "You have to take us back," he said. "The *Kuyddestor's* been hacked and hijacked, but if we can sneak onboard, Parker knows how to beat the hacker to get the ship back in the crew's hands."

"That's not happening," Asa said, ending the discussion abruptly by walking away from them over to the desk, where he took a seat and began scrolling through the console. Without looking up, he said, "Mina will take you to your new quarters. Any questions or requests can be directed to her."

"No!" said Chase. He stood and took a few steps, deliberately walking right through a coffee table in the middle of the room. It didn't escape his attention how Asa's eyes locked onto his phasing legs with a strangely hungry look. "You can't keep us here."

Asa looked up at Chase's face again, his expression resettling back into cold neutrality. "You can't go back, Chase. In time you'll see that this is the best thing that could've happened to you. The *Kuyddestor* is doomed, whether it gets destroyed by the Storrians or the Fleet or the Werikosa blow it up themselves. You'll be presumed dead by anyone who knew you, and you can take a new alias and get a fresh start at life, far away from the Fleet."

"I don't want a fresh start!" yelled Chase. Asa barely knew him—that he could possibly claim to know what was best for Chase was beyond infuriating. "I don't care how much you hate the Fleet. These aren't just soldiers, they're people. They're our friends. You can't tell us that it's best for us if we abandon them all to die."

"Chase, you don't understand everything right now," said Asa.

"Then tell me."

Asa sighed and shook his head. "We'll talk about it later. When you're ready."

Chase's voice was strained as he tried to contain the anger and frustration and desperation raging inside. "Tell me what I don't know. Or send me back to the *Kuyddestor*."

"I won't let you go back there."

"Yes you will," came a thin, scratchy voice across the room. Lilli stood, looking like a warm breeze could blow her over. "You'll help us get back onto the *Kuyddestor*, and you'll go along, too."

Asa gave her a look that could wilt a flower. "And why would I do that?"

Lilli looked at Chase, and he realized that she was on the verge of tears. "Because I've been lying this whole time. To everyone. Because I'm not really here. And if you let everyone on the *Kuyddestor* die, I'm dead too."

And then she vanished.

CHAPTER TWENTY

The act of Lilli disappearing jammed Chase's thoughts. It defied logic—this was the real her, not a traveling copy. Wasn't it? His mind raced, replaying every interaction he'd had with Lilli since they'd taken that stupid escape pod from the *Kuyddestor*. It was impossible. He'd seen her send a traveling copy all the way across a city before. But from a starship down to a planet? And all the way to wherever they were now?

Asa had gone pale, his face a frozen mask. "Where did she go?"

In Chase's mind, one thought looped in a panicky blur: *She's on the ship, she's on the ship, she's on the stupid ship.* On the ship that was under attack and at risk of being blown up with all its passengers. He took a moment to collect himself, and turned to Asa. "She's not here," he said coldly. "She never was. That was only a projection of her. Turn your ship around, and take us back to the *Kuyddestor* so we can get her."

She had told him she'd practiced sending her traveling copies, but he knew now that her ability had become much more powerful than he'd realized. It wasn't just the distance she was able to send them—she also must have developed the ability to make multiple copies at once. He cursed himself for not figuring out on his own that it hadn't been the real Lilli ever since they left the *Kuyddestor*, even though he knew it was impossible.

Mina spoke from where she stood by the elevator. "Asa, Starseeker-Four has arrived in the docking bay."

"Fine," said Asa dismissively, his eyes still fixed on Chase.

"Alix reports there were five passengers aboard the vehicle, and—"

He looked up. "What?"

"They're headed up to medical," she continued impassively.

His jaw tightened, and his guise of control slipped a bit as he turned back to Chase and Parker, standing quickly. "We'll continue this later. In the meantime, find out where your sister went."

Chase shook his head. "I already told you, she's on the *Kuyddestor*."

But Asa walked from the room without answering, leaving through a door behind his desk. Mina stayed behind, waiting patiently beside the elevator.

"What on Taras is going on?" Parker said to Chase. "Is Lilli really still on the *Kuyddestor*?"

"I don't know," said Chase. "I didn't think she could travel this far."

"Neither did I," came Lilli's voice behind them.

They whipped around to see her sitting on the edge of Asa's desk. Parker whistled appreciatively. "Impressive move, little Lil. How'd you do this?"

A glint of pride flashed in her eyes. "I told you I've been trying to push the limit on my traveling to see how much I could do with it. Going on the escape pod was a test. It was hard at first, keeping up the projection at that distance, but I got used to it pretty quickly. There's a"—she twiddled her fingers in the air—"feel to it. A frequency."

"How far are you traveling right now?" asked Parker.

"Farther than I've ever gone before. Actually I don't know how much longer I can keep it up. It'll get better if he turns the ship around." The violet circles under her eyes seemed deeper than ever.

"But I saw you make a copy on Storros," said Chase. "Can you make more than one at a time?"

Lilli nodded, and an identical copy appeared, very briefly, sitting on the desk beside her. She shrugged. "Practice."

It was fascinating and horrible at the same time. "Why didn't you tell me? This whole time I thought you were safe with us."

Lilli lowered her eyes. "I never thought you'd find out. None of us knew this was going to happen when we left the *Kuyddestor.* And then once things started going really bad, I just thought you'd be mad, and worried."

"Of course I'm worried!" Chase exploded. "You're trapped on a ship that's been hijacked!" He turned to Mina. "Will you tell Asa she's here now? We need to go back to the *Kuyddestor* immediately." Mina inclined her head slightly, which Chase took for an affirmative.

Parker stared at Lilli with a kind of fascination. "So where are you?"

She hesitated. "What?"

"On the ship. You have to tell us where you're hiding. You *have* to."

"Oh." Lilli's face started to close again, the familiar guarded expression, and Chase realized she was in the place that had been her hiding spot on the ship for the past three months.

He stepped toward her. "We need to know where you are, Lilli. How are we supposed to help you if you don't trust us?"

She ducked her head and spoke in a tiny voice. "There's a crawl space in the walls next to Uncle Lionel's—the captain's apartment. You can only get to it by climbing up a duct that looks like a dead end. Not even your girlfriend knows how to find it."

Heat flushed across Chase's cheeks. "She's not my girlfriend."

"Isn't she your friend? Who's a girl?" Unbelievably, a tiny smirk tugged at the corner of Lilli's mouth.

The teasing only added to his frustration. "Why did you need to hide? You could have done your practice from anywhere. What was the point of hiding all the time?"

She looked away, and it seemed for a second like she wasn't going to answer, but in a quiet voice she said, "I feel safer there."

"Well you're not safe now, are you? Guess it didn't work." Lilli recoiled from his words, and immediately Chase felt guilty for saying them. Because they never spoke about what had happened to Lilli—because they never spoke at all—he still had no idea how deep the damage from her past went. It was something they needed to work on. If they got the chance.

The door behind Asa's desk slid open. His bright blue eyes locked immediately on Lilli and he strode right up to her with a ferocious look in his eyes. "Is this some kind of trick? Where are you?"

She seemed to shrink before him. "I'm on the *Kuyddestor.*"

"Prove it." He took her by the arm. "Prove you're not actually hiding here and trying to trick me into returning to the Fleet."

Lilli vanished off the desk, leaving him holding air, and reappeared simultaneously beside Chase. "Good enough for you?"

The same greedy look came over Asa that Chase had seen when he'd phased through the table. "You could be doing that from anywhere. How do I know you're not somewhere besides the Kuyddestor?"

"Is that a risk you're willing to take?" asked Lilli with a hint of her old fierceness. "Anyway, you'll find out in about five minutes if you don't turn your ship around. I can't keep up this distance much longer."

"Hey, is that blood on your shirt?" asked Parker, pointing at bright stains around Asa's cuffs. "Did you just murder someone?"

Asa turned his glare on Parker. "No. You'll be happy to know that my associate saw fit to bring the injured Fleet soldiers aboard my ship."

"Maurus is here?" asked Chase with cautious relief. This had to be Ksenia's work. Whether Asa had sent a shuttle for her too or she'd figured out her own escape, she must have gone looking for Chase and the others at the mineworks and found Maurus and Vidal there instead. "Are they okay?"

"One of them is nearly dead," Asa said. "The others are fine."

Chase's stomach dropped. "Take us to see them."

"No. We'll try to return them to their ship when we go back for your sister, and should that fail, we'll jettison them somewhere."

"Jettison like shoot into space?" asked Parker sharply.

Asa gave him a flat look. "In an escape shuttle, with an emergency beacon. Better?"

"Take us to see them now," said Chase. "If you don't, I'll just walk right through that door and go anyway."

"Show me," commanded Asa, pointing to the door behind his desk. "Show me how you do it and I'll take you all there."

Feeling weirdly exhibitionist, Chase walked over to the door. He looked over his shoulder at them, and in a stinging rush passed through the door.

On the other side was a small room with another elevator. Chase waited a moment, and the office door slid open. Asa looked at Chase like he wanted to examine him under a microscope. "You've done this all your life?"

"No. I was only able to do it after the attack."

"After you were dispersed?" Asa asked.

Parker cleared his throat and pointed at the elevator. "Hey, are we going somewhere or what?"

Maybe Asa's curiosity was normal for a scientist, but his blunt questioning was starting to irritate Chase. Dr. Bishallany had never been this insensitive about how he got his ability. "It happened after my parents were killed," he snapped. "After I lost my memory."

Asa's face tightened momentarily, and he swiped his hand over the elevator console. The door opened, and he ushered them in, turning to Lilli. "And you, were you able to do your projection all your life?"

Lilli glared at him. "It's why the Fleet kidnapped me and stuck me in their medical center for three weeks."

"So someone in the Fleet knew about you beforehand?"

Lilli gritted her teeth and didn't answer.

It felt like they hadn't moved at all, but when the elevator door opened they were already at the medical bay. It was as pristine white as the docking bay, with long examination benches and rows of silent machines of all sizes. Jericho was there, moving around a long silver apparatus that looked like a submarine. Sitting at a table looking dirty and disheveled and with his burned arm encased in some sort of plastic device was Maurus. Relief flooded his face when he looked up and saw Chase and the others.

"Thank the daughters of Hesta," he said hoarsely. "We didn't know who'd snatched you up." He looked at Asa. "Though I guessed it was you once I saw the androids."

Standing behind him was Ksenia, who watched everything

with a sharp, critical gaze. She had regained her poise, despite her torn suit and disheveled hair. Her eyes traveled over all three of them, and up to Asa.

"Thank you," Chase said to her. "For bringing them here."

Ksenia gave him a gracious smile and nodded. Asa cast a quick glance at her but said nothing, and walked over to the long submarine-like apparatus. "How is he, Jericho?"

"Very touch-and-go right now," said the android mildly. "Significant internal hemorrhaging had already taken place before he arrived here, and both of his legs were shattered."

Chase looked at Maurus, alarmed. "Derrick?"

Maurus nodded. "He's in bad shape, but at least he's here." He raised his eyes to Asa. "Thank you."

Asa tipped his head. "Redemption suits you well, Lieutenant Maurus."

"Where's Vidal?" Chase asked.

"The other android took her to change into fresh clothes," said Maurus. "She was covered in Derrick's blood."

"If you don't mind, I'm going to go change as well," said Ksenia, brushing her dark hair back from her face and moving toward the door.

Asa stepped to block her. "Excuse me, do I know you?"

This caught Chase off guard. He frowned, thinking at first that Asa had made a mistake.

"No, but I know you, Asa Kaplan," said Ksenia, flashing her dark eyes. "And Chase's parents as well."

"How do you know them?"

"If they never told you the story, I'm not sure I should."

Asa shook his head, an absurdly dumbstruck expression on his face. "I don't believe you. Marcus never kept a thing from me in his life."

Marcus? Chase frowned. He didn't know much about his parents, but he'd always heard his father referred to as Henk.

Ksenia didn't miss a beat. "You'd be surprised what he kept from you. Can we debrief after I've had a chance to rinse off all this blood and lichen?"

Asa smiled at her, and with frightening speed the smile fell away and left only his intensely cold expression. "You're an outstanding liar. I can see how you were able to fool these children so easily into believing that you're acquainted with me."

A blunder like that left little doubt that she was lying about knowing Chase's parents. Still, Chase shook his head, confused. "But I saw her in Lumos . . . she'd left me a note saying that if I met her there, she'd tell me more about you and my parents."

"She told you she left the note, or you asked her if she'd left it for you?" asked Asa.

Chase paused. It took him a moment to remember, but when he did, he reddened. He had brought up the note to

Ksenia first, giving away the information before she could volunteer it.

"Oh, Chase," said Parker. "You dope."

Asa circled around Ksenia where she stood, leveling the full force of his glare on her. "Jericho, you got a DNA sample from her, I trust. Who is she?"

Jericho was bent over a console on the apparatus that held Lieutenant Derrick, but he stood up and in a pleasant voice said, "Her name is Ksenia Oriolo, according to Federation records, although there is another record matching her DNA for a Hylene Chauncy, native to Ko Aiob, District 32."

Ksenia kept her eyes locked on Asa, her mouth frozen in a defiant smirk.

Asa nodded in mock approval. "Ko Aiob. Impressive. So you pulled yourself up out of the slums and somehow found a new identity and a new life."

Chase's embarrassment at being duped began to turn to anger. "So you're a big fake? What are you doing here? How did you end up on the *Kuyddestor*?"

Jericho answered Chase before Ksenia could open her mouth. "Under her assumed identity, she was a rising star in the Federation's diplomatic ranks until she became involved in a scandal dealing with misdirected aid shipments to Banafiel. Following this she was reassigned as plenipotentiary of the Rhima terraforming project approximately two years ago."

Asa raised his eyebrows. "A punishment? How has your time in the Galloi star system treated you, Ms. Oriolo?"

For a moment she appeared to waver, and then she relaxed back against the wall. A sly smile spread across her face—she knew she'd been caught. "About as well as two years surrounded by slugs and idiots can go."

"I don't suppose you had anything to do with this Werikosa uprising on the *Kuyddestor,* did you? Considering the awfully convenient fact of your being the only Federation representative not onboard when the hijacking occurred."

Ksenia merely smiled and said nothing.

"You helped them plan the hijacking, didn't you?" said Chase, furious. "You knew they were going to attack, and that's why you were on Lumos!"

"I had business at the capital," she said in lazy defiance.

"I'm sure you did," said Asa. "Jericho, put Ms. Oriolo in detention until we can leave her somewhere more appropriate. Take the officers there as well, once Lieutenant Maurus's arm has mended."

Parker made an irritated noise. "You don't need to do that, Captain Paranoia. He's our friend."

"What are you planning to do with us?" asked Maurus.

Asa looked down at him. "I'm returning you to your starship, Lieutenant."

"You realize the *Kuyddestor* is under attack right now? You won't be able to come anywhere near that ship, and teleporting is out of the question."

"Finding a way to get you back to the ship won't be a problem. What you do once you're onboard again is up to you."

"No," said Chase. "We need to stop the hijackers before the Fleet sends another ship to destroy the *Kuyddestor*."

"That's not my concern, Chase," said Asa. "I'll send a team over to extract your sister, and we'll leave the soldiers there."

"You will not!" cried Lilli angrily.

"We can't just leave them there!" said Chase.

"You're such a coward," spat Parker.

"What do you mean, extract his sister?" asked Maurus.

Asa raised his hands. "Enough!" He opened a side door that led into a hallway, pointing for Chase, Lilli, and Parker to step outside. "Mina, the soldiers can stay in here, but keep an eye on them."

He led them down another long blue-floored hall. "I will say this once. We are not going to rescue the *Kuyddestor*. We are heading back to retrieve Lilli, and then we will leave."

Lilli vanished and reappeared right in front of Asa, forcing him to stop. "If you don't help save the ship, I'll hide and you'll never find me."

"You'll die, is that what you want?" asked Asa savagely. "Is that what your parents would have wanted?"

Chase turned on him. "Don't you dare use our parents like that! You didn't know them!"

"Wrong, Chase," Asa barked, his voice echoing down the hall. "And the last thing in the universe that they would have wanted is for you to sacrifice yourself for the Fleet."

"Why do you hate the Fleet so much? Did you work for them? Were you part of the program that created my parents?"

"Did I work for the Fleet?" Asa lowered his head, his mouth twisting into an expression somewhere between a sarcastic smile and a grimace. "In a way."

"What's that supposed to mean?" asked Parker.

"What do you know about your parents, Chase?" Asa asked.

Chase paused. "They were genetically engineered soldiers created by the Fleet. One day they escaped, and Captain Lennard found them and helped them hide somewhere."

Asa nodded. "That's right. Now ask yourself something. If you were going to go to all the trouble, expend all the research and energy and technology required to create a genetically enhanced soldier, an experimental fighting machine . . . would you only make two of them?" He shook his head. "No. You wouldn't make an army of them, not at first, but to only make two would be too risky. You'd have to run tests, find their limitations. What if something were to happen to them?"

Chase stared back, his mind stubbornly resistant to Asa's words. "Then you'd have to start over. So?"

Parker smacked him on the shoulder. "Good lords, Chase, don't you get it?"

Asa said nothing at first, allowing several moments of silence to hang between them. "There were seven of us."

Chase's mind raced. *Us?* This was not at all what he had expected. "Wait. What?"

Asa nodded. "Once upon a time, my name was Fighting Unit 2402. A triumph of genetic engineering, a physically perfected humanoid soldier—almost Earthan, but better. Just like your mother and father. We were all raised together, trained together ... and finally we escaped together."

It was like a bomb had gone off in Chase's head. He looked over at Lilli, wide-eyed, but she only frowned at Asa as she listened. A flurry of new questions burst from Chase's lips. "How did you escape? Why didn't you stay together? Did you know they had children?"

Asa lifted a finger to stop him and began to lead the way down the hall again. "For safety's sake we had to split up for a time after we escaped, but we were to remain in contact, with me acting as the hub of information. We had a plan to exact our revenge on the people who'd created and nearly destroyed us. But a few years after our escape, Henk and Caralin lost their appetite for revenge. Seems their focus went elsewhere." Asa paused long enough for Chase to realize that Asa was talking about him.

"What about the tracking chips that Lilli and I had? They were made by you."

"Your parents didn't contact me very often, but one day they sent a message requesting my help with some sort of very complex tracking chips. They didn't tell me what they were for, but I had my suspicions, so I agreed on the condition that I be allowed to build in multiple redundancy backups to the systems of my choosing."

"So you always knew where we were?" asked Chase.

"I always knew where the chips were," Asa clarified. "Although I had to promise your parents that I would only use that information in case of emergency."

"What about me?" asked Parker. "Whose son am I?"

Asa glanced at him, expressionless, and kept walking without responding.

Chase's mind was buzzing too hard to worry about Parker's question. A gap of information popped up, a huge question. "What about the others? You said there were seven of you. Did you all escape together?"

Asa nodded as he rounded a corner. "Yes. One of them you've already met."

An hour ago, Chase would have been certain that this person was Ksenia, but knowing who she was now, he had no idea whom Asa meant.

Asa hit the console on a doorway, leading the way into an office. Chase stepped inside and froze, feeling like he'd gotten all the wind knocked out of him.

Leaning against the desk with her famous perky smile was Parri Dietz.

CHAPTER TWENTY-ONE

Chase gaped at Parri Dietz, the face he'd seen a hundred times on the news feed. Asa had to be playing a joke on them. For as much as his secrecy and paranoia finally made some sense, it was impossible that his counterpart was a famous newscaster whose face had probably been seen by every humanoid in the galaxy.

"Are you kidding me?" said Parker. "This is—this is the . . . ? No."

Ignoring him, Asa walked up in front of Parri Dietz and slammed his hand on the desk hard enough to dent the surface, making Chase jump. "What were you thinking?" he barked.

Parri Dietz stood up off the desk and casually adjusted the cuffs of her silk shirt. "Nice to see you too, Asa."

"How could you bring four strangers onto my ship?" he hissed. "Do you realize what you've done?"

She tilted her blond head, utterly unfazed by his anger.

"After Mina told me they were down on the moon, I wasn't going to just leave them there. One of them was nearly dead."

"They're *Fleet soldiers*." Asa said this the way other people might say *Goxar raiders* or *Zinnjerha*.

Parri frowned at him. "They're barely older than Chase and Parker."

"She knows my name," whispered Parker, nudging Chase.

"And one of them was the Lyolian," she continued. "You know he's too valuable to just leave out there for the Werikosa to take their frustrations out on. He knows things."

"Did any of them see you?" Asa asked.

Parri gave him a pointed look. "Do you think I'd be that stupid? I hid out in the control cabin while Alix brought them onboard."

"Who's Alix?" blurted Chase.

Parri Dietz turned her sparkling smile on him. "Well, hi there, Chase. It's nice to officially meet you. Alix is my android." It was the same smile she'd given him on the *Kuyddestor*, around the time Parker's chip went missing, and in Lumos, when he was supposed to be meeting Asa's contact. She'd known the whole time who he was. His brain scrambled to reorient itself to the new reality of those situations, but still it was just too hard to believe that Parri Dietz was an escaped genetically engineered super soldier. Like his parents. Only famous.

"You can't be one of the escaped soldiers," he said. "You're supposed to be hiding."

Asa sighed. "Would you let that ridiculous guise down so they can see?"

Winking at Chase, Parri Dietz reached up with both hands and massaged her temples in a sharp circle. When she looked up again, the perkiness had vanished, and her face was transformed into something leaner, harder. Her bright eyes became heavy-lidded and dangerous, the cheery smile twisting into a wolfish smirk. Even her eyebrows looked sharper. Chase had to blink several times to reconcile the change—she was still the same person, the same face, but at the same time completely different.

Asa stood beside her. "This is Fighting Unit 2403. Or as we prefer to call her, Nika."

Parker scoffed. "We're supposed to believe *that's* enough to fool the Fleet?"

"It's never been a problem," Parri/Nika said. Her voice was different now, too, dark and liquid. "Facial recognition scanners can't even tell the difference."

"But just changing your expression can't—"

"We've gone to a little more trouble than that," interrupted Asa. "Implants of adamantine mesh under her skin change the appearance of her bone structure, reflective screens in her eyes change her irises. And of course that delightful Parri

Dietz voice we all recognize has been carefully calibrated to evoke feelings of trust and stability in almost all types of humanoid. The monsters that created Fighting Unit 2403 won't see their handiwork in the Parri Dietz that we created. People believe what they want to believe—if you present them a convincing deception, they'll do ninety percent of the work for you."

Chase couldn't take his eyes off her altered face. "Did you do all that to her?"

Asa shook his head. "Nika designed and built the hardware herself. Someone else handled the integration surgeries. She's got a busy schedule, as you can imagine, but she makes herself available when she can. Like when I need her to steal back a microchip that someone is too close to figuring out."

"Thief!" exclaimed Parker.

Chase frowned. "That whole time we thought Ksenia was the one who took the chip and left me the note."

Nika shook her head. "That was me."

"So, Chase's parents and the two of you. That's only four," said Parker. "What about the last three soldiers from your group?"

"Ah." Asa glanced at Nika. "One is around and stays in regular contact with both of us."

"And the other two?"

"They're dead." Asa's expression gave away no emotion.

Nika sat down in the command seat, rubbing her face. "Oh, this feels good. I can't remember the last time I turned off my implant mesh. If you want, Asa, I can take the two un-injured soldiers with me when I leave, drop them off some-where remote. The third won't be mobile for a while, I'm afraid. He's all yours."

"We're taking them back to the *Kuyddestor*," said Chase. "Asa's going to help us take it back from the hijackers."

Nika dropped her hands from her face. "Excuse me?"

"There's been a hitch in the plans," said Asa. "The children are under the impression that I'm going to help them take back the ship from the Werikosa rebels."

"After he just rescued you from it?" Nika asked Chase in a scolding tone.

"Rescued?" Lilli's scratchy voice turned everyone's heads. "We never needed to be rescued. We were fine on the ship—I mean, before the hijacking."

"You weren't fine," said Asa harshly. "You were captives."

"We were safe!" she fired back.

"You were brainwashed."

Lilli's face turned fiery red, but before she could start a re-sponse, Asa continued. "We've set a course back toward the *Kuyddestor*. When we get there, we'll take a cruiser and latch onto the sidewall, cutting a hole through the exterior and ex-tracting you in the thirty seconds available before the Werikosa realize what's happening. You will be where I tell you to be, when I tell you to be."

Lilli put her hands on her hips. "I won't be anywhere unless you promise to fight the Werikosa and give the *Kuyddestor* crew control over their own ship again."

Asa stared at her. "You would honestly sacrifice yourself to save that ship? I don't think you understand—"

"*You* don't understand," snapped Lilli. "I don't know you. I've never even seen you before today. I don't care if you were made in the same soldier factory as my parents. You never came to our home; they never mentioned you. I've known Uncle Lionel my whole life. He's my family. So if you want to keep me alive, you'll keep him alive too."

Impressed with the steely strength in his sister's voice—even as his gut plummeted at her suggestion that she would let herself go down with the ship—Chase jumped in. "You think that Captain Lennard is just another Fleet officer, but he's different. He knows there are some bad people in the Fleet—people bad enough to destroy Trucon and blame it on Maurus and the Karsha Ven. After all of you escaped from the Fleet, my parents were trapped and he helped them find a safe place to hide. He was their friend."

"I see," said Asa. His gaze rested on Parker for a moment, and he exhaled in a short, loud burst. "Fine. I will help you save the *Kuyddestor,* but on one condition: After the ship is secured, all of you will come with me. Your place is here, not living under the roof of the establishment that killed your parents."

"No," said Lilli automatically.

Asa clenched his hands like he wanted to shake her. "I will not negotiate—"

"Asa, you have the social finesse of a man who's spent the last decade surrounded by androids," interrupted Nika smoothly. She turned to Lilli. "But you're being foolish, my dear. Even if Captain Lennard is your family, like you say, he can't keep you safe like Asa can. Look what's happening to his ship right now."

"But that's only because—" Chase began.

"He's a Fleet captain, Chase," said Asa. "Even if he's as anti-Fleet as you say—especially if he is—he's a target. He will always be within their striking distance. And as long as you stay close to him, so are you."

Chase dropped his head and took a deep breath. He hated to admit it, but Asa was right. Of all the places in the universe to hide from the Fleet, aboard a Fleet starship was possibly one of the worst. He knew that Captain Lennard cared deeply about him and his sister, that he would do anything to protect them, but was he the best person to do that?

"Are you going to lock us up in some compound like where you had Parker?" he asked.

Asa considered this. "Not necessarily. We can negotiate."

With every second he spent deliberating on this, time was slipping away for the *Kuyddestor* crew. Chase had to make a decision. "Fine," he said. "We'll go with you. Lilli, say you promise. You too, Parker."

"We'll go with you," said Parker immediately. "I promise." Chase glanced at him, frowning. He'd expected some—okay, more than some—resistance from Parker. Was he saying this for the good of the crew, or was there some other reason he was suddenly okay with leaving the *Kuyddestor*?

Lilli balked. "We belong with Uncle Lionel," she repeated.

Chase took her by the shoulder. "I don't know if we do or don't belong on a starship. But this is the choice he's giving us, so either we promise to live here, or the *Kuyddestor* is lost—and that means not just you, but everyone on the ship. Do you really want to make that decision for them?"

With a shudder, Lilli shook her head, angry tears filling her eyes, and vanished. Chase looked up at Asa. "We'll come with you as soon as we know the *Kuyddestor* is safe."

Asa nodded and began entering information on the console in the desk.

"Well, that was interesting," said Nika dryly. "I do wish I could come along and help."

"You can't blow your cover," said Asa, not looking up from the desk. "Get out of here and go do your thing."

Nika nodded and walked toward the door. "I'll be watching and reporting," she said. "Be safe out there, soldier."

✳   ✳   ✳

As they walked back to the medical bay, Chase nudged Parker. "Are you really okay with going with Asa when all this is over?" he asked.

Parker shrugged, glancing up at Asa. "Might not be so bad this time." Something had changed, but Chase couldn't figure out what.

Vidal had been pacing beside the submarine apparatus, but she whipped around as soon as they entered the medical bay. Her eyes narrowed at Asa. "Who are you? What kind of ship is this?"

"I'm Asa Kaplan," said Asa. "And this is my personal vessel, nothing more."

"But who *are* you? All I know is that some unidentified cruiser with an android pilot rescued us from the bottom of a lunar mine shaft and brought us here."

"That's as much as you need to know," said Asa.

Parker had crossed the room to peer inside the window of the medical machine where Derrick lay. Chase joined him, but the inside was dark and there was nothing to see.

"You must have been fairly close by," commented Maurus. He still sat in the chair, but his arm was no longer encased in the mending machine, and someone had given him a fresh shirt. "I have to know, did you set up that whole Lumos thing so you could get your hands back on the kids?"

Asa ignored the question. "We're going back to the *Kuyddestor*, and I need your help figuring out the safest place to board the ship."

Vidal shook her head. "They'll blow you out of the sky as soon as you come close. If there was a way to break through the ship's scramblers and teleport on board, that might—"

"Not an option," said Asa. "Fleet scramblers are impossible to bypass. The only place you can teleport onto a Fleet ship is the teleport chamber, and that will be locked down and crawling with Werikosa."

"But how are you planning to get anywhere near the ship?"

"We'll take a small cruiser, and we'll fold right up beside it."

Maurus scowled. "That kind of precision is impossible with a fold. Between the ship's movement and the expansion factor, you'll end up splitting the *Kuyddestor* wide open and taking your own head off in the process."

"Normal ships can't do it. Mine can. We'll have to board quickly, but we'll be too close to the *Kuyddestor* for them to be able to fire on us. We'll just have to be ready for what's coming at us from the inside."

Maurus gave him a skeptical look. "We're going to need a lot of firepower."

Good thing we're planning this with a weapons dealer, thought Chase.

"Two of my androids will come with us. We'll need to get to an onboard computer to fight the hack."

"I'll take care of that part while you fight off the Werikosa," said Parker.

"Oh, you're not coming with us," said Asa quickly. "I can handle the trojan."

"Before you're fighting off a herd of angry Werikosa, or during?" snapped Parker. "I can fix the hack while you fight."

Asa shook his head, white-lipped and furious. "Absolutely not. I will take care of the trojan and get Lilli off the ship with my androids."

Vidal frowned and pointed. "She's right here." With a start, Chase saw that Lilli had rejoined them at some point, and stood sullen in the corner of the room.

Mina stepped into the medical bay. "Prep Scada-One for departure," Asa told her.

"You're going to want to move quickly," said Mina. "By my revised calculations, the *Destrier* will arrive in two hours and twenty-one minutes."

"What?" asked Maurus, shocked. "That's impossible. They

were coming from the Ichis system—it should take them at least another day."

"Looks like Asa isn't the only one whose ship defies expectations," said Parker.

"Contact them and tell them not to attack the *Kuyddestor,*" said Chase.

Asa shook his head. "I will not bring more attention to us than I have to. We can do this before they get here."

"You'll have to," said Mina. "Because the *Kuyddestor*'s just started its attack on Storros."

CHAPTER TWENTY-TWO

Asa led the entire group swiftly down the hall to a conference room, where he leaned over a console, tapping in commands. A 3D image of the *Kuyddestor* popped up over the top of the long table, spinning slowly around.

"Give us the current situation, Mina," he said.

"The *Kuyddestor* is firing missiles toward the surface of Storros, targeting its major cities," said Mina. "So far the Storrian defenses have intercepted every one, but their ships are sticking close to Storros. They won't be able to get any good shots on the *Kuyddestor*, which seems to be keeping a close orbit around Rhima."

"What made the Werikosa start their attack?" asked Vidal.

"I think if we want to know what the Werikosa are thinking, we should ask the woman who helped orchestrate this hijacking." Asa turned to Mina. "Have Jericho bring her to us."

A few minutes later, Jericho entered with Ksenia, who

walked freely beside him. She smoothed her dark hair back off her face and straightened her back.

"Ms. Oriolo, your Werikosa cohorts have begun their attack on Storros. Do you know what their plan is?"

Ksenia said nothing, one corner of her mouth tilting upward.

"How many Werikosa are on the ship right now?"

She shrugged. "I didn't have anything to do with that part of the planning."

"Who hacked the ship's computers and helped the Werikosa take over?" asked Parker.

"That information wasn't shared with me."

"Well aren't you just about useless?" snapped Vidal.

"We'll find a use for her," said Asa. He motioned for Jericho to rejoin them. "Take her down to Scada-One and prepare for departure. Ms. Oriolo, you are coming to the *Kuyddestor* with us to negotiate the surrender of the Werikosa."

Ksenia raised one eyebrow and turned to leave with the android.

"And Ms. Oriolo," added Asa, speaking at her back, "I don't know what kind of reward you were expecting to get when you helped plan this sabotage, but I would suggest you begin lowering your expectations."

After a pause, Ksenia kept walking out of the room, never looking back.

Asa turned back to everyone else, cracking his knuckles against the console. "Okay, here's the plan. Once we get access to the ship, I'll go on board with Mina and the lieutenants, while Lilli will immediately leave the ship with Jericho. You two"—he indicated Maurus and Vidal—"will try to free your trapped crew and arm them, while I go to the bridge with Mina and Ksenia to try negotiating with the rebel leader to cease the attack on Storros and surrender the ship."

"Negotiating?" asked Maurus. "You think that's going to work?"

Asa cut him a sharp look. "I can be very persuasive." He pointed at a spot low on the bottom of the virtual *Kuyddestor.* "We'll fold up against the hull here, clamp an airlock onto the hull, and use a plasma saw—"

Chase glanced over at Parker, who was also frowning. "What about us?"

"You?" Asa glanced up from his diagram. "You wait here for Jericho to return with Lilli."

"No," said Chase. "We're part of this. We're coming with you."

Asa stabbed his thumb at the console, and the 3D image of the ship vanished. "This is warfare. I will not put the two of you at risk."

Parker tipped his head at Chase. "He's never at risk. You know that."

Asa's hard blue eyes looked Chase up and down, analyzing

him with a mercilessly analytical stare. "Fine. Chase, you're in charge of making sure your sister comes with us. Parker, you stay here."

In truth, Chase didn't want Parker to come along either. It would be too dangerous for him. But this was just like the argument with Captain Lennard, when Parker fought for the right to come with the expeditionary squad to Lumos. He'd lost that battle but gone anyway, and what would Chase have done without him? "Parker should come. We'll need him."

"This is not up for negotiation," said Asa harshly.

"Yes it is." Chase glanced at Parker, and then at Lilli. "We don't trust you."

Parker continued. "What's to make us think you'll really do what you promised and not just grab Lilli and run?"

Asa glared at them. "My word."

Parker scoffed. "You run a weapons syndicate selling particle dispersers to slum lords. Your word isn't enough. Besides, I know that mainframe like the back of my hand. I've been skimming through it for months. Maybe you know a thing or two about computers, but I know exactly where to look for this thing."

"A thing or two about—?" Asa stared at him, flabbergasted. "I don't think you understand everything that I'm capable of."

Lilli crossed her arms. "Either they come with you to keep you honest, or you'll never find me."

"You can't keep using that threat," growled Asa.

"I can and I will," she responded.

Asa looked like he wanted to strangle someone. He looked to Vidal and Maurus for backup, but although Vidal appeared uncertain, she didn't say anything. Maurus just shrugged. "We can keep the Werikosa away from them."

Asa stepped back from the table. "Fine. Mina, you will guard Parker at all times on this mission. Never leave his side. I'll handle Ksenia and the Werikosa by myself."

Mina nodded. "The Storrian defense Fleet appears to be moving in on the *Kuyddestor* now, Asa. We should leave immediately."

They rushed through the hallways, skipping the elevator but somehow ending up at the docking bay in less than a minute. They had been in a different part of the ship than where they first met Asa, but after the long walk to get there, it had seemed to Chase like they must still be far from the docking bay. He looked at the walls, wondering if it were possible to build a ship with shifting hallways.

The vehicle they boarded was different than the transport vessel that Chase, Parker, and Lilli had arrived on. This one was open from the piloting console all the way through to the back, with seats lining the walls on either side of the long midsection, and an impressive array of blaster rifles, armored vests, and other advanced battle gear hanging overhead.

Ksenia sat in the passenger seat closest to the controls, watching everyone else with her enigmatic eyes.

Chase, Parker, and Lilli chose three seats together near the middle of the vehicle, while Asa headed to sit at the controls with Jericho. Mina took the seat beside Parker. "Starting your watch already, are you?" he asked her sarcastically. She didn't answer, and he shifted in his seat toward Chase and began to whisper. "So I've been thinking about the whole thing with my parents. Why Asa kept me hidden away all those years. He's acting weird, right?"

Chase frowned and shrugged. "When is he not weird?"

"Well, it made me wonder . . . what if he's my dad? Maybe something happened to my mom, so he hid me away and fed me this lie about being an orphan. I mean, where else would I get this kind of smarts? I'm the best hacker on an entire Fleet ship. You think maybe I'm the son of a genetically engineered soldier, too?"

Chase hesitated before answering. He had to admit, it kind of made sense. But he could also think of a million reasons why Parker couldn't possibly be Asa's offspring, starting with the fact that Asa had seemed to be against any of the soldiers having children. And suddenly he thought he understood why Parker didn't fight the idea of staying with Asa. "You could be right . . ." he said cautiously.

"I think I am." Parker paused and nodded. "I feel it." Beside him, Mina said nothing.

Maurus and Vidal were scanning the armory affixed to the vehicle's interior, talking quietly with each other. "Take a seat," Asa called to them, as the vehicle's engine powered up, rising a few feet off the docking bay floor. As the outer doors of the docking bay rolled open, he slid screens around on the console, speaking in a low voice with Jericho about their route.

"What kind of blasters are these?" asked Maurus. "I don't recognize any of them. Are they your creation?"

Without looking back at Maurus, he said, "Annihilation radiation is an outdated technology for blasters. These are based on xenon particles, and they are lighter, charge faster, and have a much more accurate firing radius."

"I'll bet the warlords just love them," Maurus muttered.

"Please sit down, Lieutenant," came Jericho's mild voice. "We're about to make the first fold."

As the galaxy collapsed around them, Chase closed his eyes and tried to prepare himself for what they were about to attempt. Everything would be determined in the next few hours—whether they were able to stop the attack on Storros, prevent the *Destrier* from blowing up the *Kuyddestor*, and save the crew. If they didn't all die trying.

But even if they did succeed, the price would be leaving

the *Kuyddestor* behind and going with Asa. With a deep, pulling sadness Chase realized that his brief time aboard the starship had come to an end. All the hours spent laughing with the crew in the officers' lounge, the confessions he'd shared with Dr. Bishallany and the safety he'd felt in the presence of Captain Lennard, not to mention his budding new friendship with Analora—it was all over. He thought he'd been unhappy aboard the *Kuyddestor*, but the unhappiness was his alone, and around that the ship had become his home. And now he had to leave it all and start over fresh once again. Chase watched the back of Asa's head, the way he interacted with Jericho in short, clipped phrases. Nika was right that he acted more like an android than a human most of the time, except for those moments when a glimmer of his deep capacity for anger came briefly to the surface.

Everything on Asa's ship had happened so quickly, Chase had barely even begun to process all he'd learned about the seven genetically engineered soldiers—now down to three. His parents had once been part of that team. Now that they were gone, it was no surprise that Asa felt responsible for Chase and Lilli. But did he want them to come with him because he felt linked by their shared background and wanted to protect them, or because he was fascinated on a purely analytical level by what had happened when his teammates had mixed their enhanced DNA? Lilli was right—they didn't know Asa at all. She sat beside Chase, arms crossed and eyes far away in thought. He noted how the tension in her face seemed to lessen the closer they got to the *Kuyddestor*. He wished he could ask his parents what they thought of Asa, and why they'd chosen to keep their distance from him while making Captain Lennard a member of the family.

"Alright, there's the ship," said Asa. "It looks like the Storrians have begun their offensive."

"I don't see anything," said Parker, leaning forward in his seat and craning his neck toward the front.

"Jericho, put the zoom up on the front screen."

The *Kuyddestor* came into crisp view in the window. Regular pinprick bursts of fire from its sides showed where the Werikosa were releasing its missiles, but the screen wasn't wide enough to show if the missiles were still being intercepted over Storros. Fiery bursts from the Storrian defense squad's counterattack exploded along the hull, leaving blackened stretches of metal that made Chase's heart stop.

"This is going to be harder than I thought," said Asa.

"It isn't going to work," said Vidal. "Pull back."

"No," said Asa. "This just means we won't have time to cut through the *Kuyddestor*'s hull. We need a faster point of access."

While Asa pulled up schematics on the control panel, Maurus and Vidal conferred quickly in the back of the cabin.

Maurus raised his head. "One of the thruster access hatches is probably your best bet, but trying to open one from the outside would probably be as difficult as cutting the hull."

Asa looked back and found Lilli seated along the back wall. He gestured for her to come join him, and Chase got up and nosed in.

"Can you open an access hatch from inside the ship?" he asked quietly.

"I don't even know where to find it—it'll take me too long."

"Can you find someone who can help you?"

"Everyone from the crew is locked up."

But there was one person who wasn't locked up, and she knew the ship as well as any engineer. "What about Analora?" asked Chase. "You said she's hiding in the walls. She knows the ship as well as anyone. How quickly can you find her?"

Without a word, Lilli dropped her head. Chase imagined the real Lilli, climbing down out of her hiding place and running inside the walls of the ship. But more quickly than he expected, Lilli raised her head again and nodded. "Okay. She doesn't know exactly where they are, but if you tell her which quadrant of the ship, she said it won't be hard to figure out."

Maurus had moved forward and stood over Chase. "Tell her to go to the thrusters in sector 119."

"Be careful," said Chase.

"Be *fast*," said Asa.

Lilli dipped her head again, and they waited in anxious silence. Chase watched her like a hawk, flinching every time she tensed a muscle or moved her head a centimeter. At one point she uttered a low cry of surprise. At almost the same time, Vidal cursed under her breath. Chase glanced up and gasped at what he saw in the window.

More of the Storrian defenders had arrived, and were launching a concentrated attack on the *Kuyddestor*, setting the entire side of the ship aflame. Maurus laid a hand on Chase's shoulder. "The ship's shields will absorb most of the damage."

"At least this will distract the Werikosa onboard," added Asa.

Bright light lit up the side of the window as a cluster of Storrian ships exploded. In a row, they all started to explode, one after the other, like someone was picking them off. In less than a minute, half of the Storrian defenders were gone, their flaming remains drifting away from the *Kuyddestor*. The rest had backed off, vanishing to safer coordinates.

Asa placed a hand on Lilli's shoulder. "Lilli, it's now or never. We need to make our move."

Lilli looked up. "We're at the spot, but . . ."

"What?"

"Analora's having trouble with the panel. There's a security code to open it."

"Tell her to try code 0990," came Vidal's voice. Chase

glanced back at her. She was staring at Lilli with a slight frown, but he could tell she was picking up on what was happening.

Lilli dropped her head again. "That did it," she mumbled. "Panel armed for opening."

"Jericho," said Asa.

Jericho's hand slid across the panel. "Prepare for fold."

Chase had just enough time to grab the back of Lilli's chair, but the fold was an exceedingly gentle one. When he looked up, the hull of the *Kuyddestor* hovered mere feet away from their cruiser.

"Sons of Hesta," muttered Maurus, looking out with astonishment. "You really did it."

"Activating latch systems," said Jericho. A series of mechanical sounds came from the back of the cruiser, and a very loud THUH-THUNK. "Testing latch. And secure."

Maurus led the way to the back of the cruiser, where a wide door was already sliding open to reveal the cold gray metal of the *Kuyddestor*. The outline of a round hatch was cut into the wall.

"Everyone make sure you're armed. No, not you, Ms. Oriolo." Ksenia looked like she was about to protest, but Asa had already turned to Lilli. "Tell Analora she can—"

Before he could finish the sentence, the hatch blew off the wall, knocking Maurus to the floor, and passing right through Chase, who found himself standing with his ankles vanishing into the middle of the steel panel. Looking around, he saw that Lilli had vanished from their midst, but she was already leaning out of the access hatch of the *Kuyddestor*. He squinted at her, wondering if he was finally seeing her real self or another copy. Part of him hoped it was still a copy. She was safer that way.

Asa and Vidal lifted the panel off Maurus, who looked slightly dazed, a trickle of blood coming from his hairline.

"Hurry up," said Asa. "We need to get past the safety doors as soon as poss—"

Before he could finish, a blast shook the entire cruiser, shifting it an inch off the latch. With a terrible roar, the vacuum of space sucked at the entire room, bending the panel beside the latch and pulling at them all.

"Someone's firing at us! Get out!" roared Asa, pulling Maurus off the floor. Vidal grabbed Chase by the arm and pushed him ahead of her, so that he was the first one through the doorway.

Inside the *Kuyddestor* it was almost completely pitch black, the only light coming from Asa's ship. Chase remembered that they were somewhere inside the thruster compartment. He could see Lilli, but it took him a moment to spot Analora standing beside the operations panel. It hadn't been more than a day since he'd last seen her, but she looked pale and worn. Chase grabbed her hand and squeezed it, and she threw her arms around him in a quick, tight hug. "I'm so scared," she whispered in his ear.

The others were stumbling through the hole and into the compartment, Mina bringing up the rear. "Keep going—we have to get out and seal this room up," said Maurus. "If they hit the ship one more time, we'll all get sucked out."

Analora led the way through the darkness, and they came out through a door and into a red-lit hallway. The overhead lights were flashing, and an incessant, monotonous siren blared. Asa slammed the door once they'd passed through and touched the communicator by his ear, speaking in a voice too low to hear.

"Who fired on us?" Maurus yelled over the siren. "Was that the Storrians?"

Asa shook his head. "I'm not sure. I sent Jericho back to our holding position; he's trying to figure it out."

Maurus stopped Chase as he and the others followed Asa into the stairwell. "There's probably going to be some fighting up ahead, and I need your promise that when I tell you to hide, you'll hide."

Chase opened his mouth to protest. Maurus knew he couldn't get hurt—why wouldn't he let Chase help?

"Chase, you're the leader. You have to keep the others out of danger, okay?" Maurus gave him a piercing look, and Chase realized if he went charging into a firefight, Parker or Lilli or

Analora might follow. And he'd never forgotten the lesson he learned when Parker almost died from a poisoned spike thrown from the back of a Goxar: He himself might be immune to harm, but he couldn't protect anyone.

"Head for the engine room!" shouted Vidal, taking the lead. Single-file, they ran after him down the corridor and up a narrow flight of metal stairs to the engine room level, their footsteps echoing against the low blare of the siren.

They had just passed the second stairwell door when Asa stopped and looked around. "Where's Ksenia?"

A moment later, the stairwell door exploded.

CHAPTER TWENTY-THREE

Werikosa soldiers poured into the hallway through the blown-out door, blaster rifles perched on their shoulders. Maurus and Vidal had been in the lead, but this placed them farthest away from the soldiers, with everyone else in between. Closest was Analora, who screamed and stumbled back away from the array of blaster nozzles in her face.

Chase pushed his sister back against the wall and started running forward to create a distraction. In a blur of movement, someone else got there first, shoving Analora to the ground. It was Mina, who grabbed the nozzle of a blaster and tore it away from its owner, using it to knock away a row of Werikosa before she turned and dashed for Parker, slinging him over her shoulder like he weighed nothing.

But as swift and strong as Mina was, it was Asa whom Chase couldn't take his eyes off of. Smoother than an android, faster than any human Chase had ever seen, Asa seemed to be doing six different things at any given moment. He took out a whole row of Werikosa with his blaster while leaping over one of their fallen comrades, grabbing a light fixture and using it to spin around and take out two combatants in two different locations.

This was what Asa was built for. As Chase watched him singlehandedly decimate the contingent of Werikosa soldiers, a series of questions flashed through his mind. Had the Fleet put Asa into battle? Had they used his parents for this too? He suddenly had a very different image of who they might have been, not a pair of frightened runaways like the captain had once described, but a pair of dead-talented, cold-eyed killing machines.

Something rolled into the middle of the floor with a glassy sound.

"Cover!" screamed Maurus, diving away from the object.

A second later, a sharp, deafening *POP* sounded along with a flash of blinding light, and immediately the hallway began to fill up with thick, acrid smoke. Chase heard a girl's wail and rushed toward the sound. He almost tripped into Analora, who had crawled over to the wall. Her hands were clapped against her head, and Chase pulled them away, smearing the blood that trickled from one of her ears.

Wrapping an arm around her shoulder, he pulled her up and ran away from the explosion. The smoke was spreading around them thick as pudding, and so he nearly crashed into Lilli, who mutely grabbed his wrist and led him and Analora over to a place where she'd pried a panel of the wall free. They climbed in after her and scuttled through the duct until they came to the inside wall space. As Chase slid out, he was relieved to see that Parker was already there, Mina crouched at his side. It was dark, but there were no red emergency lights inside the wall, and no siren.

"We have to get to the engine room," said Parker. "The computers there are the best place for me to start looking for the trojan."

Analora gazed ahead for a moment, thinking. "We can't get all the way there, but I know how to get us pretty close." She took off at a jog, and they ran single-file through the tight corridor until she stopped short in front of another crawl space and cried out in despair. "This was one of Dany's holes. Somebody patched it!" A round piece of metal was welded onto the end of the crawl space. Analora took a utility knife from her pocket and tried to jam it through the weld, and after a few strikes she found a weak spot, wiggling the blade in between the metal patch and the wall. When she tried to pry the patch away, her blade snapped, and after a stunned pause, she threw the knife to the floor with a frustrated sob.

"Let me try," said Chase. If there were weak spots on the weld, and it was done from the outside, enough force from the inside might be able to break it free. Taking a deep breath, he ducked his head and phased through the patch into the crawl space. Analora's cry of surprise carried through the thin metal.

Feeling his way around the black space, Chase lay on his back and positioned his feet on the patch. He worried that between his already elevated adrenaline level and the impact from hitting the metal, his feet might just phase uselessly through it, so he took a few moments to make himself focus. He envisioned how his heels would crash against the weak spot. After a couple breaths, he slammed his feet into the wall.

Half of the patch came loose, and a shaft of dim light shone into the crawl space. "Yes!" came Parker's voice. "Hold on a second." Slim fingers appeared around the edge of the metal, and a second later Mina tore the plate clean off. Through the hole Chase could see Analora's astonished face.

"Chase, did you—?" she began.

"I'll explain it later," he said quickly, and he turned and started down the crawl space. After all his effort to keep it a secret, he'd shown her what he was. At least, he told himself, she'd seen him succeeding at something and not falling from a tree or getting overrun by forest monsters.

"Analora says to push the next panel out and go to the hall," said Parker from behind. It popped out easily, and they crawled back out into the red light–bathed hall. There was no sign of Asa or any of the others.

Parker looked both ways down the hall. "Oh, we're really close." Quietly he led the way toward the engine room. The double doors were wide open, but over the sound of the alarm in the hall it was impossible to tell if there was anyone inside. Chase jogged past Parker to stick his head in first, just in case there were armed Werikosa. It was completely empty, and all the consoles were dark.

"How are you going to log into the mainframe if the crew's all been blocked from logging on?" asked Chase.

"The crew has to use their badges to log on, and their badges are DNA-coded, right?" said Parker, as he powered up the nearest console. "Whoever's locked the crew out just disabled all the DNA coding. But I had to figure out how to get past that when I hacked the mainframe earlier, so I already have a bypass set up. Now I just have to figure out where the trojan was installed."

As Parker worked, Chase paced through the empty engine room. Mina looked over Parker's shoulder, watching the code scrolling on the screen, while Analora and Lilli stood watch by the door.

"Shouldn't the others be here by now?" asked Analora.

Parker slapped the console. "The file was installed in the

engine computer," he said in a thunderstruck voice. "Right here in front of the dummies."

"Can you stop it?" asked Chase.

"I can't disable it. The whole computer would have to be wiped clean and reinstalled." He turned to Chase. "All I can do is shut down and disconnect the engine computer."

"Does that mean the engines won't work?" Chase asked.

Parker nodded. "We'll be stranded."

"Is there anything else we can do?"

"Nope." Parker turned to Mina. "I'll start shutting it down. Once I'm done, you can unplug the connectors."

Chase started pacing around the room again. As long as Parker was fixing the problem and Mina was here to protect him, there was nothing for him to do in the engine room. "Where do you think everyone else is? Mina, do you have a way to contact Asa?"

She looked up for a moment. "He's not responding to my calls. But I can hear him fighting somewhere."

Chase headed for the doors. "I'm going to go look for him."

"I'll come with you," said Analora.

"No way. Stay here. Mina, watch her and make sure she doesn't get hurt."

Analora glanced over at the android and gave Chase an offended look. "I can take care of my—"

"I'll come with you," interrupted Lilli, following him toward the doorway.

"No!" He wouldn't be able to do anything if he was worrying about Lilli the whole time. "Please, I don't need anyone's help, just let me do this on my own. Nobody else leaves the engine room."

"Even if the Werikosa break through?" asked Lilli sarcastically.

Chase gave an exasperated sigh. "If you need to do something . . . send a copy up to the flight deck and tell the crew we're onboard. Tell them we're going to end this." Before she could say another word, he gave her what he hoped was a stern look and jogged out the door.

A focused calm filled him as soon as he was back in the hallway. The red lights were flashing, the siren droned overhead, but he no longer needed to worry about making sure that the others were safe. He felt fast and strong and invincible. At the stairwell, he started running up the stairs, racing past the civilian and soldiers' levels.

He paused at the flight deck level, wondering if he should go help the crew, but Maurus and Vidal had been tasked with that. Part of him wanted to stick his head out in the hall, to see if they were okay, if he could hear any sounds of a fight, but he pushed onward. If anything was going to save the *Kuyddestor*, it was stopping the Werikosa who were attacking the bridge. And if Asa hadn't made it there yet, it was all up to him.

He got out on the bridge level, jogging past the elevator and the captain's quarters. When he came to the bridge, he leapt at the door without slowing down, tensed to jump right back out if need be, but what he saw when he got there stopped him cold.

The room was completely empty, all the tiers and chairs unoccupied. He frowned, panting as he looked around. Where was everyone? The only place on the ship to fire the ship's external missiles was here, so who was firing at Storros?

After a few seconds, he noticed a different kind of movement: the screens. On all the different screens were radar maps, moving targets, images of space and explosions, and the decimated Storrian Fleet. Thin white words appeared on one of the screens: ACQUIRING TARGET. Someone was using the ship's weapons, just not from the bridge. He had to get back to Parker and tell him what he'd seen.

Chase jumped back into the hallway. He was halfway to the stairs when Ksenia walked out of a conference room with Petrod at her side. The leader of the hijackers looked oddly meek in her presence.

Chase spoke before she'd even noticed him. "What is going on? Who's launching the attack on Storros?"

Ksenia turned to face him, and a smile stretched across her face.

"I'd like to know that myself," whined Petrod at her side. "We had no intention of actually attacking Storros!"

Ksenia laughed. "Well, I'm sorry, Petrod, the Fleet made that decision for you." Before he could react, she casually lifted a handblaster at her side and blasted him in the chest. He flew back against the wall and collapsed.

"The Fleet is trying to destroy Storros?" Chase asked in astonishment. It was Trucon all over again—the Fleet annihilating an entire world for no reason that made any sense.

Ksenia looked surprised. "Destroy? Never."

Just then Asa came walking around the corner. "Never, Ms. Oriolo? No—just hurt it enough that the Storrians will need Federation funding and infrastructure to get back on their feet, isn't that right? With just enough oversight that the Federation can worm its way into their rhenium trade."

Chase dropped his jaw, flabbergasted. "This was all for a *metal*?"

"A very rare and essential one, Chase," said Ksenia. "It's dangerous to allow one planet to have control over ninety percent of the known deposits of such an important resource. If they ever decide to withhold supply, they could hurt billions of people."

"Although they've never given any indication that they

would," said Asa, moving a step closer to her. "But you're will-ing to stage a hijacking to prevent this possibility."

"It won't look that way from the outside." Ksenia tightened her grip on her blaster. "And soon all the people who know the truth will be dead."

"I won't be," said Chase. "I'll tell."

"Tell who?" She gave him a slick smile. "You'll be coming with me. There are people waiting for you."

This made no sense. "What?"

"The people who've been looking for you aren't dumb, Chase. They knew it was likely that you were on the *Kuydd-estor.* I was told to keep an eye out for you."

"They won't lay a finger on him," said Asa fiercely. "And you're not going anywhere."

Ksenia pointed her blaster at him, but suddenly her right knee went out and she stumbled to the floor, revealing the copy of Lilli who had kicked the back of her knee. It was just enough time for Asa to leap forward and deliver a heavy blow that knocked her to the floor. He crouched over her body and seized her head violently.

Chase gasped. Pausing, Asa looked up and saw both him and Lilli watching. Without a word he let Ksenia's head drop to the floor and stood. "Let's get back to the engine room." Lilli vanished, and Chase turned for the stairs, but the sound of dis-tant running bootsteps made him look back. Asa was already starting toward the sound. "More Werikosa," he called over his shoulder. "I'll handle them. Get back to the engine room, and I'll meet you there."

Mina was waiting for Chase at the bottom of the stairs. "We have a problem."

In the engine room, Parker leaned over the console, fingers flying. Analora hovered over his shoulder, and Lilli sat in a chair beside him like she hadn't just been on the bridge level. "We got the engine computer offline, and the commands started coming from navigation. Separate infection."

"So turn off the navigation systems," said Chase.

Eyes still locked on the screen, Parker made a face. "I could, but it'll take a while and I don't know how many backup trojan access points this person installed."

"I went to the bridge and it was empty," Chase said. "The screens are flashing a bunch of commands and stuff, but nobody's there running it."

"What?" asked Parker. Chase quickly explained what he'd seen, and the interaction he'd had with Ksenia, learning that the Fleet was behind the entire attack on Storros.

Parker chewed his lip, thinking. "Wow. So the Werikosa were set up as a cover, and somebody's using the trojan to operate all the bridge controls from somewhere else. I'd say we look for the computer where the commands are originating from, but it might not even be on this ship. For all we know, some-body could be doing this from back at Fleet High Command." He looked back at the console and began typing furiously. "If we can just find out who installed it . . . I can trace it back to whoever badged in when the first trojan was added, and use that to figure out how many places it was installed." Parker stopped, frowning. "Whoa."

"What is it?" asked Chase. "Do you know who it was?"

"First instance badged in under Corporal Liadan Lahey," said Parker. "The teleport operator."

"What?" said Analora. "How could she even have done that? She's only been on the ship for a year."

Mina was already on a communicator, speaking to Maurus and Vidal. "When you get through, keep an eye out for a Corpo-ral Liadan Lahey. Parker says she's the hacker."

So the thin-lipped, sour-faced teleport operator was the culprit. "I always thought she seemed like a jerk," said Chase.

"Parker, three minutes until the *Destrier* arrives," said Mina. "Jericho is prepared to fold back to the thruster access hatch and suggests that we leave immediately."

"Give me one more minute," said Parker. "I just need to . . . ugh, no. This won't work. Not in three minutes."

Chase thought about this. "We don't need to know who's running the *Kuyddestor* right now, do we? The ship is only in danger as long as it's still attacking Storros. So we just have to stop the attack. Can you get around the trojan and turn off the missile systems?"

Parker looked up at him. "No," he said slowly. "But . . ." He turned back to the screens and frowned.

"What?"

"But I could override the safe detonation distance and set off one of missiles right inside the launch tube. That should destroy the tube enough so that the ship won't be able to fire any more missiles."

Chase shook his head. It sounded like Parker wanted to blow up the *Kuyddestor*. "Won't that destroy the whole ship?"

"No," cut in Analora. "This is a battle starship after all. One single missile shouldn't be enough to destroy the entire ship. Let's hope all it does is destroy the ship's weapon launching capabilities without setting off all the other missiles."

Chase turned back to Parker, his heart racing. "You really think that's the only way?"

Parker nodded. "We'll stop the attack on Storros . . . and hopefully we won't blow ourselves up in the process."

The three of them looked at one another. There really wasn't any choice.

Parker started entering something on the console while everyone watched. Mina stood behind them, looking at something on a communicator. "One minute left, Parker. We need to leave."

"Hang on. I'm almost finished." Finally Parker hit the last keystroke and leaned back, tapping his fingers against the edge of his seat. They stared at the screens, waiting.

A shudder shook the ship like a distant earthquake, a low, long vibration that came through the walls and the floor. Parker looked back at the screen. "Done. Launch tube has been destroyed."

Chase sat down in one of the crew seats, placing his head in his hands. They'd done it. They'd saved the ship. Now they would just need to—

BOOM!

The explosion shook the room hard, sending Chase flying out of the chair to his knees. His first thought was that Analora had been wrong, and they'd just set off the rest of the missiles and secured their own death sentence. "What was that?" he yelled. "More missiles?"

Parker stared at the screen, eyes wild. "No. Oh lords. No. It was the *Destrier.* It's here. They're firing on us."

Asa came flying around the corner into the engine room just as another explosion hit. He lost his footing and fell, smashing his face on the corner of a console and splitting his lip. "It's time to go, now!" he shouted, wiping the blood away with his sleeve.

Parker drew up a comm screen on the console, hailing the *Destrier* even as Asa tried to draw him away from the screens.

"Enough, Parker. The crew is coming out of the flight deck—let them handle this."

"They won't do this in time," snapped Parker, pulling away his arm. "*Destrier,* this is the IFF *Kuyddestor.* We have regained control of the ship, please hold your fire."

Another explosion hit, shaking them so violently Chase was certain the ship had been split in two. "But we're not firing on Storros anymore!" cried Parker. "*Destrier,* hold your fire!" He looked back at the others, his face frozen in terror. "I made the connection—why aren't they answering me?"

"Because they don't care, Parker!" shouted Asa. "They're just here to destroy the ship! We have to leave!"

This was it. This was the trap Chase had feared. Maybe it hadn't been set for them, not originally, but someone in the Fleet had seen the opportunity and placed the *Kuyddestor* in a position where it could not escape defeat. The *Destrier*'s attack had nothing to do with saving Storros.

This was about destroying the *Kuyddestor.*

CHAPTER TWENTY-FOUR

Another explosion hit the ship, and a sound of groaning metal followed, ringing through the framework from somewhere above them. Parker opened another screen on the communication console, but Asa yanked him away from it. "We're leaving now!"

"Just let me try once more on a public distress band!" shouted Parker, struggling against him. "If the Fleet won't listen, someone else will hear us. We have to try!"

But Asa kept a solid grip on Parker's arm, and Mina had both girls waiting by the doorframe already. With his other hand, Asa took Chase's arm and pulled them toward the hall.

Parker turned to Chase, his expression frantic. "Please."

With a nod, Chase yanked his arm free and dashed back to the console, hitting the send button the way he'd seen Parker do. "This is an SOS, is anyone out there? This is the IFF

Kuyddestor and we've regained control of the ship, but we're under attack by the *Destrier*. Please, somebody help!"

Asa came charging back, brutally yanking Parker along with him. "The ship is lost, Chase," he snarled. "Stop this idiocy and come with us now before it's too late! Do you want to watch your sister die here?"

Lilli stood in the doorframe looking frightened out of her wits, her wrist locked in Mina's hand. Analora was there too, tears running down her face.

Asa was right; they had to leave. Chase rose and walked out of the engine room, apologizing in his head to all the crew of the *Kuyddestor* who were being left behind to their deaths as he walked down the hall. The captain, Forquera, Dr. Bishallany, even Maurus . . . He stopped and covered his face with his hands, feeling dizzy and sick at the thought.

A voice crackled incoherently back in the engine room, echoing off the walls to reach them. Chase looked up, locked eyes with Parker, and knew he was thinking the same thing. *No more explosions . . .*

With a roar, Parker wrenched free of Asa and ran back to the engine room, Chase right beside him. A trim, hammerjawed man with silver hair had appeared on the comm screen. "Hello, is anyone there? *Kuyddestor*, please respond."

Parker hit the send button. "Who is this?"

"This is Admiral Peter Shaw of the IFF *Atreus*. What in blazes is going on over there?"

Admiral Shaw! Chase immediately recognized the name—this was the man Captain Lennard had called his mentor. "Who are you kids?" Shaw continued. "Where's Lennard?"

"The captain's locked up on the flight deck with the rest of the crew," said Parker breathlessly. "Well, he was—he might have gotten out by now. The ship's pretty messed up though. We stopped the hijackers from attacking Storros. I tried to tell the *Destrier*, but I couldn't get through to them."

Shaw squinted like he was trying to see further into the screen. "You kids stopped the Werikosa? By yourselves?"

Chase glanced over his shoulder where Asa glowered in the doorway, Mina and the girls peeking in behind him, and turned back to the screen. "We had a little help. But Parker here gets most of the credit. How did you hear us? Did we reach you on the public band?"

Admiral Shaw chuckled. "Son, you didn't just reach me. On that frequency you reached nearly everyone in the galaxy."

"Are we safe now?"

"I've ordered the *Destrier* to hold their fire." Admiral Shaw paused. "You're safe."

The relief that flooded through Chase brought on a million different feelings. He bowed his head in front of the screen.

"You boys have done an excellent job. Will you have Captain Lennard contact me once he's freed?" asked Shaw.

"Yes, we will," said Parker. "And thank you, Mr. Admiral."

A smile started to crack the corner of Shaw's mouth, and with a brisk nod he ended the comm.

Chase looked up at Parker, who slowly broke into a wide grin and clapped Chase on the shoulder. "We did it. Lords, we were lucky that guy heard our distress call."

"Captain Lennard told me about Admiral Shaw a while ago. That's his mentor—one of the people in the Fleet he said he can trust."

Asa shook his head, wiping the blood from his mouth where he'd split his lip. "So you think Shaw went against the Fleet and stopped the attack because he's Lennard's friend?" He raised an eyebrow. "Or do you think maybe he *had* to stop it because the Fleet couldn't destroy the *Kuyddestor* after your plea for help went live across the star system?"

Chase's smile faded as doubt crept into his mind. Asa's paranoia was contagious. "Does it matter? We're safe now. The *Kuyddestor* is safe."

Asa gave a one-shouldered shrug. "Until the next attack." The communicator at his side chimed. He glanced at the screen and didn't answer. "It's time to leave now. Jericho's about to fold up to the thruster hatch again."

It was too soon. Chase wanted to talk to Maurus about the

hacker, to tell Captain Lennard how the Fleet had orchestrated the whole hijacking. He wasn't ready to leave yet. He turned to Asa, the request on the tip of his tongue.

"You promised." Asa cut him off in a tone that left no room for bargaining.

"Don't worry," said Parker, putting a hand on Chase's shoulder. "We're coming."

When they came to the main stairwell, Analora turned to head upstairs. She stopped outside the stairwell door when she realized that everyone else had walked past it. "You're . . . Aren't you coming up?"

Chase hesitated. He couldn't bear to tell her that he was about to leave the ship forever. He wanted to just sneak away, to avoid seeing the disappointment of all the people he was leaving behind. "We need to go help Asa with something first."

She looked warily at Asa and nodded, and then gave Chase a quick hug. "I have to go look for my dad. I'll see you soon."

Chase returned the hug and nodded, looking away quickly. "See you soon." *Only that's not true. I'll probably never see you again.*

They continued down the hall toward the spot where Jericho would pick them up, taking the narrow stairs down to the last corridor. Ahead lay the door to the access hatch where they'd boarded the ship. Asa touched something by his ear, and then touched Parker's arm to stop him from opening the door. "Wait a minute. Jericho's still working out the fold coordinates."

Parker leaned against the wall and rubbed the angry red marks on his arm where Asa's earlier grip was going to leave some ugly bruises. "You don't have to manhandle me so much next time," he said in mock resentment. "We make a good team though, your brawn and my brains."

"Parker, I'm not your father," said Asa abruptly.

Parker flushed a deep scarlet. "I never said . . ."

"No, you didn't. But I can see what you're thinking and it's only fair to let you know. You are uncommonly intelligent; I know that now. But that's only because you're the son of two uncommonly intelligent people."

Chase looked at the floor, feeling the heat in his cheeks on Parker's behalf. Asa could have at least waited until they were back on his ship to do this. A person with normal social skills would have.

"Who were they?" Parker was barely able choke the words out. "I'm assuming the whole story about them being employees who died in a teleport accident is a big fat lie."

"Just like Henk and Caralin, I found someone to help me after we escaped from the Fleet. Your parents were biological engineers. I'd heard of them because of their vocal opposition to genetic manipulation, and I thought I might be able to trust them. They understood the depravity of what the Fleet had done in creating us, and they helped me to hide. Eventually we worked together for a time. When you were born, I made them a promise that if anything ever happened to them, I would care for you."

Parker looked up. "And?"

Asa kept his gaze straight ahead. "It was the only time the Fleet nearly caught up with me. They sacrificed themselves so that you and I could get away."

Parker turned his face toward the floor and said nothing else.

Giving no indication that he realized how he'd just shattered Parker's world, Asa touched his ear again. "Jericho, are you in position?" He reached for the door, looking around to make sure everyone was there. "Alright. Let's go."

As he took his final steps aboard the *Kuyddestor*, Chase couldn't stop thinking about the months he'd spent on the ship, the friends he'd made and the busy hum of life aboard the starship. Only silent hallways awaited his future. He glanced over at Parker, who, judging by the pained look on his face, was having even worse thoughts.

But it was Lilli who stopped first, just inside the access chamber. She looked back toward the corridor with panic in her eyes. "I won't go."

Asa turned to face her, cold and menacing. "You promised."

"Where are we going to go?" asked Chase. "What will we do?"

"You'll be safe," said Asa.

"Just like my childhood," said Parker bitterly. "Safe, and sheltered, and alone."

Lilli turned to run, and Asa reached out, lightning-fast, and grabbed her arm. "I'm your guardian. You're coming with me!"

The access hatch was open, and on the other side of it was Jericho, standing inside the smaller vehicle. Chase didn't want to go either, but they'd given their word, and Asa had kept up his end of the bargain in saving the ship, however much of it had been their own doing. But watching Asa drag his sister forcefully toward the hatch, he felt ill. And angry.

Lilli screamed in defiance, and a half dozen of her copies appeared, pulling at Asa's clothes and trying to help Lilli pull away from him. "Stop that!" Asa shouted. He grabbed both her arms and shook her like a rag doll. "Stop it!"

"Ow, you're hurting me!" she screamed. The copies vanished. "Chase, help!"

Behind them in the corridor came the sound of a door opening and then footsteps. "What's going on there?" shouted a man's voice.

Before them was his sister's tear-streaked, hysterical face.

That was all it took for Chase to make a decision.

"Help us!" Chase yelled. "The hacker's in here! He's trying to kidnap us!"

The look on Asa's face: fury, hurt, betrayal—in an instant it was seared into Chase's memory. Asa glanced at Lilli, at Parker, back at Chase. His blue eyes were bright and hard, furious and desperate.

"Freeze!" yelled the soldier over the sound of his blaster charging.

Without saying a word, Asa turned and ran. Before the soldier could fire a shot, he dove through the hatch back into his ship, and it clanged shut behind him.

Chase turned back toward the corridor. "Run!"

They raced back out of the access chamber before it could depressurize, slamming the door shut behind them. Then they stood shocked in the corridor, looking at each other, realizing what they'd just done. They had broken their promise, and betrayed the only man who knew exactly who they were and where they'd come from.

The soldier stared at all of them, holding his blaster awkwardly. "Was he really the hacker?" he asked.

"No," said Chase bluntly. He took Lilli's hand and squeezed it, and she threw her arms around his waist.

Parker looked over at Mina. "What are you still doing here?"

Mina shrugged. "He told me not to leave your side."

A haze of gray smoke filled the hallway when they reached the main level of the ship. The halls were packed full, people running to seal off the parts of the ship that had been damaged by the *Destrier*'s attack. Chase held Lilli's hand to keep from losing her. Behind them, Mina followed Parker as casually as if she'd been living on the *Kuyddestor* this whole time.

Chase strained to look through the crowd as they slipped, largely unnoticed, into the chaos. He had to tell someone the things they'd learned—about Ksenia's lies, Corporal Lahey's treachery, and most importantly, the Federation's plan to attack Storros and the *Kuyddestor*.

"Chase! Chase!" Maurus came running up behind them, breathless. "I went to the engine room to look for you and you were gone—I was afraid Asa had taken you away!"

"No, but he's gone now." Chase said nothing more, the shame of his betrayal chipping at his conscience. "Did you find Corporal Lahey?"

"I haven't seen any sign of her, but we told the MPs to be on the lookout for her. She won't get far."

A voice came from behind them. "Not far at all, I'm afraid." Vidal stood there, a grim look on her face. "MPs found her body in another section of the engine rooms, along with Chief Kobes. They were both armed, but we're not sure yet if the

Werikosa got them, or if Kobes discovered what she was doing and confronted her."

In his shock, the first person Chase thought of was Dany Kobes, far away at the academy, probably still with no idea that his father had been killed. He looked at Parker. "Then who was running the attack on Storros?"

"Once she installed the trojan, it could have been anyone as long as they had the right access. Even someone on another ship."

"But, Parker, you stopped the trojan." Maurus grabbed Parker's hand, shaking it fiercely.

"No, I didn't stop it," said Parker. "It's still running in the navigation system, and probably other places as well. We just destroyed the external weapons system so no more missiles could be launched."

Maurus looked alarmed. "Then we need to get you in touch with someone from the engine room to follow up." Ensign Cutler was standing two groups away, talking to Seto and another officer. Maurus flagged him down, and after a brief explanation sent him off to the engine room with Parker. Mina followed quietly on their heels.

Before Chase could tell Maurus about the Fleet, Seto came over and slapped him on the back. "You're back!" he exclaimed. His other arm was in a makeshift sling.

"What happened to you?" asked Maurus.

"Oh, I learned a lesson: Don't fight a Werikosa in the dark." He looked around at the four of them, rubbing Chase on the head with his good arm. "Where's Derrick? Still down on Storros?"

Maurus looked at Chase, hesitating. Chase could tell he was deciding how much to tell Seto. "He got hurt."

Seto's smile faded. "How hurt? Dead hurt?"

Good question. After all that had happened, Chase wondered if Asa would still heal Derrick's injuries, and what he would do with him afterward.

Maurus shook his head. "We don't know yet."

"Do you know where the captain is?" Chase asked Seto.

"I think he went up to the bridge to try to get things back under control. Forquera's directing teams to seal up the damaged parts of the ship. And I'm sitting on my butt waiting for the medical bay to clear up enough to get this mended." He raised his wounded arm slightly.

"I need to talk to the captain," said Chase.

"He's probably pretty busy right now," said Seto. "If it can wait..."

Chase gave Maurus the kind of look that said it couldn't. Maurus nodded in understanding. "Let's go find him," he said. Chase put his arm around Lilli, and they followed Maurus from the flight deck, leaving Vidal behind to help Seto to the medical bay.

As they walked down the hall, they passed the spot where Asa had left Ksenia lying on the floor. She wasn't there any longer, but Chase supposed she could have been taken to the medical bay. Or she could be hiding somewhere, waiting to make her escape from the ship. "Have you seen Ksenia?" he asked.

Maurus shook his head. "No one's said anything about seeing her."

Chase looked around at the walls of the ship, at the people passing by. Something didn't feel right, and he couldn't put his finger on what it was.

They rounded a corner, and there in the middle of the hall was the captain. His back was to them as he gave orders to the crew that crowded around him, coming and going in packs like schools of fish.

"Captain!" called Chase.

The captain turned around, and in three strides he had crossed the distance between them. He dropped to one knee and threw his arms open, engulfing Chase and his sister in a long, strong hug. He pulled back and looked at both their faces, his own face haggard, as if he hadn't slept in days. "I'm so glad you're both okay."

"We're glad *you're* okay," said Chase. Lilli's eyes shone.

Lennard smiled. "How did you get back onto the ship?"

"Asa brought us."

"Asa Kaplan? He's here?"

"He left. But he helped us take the ship back. Mostly it was Parker, though." Chase looked around the hall before whispering, "It was all a set-up. Everything."

Lennard nodded. "We know someone on the ship helped the Werikosa take over. Parker was right about that hacker."

"But the Werikosa on the ship never attacked Storros. They weren't even on the bridge. It was the Fleet, firing *Kuyddestor* weapons from somewhere else and using the Werikosa as an excuse. They did everything."

Lennard's hand tightened on Chase's shoulder, and his face shifted from relief to a much more serious expression. "Come back to my quarters with me. I want to hear the whole story. Starting with how you ended up back in the company of Asa Kaplan."

CHAPTER TWENTY-FIVE

The captain placed Lieutenant Thandiway in temporary charge of recovery and led Chase and Lilli back to his quarters. Maurus went with them and helped Chase explain everything that had happened from the moment they met up on Storros. Thankfully Lennard didn't say anything when Chase admitted to stealing the jump pod to go to Storros, although he did give him a look that promised further discussion later.

When Maurus explained how they had ended up on Asa's ship, he provided the details of how Ksenia had shown up at the mineworks after Mina had rescued Chase and the others, and how an unmarked vehicle with an unknown pilot and an android had picked them all up.

Captain Lennard rubbed his forehead, taking a deep breath. "So Lieutenant Derrick is still with Asa?"

"He was in bad shape, sir," said Maurus. "If he survives, what Asa chooses to do with him is anyone's guess."

"And you never saw the pilot of this other vehicle? But now we can assume that Asa has more people working with him."

"Her name is Nika," said Chase. "She's another genetically engineered soldier. Like my parents. Like Asa."

"What?" asked Lennard, incredulous. "Asa?"

Chase went on to explain what he'd learned about the seven soldiers and their escape, including the fact that three of them, including Asa and Nika, were still alive. The one detail he withheld was Nika's cover identity as Parri Dietz. It wasn't that he didn't trust Lennard or Maurus with that information, but her secret was so huge, he didn't feel right sharing it. At least not yet. A nod from Lilli when he omitted that part of the story made him feel like he was doing the right thing.

Lennard ran his hands over his face, shaking his head. "Henk and Caralin never hinted that there were others like them. I'd assumed they were an Adam and Eve project. If this is true, I need to speak with Asa."

"I don't know how we're going to find him again," said Chase. "Unless Mina can tell us where he is."

When it came time to explain how they had stopped the attack on Storros, Chase felt guilty about sharing Parker's side of the story since he wasn't there to bask in his own glory. He told them about what Ksenia revealed to him outside the bridge, and how the Federation had instigated the entire hijacking and run the *Kuyddestor* remotely like a video game.

And finally, Chase explained about how the *Destrier* kept firing, even after Parker had contacted them to let them know the ship was retaken.

"Sinjan Devore has a reputation as a reactionary and a vicious leader," said Lennard. "No wonder High Command called him in as their attack dog."

"The *Destrier* was involved in a huge massacre just off of Pranatine a few years back," Maurus told Chase. "Everyone from the Fleet side was cleared, but to me it always smelled like a cover-up."

"Though I'm not surprised it was Shaw who stopped the attack," Lennard continued. "I was his second-in-command back when we served on the *Roscommon*, and we've always had a good relationship. He was a good, fair commander, and he has enough seniority and influence within the Fleet to stand up to the people who are taking it in the wrong direction."

"He told us to have him contact you when you were free again," said Chase.

"I've already spoken with him. He's coming over later today to survey the damage."

"How long is it going to take to fix the ship?" Chase asked.

The captain grimaced. "A while. Once we get all the systems wiped clean and the engines back online, we should be able to fold back to one of the shipyards around Earth. Maybe

I can find a place there for you kids to stay while the ship's being worked on."

"No," said Chase and Lilli at the same time. Chase shook his head. "This is our home."

Lennard smiled at their outburst but didn't reply, looking down instead and scrolling through some information on his communicator. He gave a low chuckle. "Reports from the engine room say that Parker is schooling the entire division on how to hack their own ship. There's going to be a scheduled blackout later today when they flush out the trojan."

Thinking of the engine room made Chase remember what had happened to Chief Kobes. "Who's going to run the engine room now?"

"Petty Officer Bycraft is the next in command." Lennard was quiet for a while, tapping his fingers on the arm of his seat. "Luister Kobes wasn't the most personable fellow, but he'll be a tough act to follow as Chief. MPs are investigating the scene to figure out exactly what happened between him and Lahey."

"I never liked her," Chase admitted.

Maurus shook his head. "I can't believe she was a traitor. She was always so rigid about the rules."

Lennard was looking at his communicator again. "Looks like there's a problem containing the breach on level seven," he said, moving like he was about to stand.

"I'll go check it out, Captain," said Maurus. The captain nodded assent, and Maurus left with a quick salute.

Now that they had a moment of stillness to think about everything that had happened, some of the small things that were still bothering Chase began to rise to the surface of his mind. "Is somebody looking for Ksenia?"

"I put out a ship-wide alert as soon as you told me," Lennard said. "There's so much activity right now, stabilizing the ship, helping the Storrian delegation return to their planet, and detaining the remaining Werikosa, she may have found a way to sneak off already. She'll probably be protected by whoever gave her this assignment in the first place."

"What's going to happen to the Werikosa?"

"The hijackers will be taken before the Federation courts, as well as the leaders on Rhima and anyone else associated with the plot. And from what I understand, the remaining settlers on Rhima will be rounded up aboard the *Destrier* and taken back to Werikos."

Chase knew the Werikosa had forfeited any right to Rhima when they attacked the *Kuyddestor*, and he would never forget the terror of crashing on the moon in the *Falconer*, but a part of him still felt sorry for the struggling civilization. "I know it's probably the right thing to do, but it seems a little unfair. They were set up and used."

Captain Lennard gave a little shrug. "Situations like this are never purely black and white, right and wrong. All the contributing factors make things much more complex, and a fair-minded person like you will always see that. Maybe the Werikosa were manipulated, but at the end of the day, you have to remember that they were willing participants in the hijacking."

Chase wondered if he would ever be so desperate to do something like that, if the people around him were dying. Did their situation justify any of their violent actions at all, or would it be the right thing to accept their agonizing fate in silence? He remembered all the strange, laughing Werikosa children, and wondered what kind of life they would have back on their acrid homeworld. He looked up and saw Lennard watching them with a serious expression.

"What?" asked Lilli.

"I was serious about finding you a different place to hide when we go back to Earth orbit. It won't be safe for you on the *Kuyddestor.*"

Her immediate response was to scowl. "Will you come with us?"

Lennard shook his head. "My place is on the ship."

"Then that's our place too," she said.

Lennard sat back and rested his chin on his hand. "Knowing what I know now about Asa Kaplan, I almost wish you both had gone with him."

This was the last thing Chase would have expected to hear from Captain Lennard. Lilli looked positively wounded. "But you're our family," she whispered. "*You* keep us safe."

"Believe me, Lilli, there is nothing more important to me than you and Chase. But after all this, I have to question how smart it is of me to keep you both on the *Kuyddestor.*"

"Hiding didn't do our parents much good," said Chase.

"But it seems to me that Asa Kaplan's found a way to do it."

Yeah, thought Chase. *By cutting himself off from everyone and spending his life traveling constantly through the galaxy aboard a silent ship, thinking about nothing but revenge.* It wasn't a life that he wanted.

The notification chime sounded at the door. Frowning, Lennard answered the door, and it slid open on the trim, silver-haired figure of Admiral Shaw. He leaned inside before entering. "Captain, may I come in?"

The captain stood, saluting. "Admiral, I wasn't expecting you until this evening."

Shaw stepped inside and shook Lennard's hand, giving him a few hearty claps on the shoulder as he did. "I guess there's no need to stand on ceremony, Lionel. Especially after a few days like you've had." Chase automatically stood in the admiral's presence, feeling almost like he should salute, although that would have been silly. Lilli remained perched on the edge of the hard brown sofa, watching the admiral with cautious eyes.

"Sorry to surprise you like this, Lionel. I must have ticked off someone important, because I've been tasked with the thankless duty of mollifying the Storrian leadership." Shaw barked out a loud laugh. The admiral was shorter than Chase had expected, and although he gave off a strong command-ing air, the plain way he spoke made him seem less intimidat-ing. "So I did what any good leader would do and threw it all at my second-in-command, and said it was vital that I come speak with you immediately."

Lennard laughed. "Well, it's good to see a friendly face."

The old admiral looked around at the other occupants of the room with sharp eyes, landing on Chase. "You would be the one I spoke with on the comm, correct? What's your name? Where's the other boy?"

"I'm Cor—Chase," he said, stopping himself at the last sec-ond from giving a fake name. Somehow it seemed wrong to lie to the admiral. "Parker's out helping in the engine room."

The captain motioned for everyone to take a seat, and Shaw nodded at Chase as he lowered himself into an arm-chair. "You wouldn't believe what a shock I got, hearing your young voice crying out SOS on the public band. Captain Devore said the *Destrier* never received your message with the all-clear. You boys truly saved the day." His gaze shifted over to Lilli on the couch. "Lionel, who are these kids?"

"Orphans from the Trucon disaster. Some of our crew found

them stranded in a gray sector on Qesaris, and rather than place them in the already overcrowded refugee camps, we informally adopted them. They have great cadet potential."

"Obviously. How do you like living on a starship, son?"

"It's . . . it's great," said Chase.

The admiral turned his attention back on Lennard. "Sounds like it was a very lucky stroke indeed that you got these kids on your ship." There was something strange about his tone that seemed to imply more than he was saying, but Chase tried to brush it off.

The notification chime sounded again, and with a slight frown Lennard rose and hit the entry key. Round-faced Ensign Cutler entered, snapping a salute.

"At ease, Ensign," said Lennard. "What brings you here?"

"I did, actually," said Shaw casually.

From one second to the next, the entire atmosphere of the room changed. Lennard started to move toward his desk, but before he'd taken more than a step, Shaw whipped out a handblaster and pointed it at him. Meanwhile Cutler turned around and pressed a finger-sized silver device against the door. It made a quiet *beep-beep* as he did, and a shot of adrenaline rushed through Chase. He jumped to his feet.

"Sit down, son," said Admiral Shaw. The friendliness in his voice had completely vanished. "Nobody's leaving. We'll get this over with quickly."

At those words, a cold chill settled over Chase.

"What is going on here, Peter?" Lennard's tone was stony. "Cutler, what did you just install on my door?"

"Ensign Cutler here has sealed up the exit with one of his special hacks. Nobody comes in or out until he says so."

Lennard loomed over the small ensign. "Cutler, am I or am I not your superior officer? Open the door."

Cutler stood completely still, looking past the captain.

Shaw smiled. "As a hacker, Robin's abilities are absolutely unparalleled. I found him a few years ago on Ueta, toiling away on code to run the equipment on his parents' farm. A pure natural genius. And so easy to work with. You may as well stop trying to swipe your communicator, Lionel. He's got a jammer in that front shirt pocket." He turned to Cutler. "Did you give Ms. Oriolo her return ring?"

"I did, sir."

Chase sat forward. "You helped Ksenia get away?"

Shaw chuckled. "In a sense. Where did you program the ring to send her?"

Even Cutler couldn't hold back a smirk. "She should be orbiting somewhere over the northern hemisphere of Werikos right now."

"You teleported her into space?" asked Lennard, horrified. "To her death?"

"She turned out to be . . . unreliable," said Shaw with a shrug.

"You killed Lahey and Kobes too," Chase blurted out as the realization occurred to him.

"We prefer not to keep people around once they've outlived their usefulness. Although, Chief Kobes . . . ?" Shaw cast a questioning look at his sidekick.

A tiny, smug smile tugged at the corner of Cutler's mouth. "Taking out that nasty old bear was just a job perk. At some point he figured out a little too much. More than Lahey ever did, actually."

Lennard's eyes were paler, colder, and more furious than Chase had ever seen. "So, Peter, you're a part of this after all. I have to say, I'm extremely disappointed. So why didn't you just let the *Destrier* finish what it started?"

"It seemed imprudent after half the galaxy had heard a young boy aboard the ship screaming for help," said Shaw in a tart voice. "One of those pesky Universal News correspondents rebroadcast him immediately, put him all over the newsfeed." *Nika.* It had to have been her. "And to be honest, I was always against destroying a big beautiful ship like the *Kuyddestor* when all we needed to do was replace a few key personnel."

"And what happens now?" asked Lennard.

"High Command's concerned with you. Seems you've gotten in a little over your head. Telling lies, protecting criminals, harboring missing Fleet-owned medical experiments." He looked at Chase and Lilli as he said this.

Chase moved closer to his sister as his anger flared up. "We're not owned by the Fleet. And we're not experiments."

"High Command tried to make me complicit in covering up the destruction of an entire planet," said Lennard fiercely.

"Trucon?" asked Shaw. "If you'd stuck with your orders and hadn't decided to take up the side of that Lyolian, you wouldn't be in this position right now. I've been sent to demote you in person. We're withdrawing your command of the *Kuyddestor*, effective immediately."

Chase looked to the captain, confused. The Fleet was only going to demote him? Compared to what he'd expected, Chase was surprised to hear this. And uneasy.

"If I refuse to relinquish command?" Lennard's voice was eerily calm.

"I don't think you'll have much of a choice."

Pounding and shouting sounded from out in the hall, followed by the rumble of blaster fire against the door. Chase glanced at Lilli, whose face was fixed and furious. She must have sent out a copy to raise the alarm. Shaw glanced back toward the noise. "Looks like it's time for us to get going. I'm taking these two children with me back to the *Atreus*, so I can get them back where they belong."

So this was the sacrifice Lennard was being forced to make. Chase took a step back. "No. We're not going anywhere with you."

Shaw pulled a few rings from his pocket, silver and thick like his own return ring. He handed Lilli a ring, which she took delicately between forefinger and thumb. *Please be a copy. Please be a copy.* But Chase knew she couldn't be a copy. She'd fought Asa tooth and nail to stay on the ship, and hadn't left Chase's side since. She glared at the admiral, holding his gaze for a moment, and opened her fingers again, dropping the ring on the floor. It made a quiet *ting* when it hit. And then she vanished.

Chase nearly shouted in joy. He couldn't help smiling, especially when he saw the confusion on Shaw's face.

"What did she just do? Is that her thing?" He turned to Cutler. "Get her back."

The ensign looked just as confused. "I don't know where she went, sir."

"Fine. We can get her later. The boy's the more important one anyway." Shaw turned on Chase, but this time instead of handing over the ring, he grabbed Chase's hand and jammed the ring on his index finger himself. Chase looked past him, at Captain Lennard, who quickly shook his head. *Don't phase.*

If he struggled against Shaw on this, if he phased away, there would be a fight. But if he pretended to go along, Shaw would teleport off the ship, not knowing until it was too late that it hadn't worked on Chase. It would hurt, he knew, or possibly make him pass out again like the last time he'd tried teleportation, but by then Shaw would be long gone, and they might have time to get away, or at least defend themselves better. So he left his hand in Shaw's cold grasp, and steeled himself against what he knew was coming.

"See you in the stars, Lionel," said Shaw, pressing the return function on his ring. "Here's your demotion." At the same moment, Cutler drew something from his pocket and tossed it on the floor with a glassy crash.

And then the teleportation began.

The pain was immediate, a giant wave that felt as if his body had been ripped in half. Chase thought he was ready for it, but he gasped and collapsed to his knees, tears springing to his eyes. Every single molecule of his body was trying to tear itself apart, and blackness rushed in to soothe him. Clinging to consciousness with everything he had, he resisted his body's attempt to pass out. *Focus, focus, focus!*

He was trying so hard not to teleport and not to pass out that he didn't notice the yellow fumes rising from the floor. He didn't feel Lennard grabbing him under the shoulders and shoving him toward the locked door.

"Get out!" the captain roared. "Get out of here!"

Long afterward, when Chase reflected on this, he would be ashamed of how easily he went, barely thinking, grasping at safety even as the thick vapor burned his eyes. Not acknowledging that only he could pass through the locked door. Dazed, hurting, hardly able to see, it took him two tries to phase through the door and into the hallway.

Outside Lennard's quarters there was a full riot. Frantic people crowded around the door, beating at the entry key console. Hands reached down and helped Chase off to the side, where he lay on the floor, reeling and only half-conscious of the commotion going on around him, of Parker's white face hovering over him.

A thread of urgency cut through his daze, a growing awareness: Something was wrong with the captain. They needed to get inside the quarters, past Cutty's lock, and help him. Chase tried to rise, weak and half-delirious from pain, but someone pushed him back down. The world swam, darkened, turned into isolated flashes of image and noise.

A flash of people firing their blasters at the door.

A glimpse of Mina, kicking at the door, over and over again. The cracking noise when it finally crumpled and came loose.

The gasps of horror and stifled cries. And a moment later, the high-pitched scream—Lilli's scream.

And he knew they were too late.

CHAPTER TWENTY-SIX

And just like that, everything had changed.

Chase lay in the white silence of the medical bay, staring at the curtains. He didn't know when he'd awoken. Or if he'd really been unconscious. It felt as if he'd been there forever, just staring, not thinking. Or feeling.

The truth lay like a lump in the middle of his mind. He approached it from the sides, probing it, challenging the reality of his hazy memory. And every time the realization hit—*the captain has died, the captain is dead*—his mind leapt away from it and shut down again.

Shapes moved around him, people he thought he knew, but he just kept his eyes focused on the curtain, ignoring everything else. The less he noticed, the less he thought. And not thinking was a good thing.

It was Parker who finally reached him. In the middle of the

night, when the medical bay was quiet but for the whisper of a few machines, Parker appeared between the curtains to stand beside Chase's bed, Mina right behind him.

"Chase, you need to get up." His eyes were rimmed with red. "I don't know if you're in shock or what, but you've got to snap out of it. Things are happening, and I need your help. It's not your fault, what happened. It's like Asa said. The captain was a target. They were going to get him one way or another."

Chase turned his head away. That wasn't enough of an excuse. He should have been able to do something. He could have distracted the admiral with his phasing, led him on a chase, anything. Even though a little voice in his mind told him the captain had been doomed as soon as Ensign Cutler showed up.

"You need to get up, Chase," Parker repeated. "Lilli's even worse off than you are, and Forquera wants us all to meet with him on the flight level right now. I can't do this all myself. I need your help."

Lilli. Chase hadn't let himself think of her yet, but at the mention of her name, her scream echoed through his memory. She would be taking this so much harder than Chase. He focused his eyes on Parker.

"There you are, buddy." Parker gave him a watery smile. "We need to get Lilli and get down to the flight level, okay?"

The nurse on duty looked up from his desk as Chase, Parker, and Mina stepped out from behind the curtain around Chase's bed, but said nothing. How much did he know? How many people had seen Chase phase through the captain's door?

Lilli was two beds over in the medical bay, curled up in a ball, clutching the pillow. Chase whispered her name a few times. Her eyes were open, but she wouldn't look at anyone. Mina pulled off the blankets, and Lilli curled a little tighter. With surprising gentleness, Mina loosened Lilli's grip on the pillow and scooped her up. Lilli didn't fight it.

Chase turned to Parker. "You're sure this is really her? Not a copy?"

"I don't think she has the energy to travel right now. But I checked her hiding spot, and it was empty."

They walked down the silent halls of the ship, passing nobody. Chase looked around at the walls, seeing the ship from a new distance. It was the captain who had made him feel like they had a home on the *Kuyddestor*. Now he felt like a visitor.

Forquera was waiting for them in a debriefing room near the flight deck, sitting on the edge of a table and frowning at the floor. His dark face was set in hard, determined lines. The *Kuyddestor* was his ship now, along with the risks of filling Captain Lennard's shoes. Chase realized he had no idea if the admiral had tried to come back or contact the ship again.

"What happened with Shaw?" he croaked. "Did he come back?"

Forquera shook his head. "The *Atreus* left almost immediately after the attack on the captain."

"Why didn't they try again?" His voice rose, spiraling quickly. "He wanted me and Lilli. He said he was just going to demote the captain. Why did he do this? What was the point?"

Forquera shrugged angrily. "It was a move. A power play. We escaped destruction by the *Destrier*, but they still showed us who's in control."

The door opened, and Maurus walked in, carrying a large duffel bag. He dropped it on the floor and turned to the group, face flat and expressionless, shoulders slumped.

"What's the bag for?" said Parker in alarm.

"You haven't told them yet?" asked Maurus.

Forquera took a breath and looked them over. "You can't stay on the ship." He paused to allow for any outbursts, and then he continued. "It's not safe here for you. It's not safe for anyone, to be honest, but for you children and for Lieutenant Maurus, staying on the *Kuyddestor* will mean your deaths, particularly once we're in stationary repair orbit by Earth."

"But you'll still be in danger, won't you?" asked Chase. "Everyone will be."

"I'll be okay. I know my way around a lion's den. There are only a few of us onboard who know the full truth—some of the bridge team, Dr. Bishallany, Lieutenant Vidal, and myself. We'll be careful. We'll protect the rest of the crew."

"What about us?" asked Chase. "Where will we go?"

"I've given Lieutenant Maurus a plan. He's taking you somewhere where you can blend in and hide. I have an old friend who will be able to help you. He has unusual methods, but he's effective. I'll tell him to meet you there once it's safe to contact him."

Chase hung his head. This was happening, and Forquera was right—it was the only choice for them. They couldn't stay on the *Kuyddestor*. And he didn't really want to anymore. Nothing was the same—any safety or sense of home he'd finally found on the *Kuyddestor* had been ripped away. "Okay. I have to go pack some stuff, I guess. And I want to say goodbye to Analora."

"Your things have been packed. Your rooms are already bare. And Miss Bishallany left a day ago."

"She left?" He couldn't stop his voice from cracking on this. She hadn't even come by to say goodbye.

"Her father sent her away as soon as he could. I'm sorry." Forquera stood. "Your ship is ready, Lieutenant. I've cleared the flight deck."

"We're leaving now?" This was happening too quickly. He needed to say goodbye. *To what?* a voice in his mind asked.

"The report I file with High Command will say that Lieutenant Maurus went AWOL shortly after the captain's death.

I won't mention the rest of you, since you were never officially on the ship."

"And the Fleet will no doubt find a way to spin the story and implicate me for murdering the captain," said Maurus, not trying to hide his anger. He snatched up his duffel bag and swung it on his back. "Let's go then."

The flight deck was empty as they crossed it, all the flight crew sleeping in their quarters or sent away. Except for one person.

Vidal stopped in front of each of them, caressing Lilli's cheek sadly, giving Parker a hug. Chase she gave a sealed envelope and a smile. Then she hugged him, too, and he had to stop breathing for a moment to hold back the sob in his throat.

She stopped in front of Maurus, glanced at Forquera, and threw her arms around his neck anyway. Chase was right beside them, and he heard the words she whispered in his ear.

"Just ask, and I'll come with you."

Maurus pushed her hair out of her face with a sad smile and shook his head. "Take care, Rusandra. I hope we meet again."

"Lieutenant Vidal, the spaceway?" asked Forquera.

Her face bright red, she hurried over to an elevated command console at the back of the chamber.

"Is that our ship?" asked Parker. He was looking at a strange blue vessel parked at the end of a row of transport vehicles. "That looks Storrian."

Forquera nodded. "It is. We salvaged it after the firefight and got it running again. I still want you to stop and trade vessels at least twice before you approach your destination."

Maurus nodded. "I know."

The gigantic doors of the spaceway began to roll open, and one by one they climbed up into the Storrian ship. It was snug inside, but comfortable. Mina placed Lilli on a seat between Chase and Parker, where she stared blankly out the window.

"What's in the envelope?" asked Parker.

Chase ripped it open and found a note.

> Chase–
> I'm so sorry about everything that happened.
> You're still in sickbay and my dad won't let me
> stay to say goodbye to you, so I'm giving this
> note to Vidal. He's sending me back to my
> mother, where I will be safer. If you ever find
> yourself near Jypras, please come visit me.
> Your friend,
> Analora
> P.S. Don't worry, I'll keep your secret.

He looked up, somehow sadder after reading the note than he'd been thinking she'd just left. He folded it up and stuck it in a pocket.

Maurus powered up the vehicle, and slowly they drifted toward the spaceway. They were all silent as they entered the colored tunnel, and the doors behind them drew shut.

"Spaceway doors open for departure," came Vidal's voice from the console. "Be safe, Maurus."

He hit the power, and they shot out of the tunnel and into space. Rhima loomed before them, big and green and terrible— though not as terrible as the monstrous starship that orbited above it, far away in the distance.

"Is that the *Destrier*?" asked Chase.

"Yes," said Maurus in a clipped tone. "They're clearing out all the settlements on Rhima. How many of the Werikosa will actually make it back to their homeworld is anyone's guess."

For a brief moment Chase envisioned Bawran standing bare-chested and defiant before a tribunal of wrathful Storrians. What would his punishment be? He wondered if the settlement they'd been at was already empty, all the Werikosa children on a one-way trip back to their toxic homeworld, along with all the other Werikosa who had tried to call Rhima home while the Federation manipulated their desperation. He wondered briefly again who was in the right in all this, and the thought made him tired.

Then they folded into deep space, and everything was gone.

Somewhere far from the Galifax star system, Maurus sat at the controls, holding the yoke with one hand as he plotted out a course. His hair hung limp in his face. Mina sat beside him in the copilot seat.

"Where are we going?" asked Parker.

"To the Segrond system," Maurus replied.

"You're talking about Ko Aiob, aren't you?" asked Parker.

Maurus nodded slowly. "It's one of the best places in the galaxy to hide."

"What is it?" asked Chase.

"A planet full of slums," said Parker. "Every species that can't find a home somewhere ends up there."

"Like Qesaris?"

Parker gave a little snort. "Qesaris is a paradise compared to this place. So I hear."

"The Ganthas colony planets are regulated," said Maurus. "Ko Aiob isn't affiliated with the Federation."

"Why not go to Lyolia?" asked Chase.

"My homeworld is on the brink of a global civil war, Chase. None of us would be safe there. My people are dying in the streets, and rebel attacks have forced our leader to go underground."

Chase listened, absorbing the information on a superficial level while beneath that, the horrific scene in the captain's quarters replayed itself in his head, over and over again. How easily he had escaped and left the captain to his death. Those few moments that he could never repeat and never take back had shattered his hard-won life, thrusting him yet again into a new reality.

"Are we ever going to see any of them again?" he asked abruptly.

Maurus gave a bitter laugh. "Who knows? Probably not. My Fleet days are over. Cursed Hesta, my days as a respectable citizen are over. I knew there were some seriously bad things starting to happen, but I had no idea our enemies were this vicious, this . . . reckless."

These are the people who orchestrated the destruction of an entire planet—murder is nothing to them, thought Chase. They should have been more cautious. He vowed never to make that mistake again.

"Alright, I've got a course planned out," said Maurus. "We'll make for the Orag-13 system first, and try to swap ships there on one of the Ambessitari colonies. If we keep our heads down and move fast, we should be able to stay one step ahead of the Fleet."

"I don't want to be on the run my whole life," said Chase. He thought of Asa and his paranoia, his life hiding among the underbelly of society, of Nika and the precarious line she danced along. He wouldn't be like them. But he had learned one important lesson from Asa: that giving his trust was a dangerous thing. Captain Lennard had trusted his crew, his long relationship with Admiral Shaw. And now he was dead.

He looked at Lilli, who huddled between him and Parker, a stream of tears running down her cheeks. They'd taken the last piece of her former life, the only person left who really knew her. He couldn't stand the idea of her living on the run as well.

Something fierce was starting to grow in him, a terrible thirst. Was it for justice or for revenge? Was there a difference?

As Maurus announced the fold, Chase wrapped his arm around his sister's shoulder. He held her tightly as they shot into space and started building his plan for how to set them both free.

ACKNOWLEDGMENTS

If writing a first book in four years is an achievement, finishing a second one in less than a year feels like a bit of a miracle, and for that, I have the following people to thank profusely:

My fantastically talented agent, Joanna Volpe, as well as Jaida Temperly, Danielle Barthel, Kathleen Ortiz, Pouya Shahbazian, and the rest of the incredible New Leaf team.

My lovely editor, Liz Szabla, as well as my publisher, Jean Feiwel, for their guidance and support.

The delightful team at Macmillan, especially Anna Roberto, Mary Van Akin, the brilliant art department, and the indomitable publicity team.

My indisputably awesome writing group: Liz Briggs, Jessica Love, Kathryn Rose, Dana Elmendorf, and Amaris Glass, for their encouragement and cheerleading.

My fellow 2014 debut authors of the OneFour KidLit group, as well as the wonderful and welcoming community of kidlit authors in Los Angeles.

A special thanks to Kristen Kittscher, for her time and help in prepping this newbie for what turned out to be some pretty awesome school visits.

All my irreplaceable L.A. friends who came out in enthusiastic support of *The Lost Planet*.

All the former classmates, teachers, and others from my hometown, Sault Ste. Marie, Michigan, whose sincere excitement over my getting published has made my day multiple times over.

All the fantastic readers of *The Lost Planet*, who are honestly the biggest reward in this whole endeavor.

Mom and Dad, because I will always owe everything to you for providing me with a most excellent childhood.

And finally a huge heaping thank you to my dear Bülent. Here's to all the adventures that still lie ahead of us.